Sarah's breath caught in her lungs.

A long-haired man had stepped out from behind the team. Had he forgotten this was his wedding day? He wore a brown buckskin coat with a long, swinging fringe along each sleeve and a necklace made of animal claws. *Animal claws?*

She felt suddenly rooted to the spot, but managed another tentative step forward. Briggs bent forward to check a hoof on one of the horses.

He dropped the horse's hoof and looked up. Sarah's gaze met his sea-green eyes and a shiver of trepidation skittered through her. He seemed disappointed, as if she was not at all what he had expected.

The sun moved behind a cloud, bathing Briggs in shade as he sauntered slowly toward her. Tall and muscular, he moved with surprising grace. *"You're Sarah MacFarland?"* he said.

She swallowed nervously, then struggled to keep her voice from quivering. "Yes."

Dear Reader,

Have you ever been tempted to turn Mr. Wrong into Mr. Right? In each of our books this month, you'll delight in the ways these least-likely-to-marry men change their tune for the right woman!

We are thrilled to introduce debut author Julianne MacLean, who has written a fast-paced and sexy Western, *Prairie Bride*. Recently jilted, angry Kansas farmer Arthur "Briggs" Brigman was the last person *anyone* suspected would advertise for a wife. Not surprising, though, when his beautiful Eastern bride shows up, determined to hide her past, Briggs is far from a charming groom. Don't miss the sparks that fly between these two under the wide-open prairie skies!

Ruth Langan returns with *The Sea Witch,* book one of her medieval miniseries SIRENS OF THE SEA. Here, a female privateer and a dashing sea captain team up—in more ways than one!—to thwart a villain's plot against the king. In *The Paper Marriage* by mainstream historical author Bronwyn Williams, a tough-as-nails American mariner marries—sight unseen—a young widow in financial trouble in exchange for help raising his adopted daughter. Don't miss what happens when he begins to fall in love with his aunt's friend while waiting for his "wife"!

And be sure to look for *Prince of Hearts,* a wonderful medieval novel by talented newcomer Katy Cooper. In this emotional story, Edmund Tudor, the king of England's youngest brother, must choose between his love for a noblewoman and his duty to his brother's kingdom.

Enjoy! And come back again next month for four more choices of the best in historical romance.

Sincerely,

Tracy Farrell,
Senior Editor

Prairie Bride

Julianne MacLean

HARLEQUIN®

TORONTO • NEW YORK • LONDON
AMSTERDAM • PARIS • SYDNEY • HAMBURG
STOCKHOLM • ATHENS • TOKYO • MILAN • MADRID
PRAGUE • WARSAW • BUDAPEST • AUCKLAND

ISBN 0-373-29126-4

PRAIRIE BRIDE

Visit us at www.eHarlequin.com

Printed in U.S.A.

Available from Harlequin Historicals and
JULIANNE MacLEAN

Prairie Bride #526

For my wonderful husband, Stephen.

Acknowledgments:

To The Kansas State Historical Society
and The Kansas Heritage Center.

To my agent, Paige Wheeler,
and editors Melissa Endlich, Margaret O'Neill Marbury
and Tracy Farrell.

To Jo Beverley, Lorraine Coyle,
Joyce David, Deborah Hale, Cheryl Leger,
Susanne MacDonald-Boyce, Ruth MacLean,
Jackie Manning, Georgie Phillips, Janelle Schneider,
Julia Smith and Norah Wilson.

To Tory Leblanc, for your wisdom and encouragement.

To Mom and Dad, for being great parents.

Finally, to my cousin, Michelle Phillips,
who writes as Michelle McMaster,
thank you for being my lifetime soul-sister.

Chapter One

Kansas, 1882

Exhausted, knowing she would not sleep for many hours, Sarah MacFarland leaned forward to peer from the train window. The shrill steam whistle blew. Heavy iron wheels chugged and squealed beneath the soles of her feet, faster and faster, mimicking the rhythm of her heart.

Tonight she would lose her virginity. For the second time.

Sarah sank back in her seat and massaged her pounding temples. She prayed silently that it would all go well, that she had done the right thing, coming out west. Searching for reassurance, she pulled open the drawstring on her black purse and withdrew the newspaper advertisement.

Farmer, Arthur Brigman, seeks gentle and peaceful wife for simple life on Kansas prairie. Must agree to daily toil and plain home.

Marriage and a simple life was what she'd always wanted, she reminded herself, as she watched two children chase each other up the aisle, screeching with laughter. A troublesome guilt slithered up Sarah's spine. Never in all her dreams had she believed she would reach her goal of marriage through deceit. But she had no choice, really.

She folded the wrinkled piece of paper and slid her fingers along the crease. If only she knew what to expect of her future husband. If only she knew what he looked like.

Stuffing the ad back into her purse, accidentally elbowing the sleeping woman beside her, Sarah decided with conviction that a man's looks were of little importance to her now. She had learned her lesson in Boston. This time she would act with common sense. She gazed out the window at the ocean of golden prairie grass. The rippling land seemed to stretch on and on forever, colliding violently with the cloudless sky.

A person could easily disappear in it.

She tilted her head back, closed her weary eyes, and imagined her new husband. Perhaps Arthur would be waiting for her with a black buggy and a handsome black horse. He would touch the brim of his hat when their eyes first met. Surely he would know her the moment he saw her. She envisioned him wearing a new wedding suit—a gray one with a matching fedora—something similar to the one her father used to wear to church on Sundays. She wondered if Arthur was clean shaven. Papa had always worn a wide, bristly mustache with the ends waxed into a curl. And gold spectacles. She smiled as she remembered how he used to smoke a pipe on Saturdays after supper. Perhaps Arthur would do the same.

All of a sudden, that tenacious guilt returned and

stabbed at her dreamy thoughts. She had not been completely honest with her future husband. She had kept many things from him. Sarah had come here in search of more than a simple home. She had come in search of safety. Sanctuary.

A baby at the back of the train began to cry. Sarah opened her eyes. She hoped Arthur would never know how far she had plunged from her father's virtuous pedestal. And she hoped her husband would forgive her for deceiving him on their wedding day.

"I still think you're making a big mistake," George Brigman said, his eyes perusing the dark, damp interior of the sod house.

Arthur "Briggs" Brigman glared with irritation at his brother, who brushed at the top of a wooden box before sitting down. Heaven forbid he should soil his new suit while he handed out his opinions.

Trying to ignore George's advice, Briggs looked around his one-room dwelling. Rain from the day before had soaked through the walls to the inside. Mud dripped from the ceiling with a tedious *tat-tat-tat*. The smell of wet earth wafted out of every crevice, the dampness seeping under his clothing.

What a fine mess for his new wife to come home to.

George stomped his foot on a grasshopper, kneading it into the dirt floor. "You're not over Isabelle yet."

Shrugging into his fringed buckskin coat, Briggs winced at the sound of Isabelle's name. He hoped after today he wouldn't hear it again.

His gaze searched the dugout for his worn leather gloves. Taking three easy strides, he swept them up from the nail keg by the door and tapped them against his thigh. He wondered if he should have shaved. Too late now, he decided. He'd been working since dawn in the cornfield and hadn't realized the time.

"You're not listening to me," George continued. "It's only been three months, and you're hardly set up for marriage."

"I'm set up fine. I have land and I have a house." He spread his arms wide so the fringe on his sleeves dangled. "What more could I need?"

"You call this a house?" George walked to the sod wall and plucked out a long blade of limp, brown grass. "You advertise in a city paper for a wife and you expect her to live here?"

Briggs clamped his jaw at the insult. He was proud of what he'd accomplished over the past year. He owned this land and all the corn and wheat and other crops planted on it. As soon as the harvest machine came, he'd make a handsome profit off his wheat and rye.

"I said I was looking for someone who could handle the prairie. That someone answered, so there's nothing else to talk about. I need help around here. I need a wife. And I'm done sitting alone on my land like the hermit everyone thinks I am, pining away over..." Still uncomfortable speaking her name, he reached up to rub the back of his neck, warm under the blanket of his thick, shoulder-length hair.

"You were never one to care what other people thought," George pointed out, a little too perceptively for Briggs's present mood.

He took a deep breath, searching for patience. He succeeded only in reminding himself of the ever present smell of dirt and grass. Everything was so darn wet.

"I am over Isabelle," he said. "I was over her the moment she took me for a fool and broke our engagement." He turned his back on his brother. He didn't need this. Not today. They had a long drive ahead of them and he had vows to think about.

"Look at you," George snorted. "You're covered with dust. You look like you just walked off the field. Why don't you at least borrow one of my suits?"

Briggs looked down at his faded beige trousers and shabby leather boots. "I did just walk off the field. This is the way I dress and your suits would never fit me. You know that."

"We could stop off at the clothier—"

Briggs raised an eyebrow, wishing George would stop making suggestions about his wedding attire. Briggs had never intended the ceremony to be anything more than what it was. A legality.

A moment of silence passed while Briggs threw an old gray blanket over the narrow bed and fluffed up the single pillow. Suddenly, his gut wrenched. He was in the habit of living alone. Soon he'd be sleeping here—sharing his bed—with a complete stranger.

"You don't have to marry this girl today," George continued. "You don't even know what she looks like."

"It's not about looks, George. In fact, a pretty face clouds a man's judgment. What I need is a capable woman who's not so concerned with fancy clothes and hats and all that other stuff women like." Briggs flipped his hair out of his face. "She's going to live out here, miles from town, lighting fires with dry cow dung."

George's disapproving gaze swept the room, then he pushed his gold spectacles farther up the bridge of his nose. "It's not too late to change your mind. You could get to know her first, maybe court her a little."

"I don't have time to court. I'm thirty years old. Besides, if I felt like courting, I'd court someone here in Kansas, instead of bringing her all the way from…uh…" Briggs drew his eyebrows together, trying to remember which newspaper advertisement she'd answered.

"Boston!" George finished for him. "You brought her from Boston!"

"Right. Boston." He rubbed his stubbled chin between his thumb and forefinger. "Now let's get on the road or we'll be late and she'll be standing around at the station wondering if she got off in the wrong town."

Briggs followed George through the narrow door, watching his brother duck so his gray fedora wouldn't graze the low frame. "I'm sure she'll be wondering that, regardless, when she sees this place," George commented.

The two walked into the wind toward the unpainted wagon, aged the color of a thundercloud. Hoisting himself into the hard seat, Briggs flicked the reins and they lurched ominously into motion. He turned the wagon through the yard toward town with George's horse in tow.

Briggs sighed. Maybe George was right. Maybe he should have waited—at least until the harvest was in. But what was done was done. He'd made an agreement and he wouldn't go back on his word. The girl had insisted on coming right away. She'd traveled across the country and he had promised her a marriage certificate the day she arrived.

Briggs squinted up at the blue sky, removed his well-worn Stetson hat and swabbed his forehead with a sleeve. Marriage. He'd never imagined it would come about like this. But recalling his *first* proposal, he decided it was better this way. He'd made a mistake in choosing Isabelle. She was completely wrong for the kind of life he'd always wanted, but he'd been struck blind by her beauty and charm. Isabelle could never have been a farmer's wife. He should have known that from the start.

Perhaps things turned out for the best, he thought, absentmindedly steering the wagon through a deep rut. There was no denying he'd suffered when Isabelle left him. Anger had beaten the drive out of him for days, but it was anger directed at himself for being so foolish. His brain had been in his trousers when he'd proposed.

Not this time, he thought proudly, watching one of the horses swat its long tail at a bee. This time, Briggs had a clear set of newspaper-print requirements and a pretty face was not among them. This time, the marriage would be built on respect and a mutual desire for companionship—things that would last through the years.

George's voice penetrated Briggs's thoughts. "Did you get her a wedding gift?"

"A wedding gift? Isn't it enough that I paid her fare all the way from Boston?"

George shook his head in that slow way of his. "A woman likes something she can hold on to. A gift that'll mean something in twenty years when she digs it out of the closet. Why don't you give her the necklace?''

''Are you out of your mind?'' Briggs exclaimed. ''What would I do about the engraving on the back? Draw a line through *Isabelle* and write in the other one's name?''

''Sarah.''

''I know her name.''

''It would be nice if you could use it when you meet her.''

''I will. I will.''

''And I don't want to hear you complaining if she's not the most beautiful woman you've ever seen. You like the pretty ones and that's why you fell so hard for Isabelle when she wasn't—''

Briggs shot his brother a glare. ''I hope my wife's got hips as big as a barn and arms stronger than Big Joe MacKaskill's. She'll need 'em if she's going to haul water from the creek till I get a well dug.''

''And when do you plan on doing that?''

Briggs clicked his tongue at the horses. ''When I get around to it.'' George didn't respond, and Briggs could feel his disapproval like a pesky fly. Being a city person and a lawyer, George could never understand how much work went into farming. Or how rewarding it could be.

''I just hope you're nice to her today.''

''I will be,'' Briggs replied defensively. ''And I don't want to hear any more about it.'' The wagon lurched and swayed over a bump in the road. ''Yah,'' he called to the cumbersome horses, flicking the reins and realizing that, come sundown, he'd be a married man.

His chest tightened at the thought of meeting this

strange woman. He sure hoped he knew what he was getting into.

"Next stop, Dodge City!" the conductor called out, whisking his fingers over the back of each seat as he staggered down the aisle.

Knots twisted inside Sarah's slender body. She sat forward to see, for the first time, the place that would become her home. It was real now, no longer a fantasy. She checked to ensure her dark hair was neat and tidy, all her buttons were fastened, then pinched her cheeks to summon some color.

"You look lovely," the woman beside her said. "I'm sure he'll fall in love with you the moment he sees you."

Sarah forced a smile. "How did you know?"

"I saw you reading that ad, and it's not hard to tell how nervous you are. But don't worry. You're a beautiful young woman. He'll be pleased, to be sure."

Sarah watched the dust-covered wooden buildings pass by the window as the train chugged into Dodge City. Sagging boardwalks sighed with fatigue under the persistent eddy of cowboys and townsfolk. The wide main street, muddy from a recent rainfall, lay battered with deep hoofprints and wagon tracks.

The train screeched to a tuckered-out halt at the station. Outside the window, a crowd was gathered on the platform, mostly men puffing pockets of cigar smoke out from under their hats. Sarah took one last quick look, swallowed her apprehension, then reached for her valise.

Inching into the aisle, Sarah carried her bag toward the door. When she reached the steps, she squinted into bright sunlight, then quickly raised a hand to shade her eyes. She searched the unfamiliar faces looking up at her. Where was the man who had promised to meet her? The man who would soon be her husband?

She took an uneasy step down. Just then, a gust of wind blew into her face and sucked her hat off her head, sending it somersaulting across the muddy station yard. "Oh, dear!" she cried, as she clumsily reached up to hold her knotted hair in place.

At that moment, she spotted him. He was pursuing her hat. Her spirits suddenly surged with delight. It was him. She knew it. He wore spectacles, a gray suit and a fedora, just as she had pictured him. He looked very much like her father.

He picked up her hat and wiped it meticulously with a crisp white handkerchief. When he seemed satisfied it was clean, he turned and walked directly toward her. "Sarah MacFarland?" he asked, reaching her and taking her heavy valise.

"Yes, I'm Sarah." She placed her hat back on her head and poked the pin into place.

"Please, come this way." He led her past a small group of men. "Allow me to introduce myself. I'm George Brigman."

Sarah peered at him, confused. Then her stomach dropped. "George? I thought you were…uh. Is Arthur your middle name?"

He stopped and laughed and held out his hand. "You've got it wrong, I'm afraid. I'm George, Arthur's brother. But I wouldn't call him Arthur, if I were you."

"Why not?" Sarah asked, shaking his proffered hand.

"Everyone calls him Briggs. No one's called him Arthur since…" He paused. "Well, I wouldn't try it."

Sarah felt an uncomfortable jolt of apprehension as she let go of George's hand.

"Please, the wagon is this way." George led her around the back of the depot.

As they walked arm in arm, Sarah wondered why Arthur—or Briggs, rather—hadn't come to meet her himself. Perhaps he was shy. That must be it, she told herself while fighting a dozen and one fears. That's why he had advertised for a wife instead of courting one.

Well, shy was just fine with her. In fact, she preferred it that way. A nice, quiet, reserved husband. Yes, that would be delightful.

George nodded his head toward a wagon. "There he is."

Sarah stopped to look, but all she saw was a beat-up box on wheels, hitched to two prehistoric-looking horses with hairy hooves. "Where?" she asked, shading her eyes.

Just then, a long-haired man stepped out from behind the team.

Sarah's breath caught in her lungs. Her first impression was that he was clearly in need of a bath and a shave. Had he forgotten this was his wedding day? He wore a brown buckskin coat with long, swinging fringe along the sleeves and a necklace made of animal claws. *Animal claws?* He looked nothing like George at all.

Fighting the nausea which had suddenly rooted itself in her stomach, she took another tentative step forward. Briggs bent forward to check a hoof on one of the horses.

"I don't think he's seen us yet," George said, sounding apologetic.

In her opinion, Briggs was more concerned with his horse than her arrival. But the extra moment gave her time to rein in her emotions and reconsider this situation. It was wrong of her to judge him based on his appearance. She hadn't met him yet. He could be a very polite fellow.

He dropped the horse's hoof and looked up. Sarah's gaze met his sea-green eyes and a shiver of trepidation skittered through her. He seemed disappointed, as if she were not at all what he had expected.

The sun moved behind a cloud, bathing Briggs in shade as he sauntered slowly toward her. Tall and muscular, he moved with surprising grace. "*You're* Sarah MacFarland?" he said.

She swallowed nervously, then struggled to keep her voice from quavering. "Yes."

George broke in. "Sarah, this is my brother, Briggs. And, Briggs, this is Sarah."

The large farmer swept his steely gaze down her body, then back up again to her tall purple hat. "Somehow I can't imagine her hauling water," he said to George.

"I can haul water," Sarah mentioned uncertainly, but no one seemed to be listening.

George shrugged at Briggs, and Sarah was sure his eyes said, *I told you so.*

"Put her bag in the wagon and get in," Briggs said to his brother.

While George climbed into the back, Sarah stood wondering why this man was so displeased with her. She'd tried to appear pleasant. For pity's sake, she'd done everything she could to primp and make herself beautiful for him.

"Let's go." He climbed into the high wagon seat. "The courthouse closes at five." When she hesitated, he frowned down at her. Heat stole into her cheeks and she suspected she'd turned a vivid scarlet. "Are you coming?"

Something inside her wanted to say no and make a mad dash for the hills, but the hills, she thought ridiculously, were quite a distance from here. She stood motionless, letting her eyes wander the flat, windy town.

The sun poked out from behind a cloud, and she had to shield her eyes again to look up at Briggs's large silhouette. This man was less gentlemanly than she would have liked, to be sure, but she was in no position to be fussy. She would rather take her chances here than back in Boston with Garrison, who could be on her heels at this very moment. At least if she married Briggs, it would be legal and she would change her name. If things didn't work out, some time would pass and her trail would become a little less visible. Garrison wouldn't be able to find her.

Of course, she hoped it *would* work out, that she and Briggs could get to know each other and some-how have a good life together. One day, she would tell him the truth, after some time had passed....

Raising her skirts, she scrambled awkwardly into the seat beside him.

"Yah!" he called out, flicking the reins. Without warning, the wagon jerked forward and Sarah's head snapped back. She bounced and jiggled, using all her muscles to avoid toppling into Briggs's lap as he turned the wagon around and headed across the wide street.

He spoke not one word the entire way, and Sarah wondered miserably if she'd just escaped one dreadful situation only to arrive smack-dab in the middle of another.

Chapter Two

With his backside planted firmly on the crooked wagon seat, and his fists clamped around the worn leather reins, Briggs refused to do anything but stare straight ahead. His head throbbed with a tension he'd not felt in months. How in tarnation had he gotten stuck with such a beautiful woman? He needed someone who could gather fuel, empty the stalls and milk the cow! Not to mention helping out with the harvest, and when it came time to slaughter the pig...well, that went without saying. Hadn't she understood his ad? What was she going to do when she saw the sod dugout she'd have to live in?

Worse yet, she was exactly the type of woman Briggs had always found attractive. Her midnight-black hair was pulled into a loose bun on top of her head. She had big brown eyes a man could lose himself in, skin the color of fresh cream and lips the color of raspberries. He didn't want to notice those things because the minute she set eyes on his sod house, she'd no doubt demand to be sent back home. He'd be a fool to think otherwise.

When they turned up Railroad Avenue, the wagon

struck a rock and leaped into the air. Beside him, Sarah bounced like a jumping bean and nearly landed in his lap. "Sorry," she said, then quickly righted herself.

All of Briggs's muscles went rigid. His body tightened with a maddening awareness and an arousal in his groin that he struggled to ignore, but it was no easy task. She seemed so delicate, like a butterfly on a sudden unexpected gale.

George moved to the front of the wagon bed and sat directly behind them. "Are you tired from your journey, Miss MacFarland?"

"Just a little," she answered, politely. Her leg—somewhere beneath all those purple skirts—bumped Briggs's, but she quickly drew it back to a proper distance, much to his relief.

"Well, you'll be pleased to know your travels are over," George said. "Until tomorrow, anyway. Then it's a six-hour drive out to the claim."

Briggs whipped around. "What do you mean, tomorrow? There's a full moon tonight. We're heading back this afternoon, just as soon as the judge gives us the certificate."

George pulled out a white handkerchief and blew his nose. "Well, I took the liberty of booking you a room in the Dodge House for tonight. It's the best hotel in town, and I thought it would be a fine wedding gift, after Miss MacFarland's long journey."

Briggs made no effort to hide his irritation. This ceremony wasn't supposed to be romantic. Briggs had planned to be up and fed and in the fields tomorrow by dawn. Now he'd have to spend the morning on the road, wasting even more precious daylight hours.

"Thank you so much, Mr. Brigman." The appreciation in Sarah's voice smacked Briggs like a brick. He turned to look at her, seeing for the first time what a wonderful smile she had. Her eyes were twinkling— at George—and her teeth were as straight and white as pure ivory. Was there nothing ugly about her?

"Y-you're welcome, Miss MacFarland," George stammered like a schoolboy. "And you can call me George."

Briggs shook his head at his brother's syrupy tone.

The horses trotted to a stop outside the redbrick courthouse. Briggs set the brake, wrapped the reins around it and hopped down. As he rounded the two-horse team, he watched Sarah clumsily wiggle down. She clutched at the splintery side of the wagon, her other hand holding her outrageous feathered hat to keep it from blowing off. Her little nose crinkled as she tried to gather her skirts at the same time.

Briggs shook his head at the spectacle—she just looked so plumb ridiculous!—until he noticed George clambering out of the wagon to assist her.

Well, he'd be damned if he'd let his brother beat him to it. Briggs hurried toward her and stopped just behind that wiggling backside. He watched her for a second. One tiny foot was on the ground, the other leg was bent at an impossible angle with the other foot still on the floor of the wagon. "Lean back," he instructed.

He wrapped his hands around her narrow waist and lifted her dainty frame to the ground. Holding her so close, he noticed the clean scent of her hair and the faint hint of rosewater on her skin. He had to fight the inclination to enjoy it.

"Thank you, Mr. Brigman." Sarah's face flushed pink as she smoothed her skirt.

It was one of those things that charmed him—a woman smoothing her skirt. But almost as quickly as the feeling came, he squashed it like a bug under his boot. "Well, don't expect assistance every time. You're going to have to get used to things being difficult."

Her jaw dropped in surprise and he wished he'd kept his thoughts to himself. But at some point, his wife was going to have to learn to put away any tendencies toward vanity if she was going to survive out on the plains with prairie fires, wind storms and grasshoppers. He had no intention of letting her spend precious hours of the day in front of the mirror, fussing over herself like Isabelle had done.

They started up the stairs together and headed toward the front door. All the while, Briggs could feel a slow, heated panic moving over him. After all his preaching to George about the problems with a pretty wife, what in the world was he about to do?

Feeling dizzy, Sarah gaped at the large brick building. Halfway up the steps, she grabbed hold of the handrail. She could not go through with this. The man beside her was not at all the kind of man she imagined she'd be wedding. Why couldn't it have been someone like George?

Panic stormed at her from all sides as they entered the building and climbed the creaky stairs to the second floor. They reached the office at the end of the hall and Briggs ushered Sarah through. As she approached the distinguished judge seated behind a large mahogany desk, she realized she was another step closer to going through with it. Sarah heard footsteps behind her and felt Briggs's looming presence like a net about to be tossed over her head. He was standing too close to her, trapping her in this stuffy office. She couldn't breathe! She had to call this off. It wasn't too late until the papers were signed.

Turning on the oriental carpet to face him, she sucked in a quick breath. He was standing before her like a huge, stone wall. She swallowed, staring at his animal claw necklace, realizing he was taller than she had thought. The top of his white linen shirt had fallen open. She could see his bare neck and it made her mouth go dry. He flipped his long golden-brown hair back, revealing tiny beaded designs on the shoulders of his faded buckskin coat.

"You all right?" he asked. "You look like you need a glass of water or something."

Nodding, she dropped her gaze to the floor. She wished she were anywhere but here.

"George, get her something, will you?" Briggs led her to the crimson upholstered sofa where he rested his hands on her shoulders and sat her down. He knelt before her, then picked up a few papers from the desk and fanned her with a gentle breeze. She looked up to meet his gaze.

Perhaps, she thought as she stared into those deep-green eyes, there was some kindness in this man after all. Surely this was the right thing to do. Women traveled west all the time to marry men they'd never met. He'd said in his advertisement that he wanted someone who would enjoy a simple life on the prairie and that's exactly what she had wanted, too, wasn't it? She just hadn't imagined, in all her girlish fantasies, marrying anyone so rugged. So much like this rough, untamed land.

George hurried into the room with a glass of water

and handed it to her. She self-consciously sipped, feeling the eyes of each man watching her, waiting and worrying.

"Perhaps some air would do you good," the judge suggested, opening the window. A fast prairie gale dashed inside and swept some papers off the desk. The white sheets floated and rocked in midair before Sarah's eyes. She felt dizzy, like she was rolling right along with them, falling and swirling into a dark, unfamiliar canyon.

"Darn wind never stops." The judge pressed his palms to the desktop to hold down what was left.

Still kneeling in front of her, Briggs waited for her to finish the water, then took her empty glass and set it on the desk. She stared blankly at his strong facial features—the square jaw, the dimpled chin, the long lashes like an awning over his green eyes. His lips were full for a man's, and she found herself wondering with a strange inner excitement what his kiss would taste like.

He touched her forehead with the back of his hand, and Sarah instinctively jerked back. Briggs hesitated, his eyes narrowing with a dozen questions.

Surprised at her impulsive reaction, she tried to relax and allow him to examine her. He seemed to sense her readiness, and again he touched her forehead. The hand was gentle.

He lowered it to rest on his knee. "You're a little warm."

"It's just the heat."

The judge laughed, his voice deep and booming. "Happens all the time," he joked. "But usually it's the groom. Some days they drop like flies, facedown onto the rug."

George joined in the judge's laughter, but Briggs kept his attention focused on Sarah. "You all right, now?" he whispered privately to her. "It's not too late to change your mind."

Suddenly her skin beneath her clothes erupted in strangely pleasant goose bumps. She felt protected and cared for—something she hadn't felt in a very long time, not since her parents had died. With that sensation, her heart began to slow its speedy pace and her instincts told her clearly that beneath the hard exterior, this man was decent and kind and would make a fitting husband.

It was all she needed to lift her up off the sofa. "I'm fine," she heard herself saying. "Let's go ahead."

Standing in front of Judge Fraser, gazing into the depths of Sarah's coffee-colored eyes, Briggs was surprised by his sudden lack of cold feet. She'd seemed so innocent just now, sitting on the sofa looking up at him, desperate for him in a way he couldn't quite understand. Isabelle had never looked at him like that. No one had. He felt an inexplicable need to take Sarah into his arms and tell her everything was going to be all right.

Briggs glanced at the judge and reminded himself of his vow to avoid the kind of heated attraction he had felt for Isabelle. After the lesson he'd learned, he hadn't thought himself capable of it ever again.

So why was his body betraying him with such a powerful surge of excitement?

The judge turned a page and startled Briggs out of his thoughts, reminding him to listen to these important, lifelong words. "Repeat after me," Judge Fraser said, his gaze directed at Briggs. "I, Arthur John Brigman, take you, Sarah Jane MacFarland..."

Feeling as if he were floating, Briggs repeated the words, ending with "to love and to cherish, until death us do part."

Great God, what was he saying?

Until death us do part!

To love and to cherish!

He tried to remember Sarah's letter a few weeks ago. It had convinced him she was the right woman. She'd mentioned her parents' recent death, her loneliness, and he'd thought even before meeting her that she possessed a family loyalty that Isabelle had not. Wasn't it possible that another woman would be everything he had wanted Isabelle to be? Wasn't it possible he could trust her?

He listened to Sarah's shaky voice repeating the same words he had spoken; he sensed her anxiety, but there was no turning back now. As he slipped the ring onto Sarah's slim finger, he promised himself he would build her a real farmhouse just as soon as he brought in the harvest. With any luck, they'd move in before the first snow. He would finally sell that necklace he had bought for Isabelle. His hopes and dreams belonged with Sarah now.

The judge said his final words and Briggs gazed down at Sarah's expression in wonder. Her eyes were wide and unfathomable, her cheeks flushed like two strawberries. They were man and wife now, he realized, and his heart pounded hard enough to knock him over.

Briggs felt George nudge him in the back, then looked at the judge and realized they were both waiting for the kiss. His stomach flipped. He let his gaze fall back to Sarah's frightened face. How was he to do this?

Taking a deep breath, praying for a lifetime of courage, he leaned forward and pressed his lips lightly to hers, all the while resisting the sizzling desire to let his tongue wander inside.

He would have liked to linger there a while, but when his body began to respond too eagerly, he pulled back. Such things should be enjoyed in private, he knew, and thankfully that moment was near. Simply the idea of it was enough to make him weak with anticipation for the night ahead.

Chapter Three

Sarah glanced across the small round dinner table at her new husband and could barely swallow. One part of her wanted only to move on to the wedding night and get it over with as soon as possible. Another part of her wanted to put it off forever. Surely when Briggs came to her in the dark, he would know he was not the first. Garrison had told her men knew these things....

She had to be strong, she told herself. She had to get through this. Perhaps her previous experience would not make a difference to Briggs. After all, there was no love between them. He merely wanted a helper on his farm.

Silverware clinked against china plates all around them. Conversation hummed and laughter bellowed from the back corner of the restaurant. Sarah shifted in her chair, then cautiously looked again at Briggs to see if he'd noticed how little she'd eaten. To her dismay, he was staring at her over the vase of petunias.

Their eyes locked. For that brief second she wondered what in heaven's name he was thinking. Then without warning, self-consciousness came hurling at her. She dropped her gaze, picked up her fork and scooped up some mashed potatoes swabbed in dark gravy. Chewing furiously, she knew her face had gone as red as a ripe tomato. Briggs probably wasn't surprised. Her behavior was what a husband would expect from a naive bride on her wedding night.

But Sarah knew fully what to expect from a husband, and the agony of that coming moment sent a ripple of fear up her spine.

After dinner, she dawdled over her coffee while they discussed nothing more interesting than the weather and Sarah's long journey. Soon the conversation slowed to an agonizing end. Her coffee was cold and Sarah knew her time had come. She breathed deeply, trying to calm the nervous knots in her belly.

Briggs slid his chair back across the floor. "Are you finished?"

Sarah gulped back her blistering panic, forced a smile and nodded.

"Shall we go, then?" he asked, holding out his hand.

She placed her hand into his and allowed him to help her out of her chair. They walked arm in arm upstairs to room 21, where he inserted a large metal key into the lock and pushed the squeaky door open. Standing in the hall, unable to take even a small step forward, Sarah peered inside.

One flickering kerosene lamp produced a smoky light. A tall rosewood dresser stood against the far wall, holding a blue-and-white chamber set. But the most notable piece of furniture was the intimidating wrought-iron bed. Why did a woman have to go through this in order to be married? she wondered miserably.

"Make yourself at home," Briggs said, gesturing with an outstretched arm and probably wondering why she was hesitating.

After a few seconds, she took that giant step over the threshold. Once inside, she turned around, her hands clasped tightly in front of her. Her rugged-looking husband was leaning one shoulder against the door frame, both his hands in his front coat pockets. He swept a seductive gaze down her body, then let it return to meet hers. There was a tingling in the pit of her stomach, but what was causing it? Fear? Dread? Or was it an indecent thrill? It seemed incomprehensible that she could feel anything but misery at this moment.

"Aren't you coming in?" she asked, feeling the weight of his stare, wanting to put this night behind her, along with all her mixed-up emotions.

He stepped back into the hall. "Not just yet. I thought you might like some time to yourself after your trip. I reserved the hotel tub for you." He rubbed his jaw. "And I thought I might get myself a bath and a shave, too. George is expecting me at his house. It's just a few blocks away."

Sarah let a sigh escape. Would the waiting never end?

"I'll come back in an hour?"

She nodded without thinking, then watched him close the door. With knees trembling, her breath coming in short gasps, she listened to her husband's heavy footsteps fade down the hall. Then silence boomed in her ears.

She collapsed onto the bed, burying her face into

the pink flowered quilt. Odd that she noticed the bed didn't creak, but when she remembered the embarrassing racket the other bed had made, she realized it was not so odd she would notice such a thing. It was a sound she would not soon forget.

Outside the hotel, Briggs stood a moment, staring up at the star-speckled sky. He listened to the saloon piano clanging a tinny tune down the street and found himself missing the quiet night hiss of prairie grass.

So much for avoiding beautiful women in fancy skirts and feathered hats, he thought as he breathed an autumn scent in the late August air. He'd sat at dinner, watching his wife fidget in her chair like a child in church, trying to hide that goosey grin and failing terribly. She was nervous about tonight, poor thing. She was plumb scared out of her wits.

He was, too, he supposed. He'd never been with a virgin before.

All of a sudden, a case of the jitters hit him. He hoped he would make it pleasant for her, even though he knew he probably couldn't, no matter how hard he tried. Women didn't usually enjoy it the first time. Or so he'd heard.

He pulled his gaze from the blanket of stars overhead and started walking toward George's house. Maybe the bath would relax him a bit. He sure as hell hoped so.

Sarah sat up in bed wearing her pink cotton nightdress, buttoned tightly at the neck. Good Lord, she felt like she was choking. Waiting in the empty silence, listening for those footsteps down the hall, she fought the cold fear in her heart. Visions of the marriage act clouded her senses as she fiddled nervously with the pink satin ribbon at her collar. The nightdress had been a gift from Garrison on that horrible night and it stung that she must wear it now. But what else was she to do? Wait naked in bed for her husband? Certainly not.

By the time she heard those boots tapping softly down the hall, she was nearly frozen with fear. The key clicked in the lock, the doorknob turned, and the door slowly creaked open.

The time had come. She was alone with her new husband.

"Sorry I'm late," Briggs said quietly, closing the door behind him. He stared at her only briefly, then turned and shrugged out of his coat.

Sarah said nothing. She couldn't. All she could do was sit up against the pillows, biting her thumbnail, taking in the details of his appearance in the flickering lantern light.

He turned his back to her while he pulled the animal claw necklace over his head, set it lightly on the chest of drawers, then unbuttoned and stripped off his loose white shirt. Sensations of awe exploded within her at the sight of his bronze, muscular back. He was large and strong. Stronger than Garrison. He would be heavy on top of her. She would feel trapped....

Looking away, she shivered, remembering what had come after Garrison had removed his shirt. At least this time, she would know what to expect. Unpleasantness. And who knew what else, when Briggs discovered she'd kept something from him?

Briggs took three slow, sultry steps toward the bed. "There's no need to be afraid. You look as if you've just been sent to the hangman."

Her voice shook as she grasped desperately for words. "We hardly know each other."

He came closer, tilting his head. He looked different from before, when he'd first looked at her with those callous green eyes. Now his expression was reassuring, compassionate.

But no amount of compassion would change what he was about to do to her.

"I'll try to be gentle," he said tentatively, as if he wasn't sure he could be.

He raised a knee to the bed and crawled catlike across her to lie on the other side. A faint scent of musk touched her nose.

"I hope that by tomorrow we'll know each other better," he added in a soft voice. He settled down and cradled her chin in his large hand. "Can I kiss you, Sarah?"

Trembling, she nodded, then closed her eyes to prepare for the feel of his lips upon hers. Her heart throbbed painfully inside her chest, her mind alive with horrible expectations. But when his hand caressed her cheek, then moved gracefully to her ear and played in the wavy locks of hair she'd just finished combing, she found herself feeling warm and a little less afraid.

Then his lips moved over hers like a whisper, carefully at first. She quivered at the sweet tenderness of it all, the flavor of his mouth, the unanticipated desire she was feeling. His lips parted hers in a smooth, sweeping motion, and his tongue moved into her mouth. A sensual response awakened deep within her. Her body was relaxing, her muscles letting go of their resolve. *If only the rest of it could be as satisfying as this soul-reaching kiss,* she thought. If only they need not go further.

Briggs drew back and wet his lips, his hand still playing in the tendril of hair over her ear. "That was nice," he whispered. "Would you like me to lower the lamp? Or would you prefer I leave it burning?"

"No," she blurted out too quickly. "I think I'd like it to be dark."

He leaned away and lowered the wick in the lamp beside them. The room went black, and Sarah said a silent thank-you to be spared the expression on his face when the truth struck its inevitable blow.

She felt him lift the quilt to climb under, and gathered from his movements that he was removing his trousers. "Lie back, Sarah," she heard, as if from afar. "Come. Get under the covers with me."

Her eyes adjusting, she sat forward while Briggs removed some extra pillows and tossed them to the floor. She reluctantly inched down until her head rested on the pillow. For a moment nothing happened. She had lain on her back and her husband was simply lying there on his side, resting his cheek in his palm, propped up on one elbow.

"What's wrong?" she asked, worrying he could see she was hiding something.

"Nothing. I just wanted to look at you." He gracefully rolled on top of her.

Sarah gasped with sudden dread, but caught her breath when Briggs lingered there, his hands again twirling through her hair splayed out on the pillow. After a few seconds, as if he were allowing her heart time to slow its rapid pace, he lowered his face to hers and kissed her again. Ah, the kiss. She did like the kissing.

Butterflies danced within her as he brushed his lips across her cheek, down her jaw, then nipped at the sensitive skin at her neck. Gooseflesh tingled down her left side. What was all this? Why was he putting off the inevitable?

He pulled gently at the ribbon on her nightdress and unfastened the tiny top buttons. His lips journeyed slowly across her collarbone as she stared through the darkness at the ceiling.

"Try to relax," he whispered, pulling the nightdress down over her shoulders. "You're tense." He looked down at her and she feared he would see into her soul and know everything.

"Would you like me to stop? If you're not ready…"

"No! I mean, I want to be your wife. In name and in body."

He looked at her a moment, then kissed her again, his warm tongue twirling around hers. Emotions skittered through her body, her blood became liquid candy in her hot veins.

He sat back on his heels and removed her nightdress. Then he settled his weight upon her. "Sarah, I'm glad you came. I didn't think I would be, but I am."

For a brief moment, while nothing but his body and his words seemed real, she was glad, too. She nodded in agreement.

Then Briggs shifted, and all at once she could feel the silky tip of him poised where pain had been last time. Sarah instinctively squeezed her legs together.

"Is everything all right?" he asked, pausing to gaze down at her.

She had no answer to give. Her fears had returned

with the reality of what they were about to do. "I'm just nervous, that's all."

He kissed the tip of her nose. "It'll be okay. Just relax."

But how could she?

Slowly, finally, he thrust into her.

All movement stopped.

He was inside her.

Seconds ticked by. She opened her eyes, panic overwhelming her. Did he know? Would he be angry?

Finally he began to move in an easy rhythm and relief coursed through her. She told herself the worst was over and it was all right to relax now, and soon she felt an unfamiliar pleasure. Her muscles loosened and tingled, her skin seemed to melt into his as they made love in the darkness. Oh, it had been nothing like this the first time. It had been nothing like this at all!

Her head began to spin and she shut her eyes and couldn't stop herself from shuddering unexpectedly with an overwhelming sensation throughout her body. Surprised and confused, she felt Briggs tense in her arms. A sound escaped him—a sound that could only mean pleasure as she had just known it. He throbbed within and she knew they had finally completed the marriage act.

He relaxed on top of her, heavier now. Their bodies seemed glued together with heat and perspiration as they lay there in silence.

All of a sudden, Sarah felt awkward. Her arms were around him, her fingers spread on his hot, slick back. He was still inside her. She didn't know what to do, what to say. Then the awkward moment came to a sudden end. Briggs withdrew and rolled off her, leaving her exposed to the chilly bedroom air.

Briggs lay motionless in the dark, listening to his wife's unsteady breathing, feeling her lie so very still beside him. He draped his wrist over his eyes. He had thought...

He didn't know what he had thought. Why must he be so surprised? He knew nothing about this woman in bed beside him. Why should he have expected her to be a virgin? She had never promised such a thing in her letter. He had simply assumed it because she'd said she had attended church regularly and lived with her parents until their death. And the look in her eyes, the nervousness when he'd walked into the room earlier...she had seemed so innocent.

How can a man know what a woman is about? he wondered.

He can't. It was as simple as that. He should never have presumed anything about Sarah. He simply had to accept that he had been second in line. She'd had a lover. Perhaps she'd had more than one.

But why all the trembling? Was it an act? Had she wanted to trick him?

Oh, he didn't want to think that. He sat up and dropped his feet to the cold floor. His fingers squeezed the edge of the mattress as he found himself wondering many things. Where had this woman come from and who had touched her before he had? Why couldn't he have just taken her without expecting to feel something in the process?

Briggs felt a hand on his shoulder and tensed. "What's the matter?" Sarah asked, her voice shaky with a worry he now fully understood. ''Why aren't you sleeping?''

He stared blankly, searching his mind for words, but it was no use. He could think of only one thing. He never should have let down his guard.

Chapter Four

Rolling onto her side and sinking into the center of the soft mattress, Sarah tried to focus on Briggs through inky darkness. He sat on the edge of the bed, his broad back to her, his hair disheveled. Her mind slashed through a brambly thicket of unanswered questions. Had he known? Did it matter to him?

She hugged the quilt to her chest. "Is everything all right?"

"It's fine," he said, his voice frightfully cool.

"Why don't you lie down?"

"No." He rose to his feet, the beauty of his body stunning Sarah to speechlessness in the wake of her terrible anxiety. All she could do was stare in awe at the strong arms, the firmly muscled back, and the sinewy thighs as he picked up his trousers and pulled them on. "I can't sleep."

Sarah leaned up on one elbow, knowing he was lying to her. She remembered how his movements had stilled during their lovemaking. He had recognized her secret, and now he could not even bear to lie next to her.

"Briggs, I—"

"Why don't you get some sleep? You've had a long day."

Something passed between them. He wanted her to see that he knew. His dark expression ordered her not to speak, not to explain anything. He did not want to hear it. Not now. Maybe not ever.

He pulled his shirt over his head. "I'm going for a walk."

Scalding tears threatened, but Sarah blinked them away. Weeping into her pillow would do her no good at this point. She had to be strong if she wanted to fix things.

She lay back down, wondering what would come next. Briggs moved like a shadow across the room and she knew he wanted and needed to be alone. With any luck, she rationalized, his anger would soften after a few hours. Surely when he considered it, he would remember that their courtship consisted of one short letter. If he'd wanted a virgin for a wife, he would have specified that in some discreet way. The only thing he specified was that she be a willing worker, which she was.

Hoping with quiet desperation that Briggs would view the situation from that perspective, Sarah sat up and watched him shrug into his buckskin coat. She noticed with some relief that he was leaving his claw necklace on the chest of drawers. At least he planned to return.

"Are you sure you wouldn't like me to come with you?" she asked, still clinging to a sliver of hope that he was not angry.

"I'm sure. Get some sleep." Without looking back, he walked out of the room and closed the door tightly behind him.

* * *

The next morning, Sarah opened her eyes to bright sunlight spraying through the white lace curtain, painting dappled shadows on the pink patterned quilt. The exhaustion from endless days on the train seemed determined to linger inside her weary bones and muscles. She stretched her arms over her head and pointed her toes, trying to recall what it felt like to be free of misgivings, then realized with a jolt of alarm that her husband's side of the bed was empty.

Sarah bolted upright. Was he so angry he'd left her for good?

Her eyes darted to the chest of drawers. The claw necklace was gone. Tossing the light sheets to the floor, she got out of bed and crossed the room to her valise. She flipped it open and pulled out what was on top—the purple gown she'd worn yesterday. She had to find Briggs and make things right. She wanted—she needed—this marriage to work. Just then, she heard a key slip into the metal lock in the door.

Good Lord. What if Briggs had abandoned her and the hotel manager had come to throw her out? She wasn't dressed yet!

There was no time to pull the dress over her head. She could only hug it fast to her body, hiding all but her bare shoulders.

A knock sounded, but the intruder pushed the door open without waiting for her to request otherwise. Now finding herself staring at the brown fringed coat and long golden hair that could belong only to her husband, Sarah exhaled a long-held breath and barely heard him when he spoke to her.

"Wagon's ready." He stepped all the way into the

room and closed the door behind him before looking up from under the rim of his brown cowboy hat. His icy gaze flicked from her eyes down to her feet, then back up to her eyes again. ''Hurry and dress yourself. I want to get on the road.''

With that, he was out the door again, leaving Sarah frozen in her place, her heart pounding like a hammer while she looked down at herself clutching the silk and lace against her skin, wishing she could go back in time and change what she had done.

Briggs stood by his wagon, one hand on his hip, the other raking through his long thick hair. He watched and listened with annoyance to a pack of dogs across the street, barking and howling at each other. He wished they would quiet down for just one minute so he could think about how he was going to stay married to this stranger he had taken as a wife.

Even now he was hoping he'd been mistaken about what he'd discovered last night. What he needed was an explanation about why she'd put on that gifted performance. If he didn't like what he heard, he would just have to stop caring about it. He'd done it before—stopped caring. He could do it again. He'd never intended any of this to matter in the first place.

Ten irritating minutes passed before he spotted Sarah walking out the front door of the hotel, shading her eyes with her white gloved hand while she perused the street looking for him. For a moment he just stood there, letting her search, until she finally spotted him and seemed to sigh with relief. He noticed she wore the same dress she'd worn yesterday—the lacey purple thing with the oversize bustle, which would no doubt get flattened when she plopped herself down to milk Maddie.

Gathering his resolve, he approached and took her bag. "Here, let me take this." He carried it to the wagon, then helped her into the seat.

"I came right down, thinking you were in a hurry to go," Sarah said, adjusting her skirts around her. Briggs looked into those deceivingly innocent brown eyes and felt an inexplicable stab of regret. Why couldn't things have gone smoothly and without any surprises?

Staring up at her, he noticed her eyes had that sweet twinkle in them again, the same twinkle that had completely charmed him the day before. He hated to think she was looking adorable on purpose, to manipulate him in some way. Surely he was being too suspicious.

"I have to return the key," he said. "Wait here."

He walked back into the hotel and stopped at the front desk, but no one was there. Waiting impatiently, he tapped his boot against the bottom of the counter and turned the cold metal key over in his hand. He stared listlessly at it. Perhaps he should look at the room one more time. Just to know for sure.

Trying not to be too hopeful—that would only lead to disappointment—he climbed the stairs, walked down the hall and slid the key into the lock. When he opened the door, he hesitated, his heart booming as if inside his head. He stared forlornly at the bed, its intimidating pink quilt pulled up and tucked tightly under the pillows. This was foolish, he thought again, but he had to do it.

He walked to the bed, grabbed hold of the blankets,

took a deep breath and ripped them back. A pristine, white bedsheet stared back at him.

The hopes he had tried to keep at bay plummeted before him. What had he expected? To find he had been wrong, and the evidence would be written like a freshly painted sign on the sheet? He'd walked all over Dodge last night wondering if it was possible that he had simply not understood the realities of virginity. After all, he'd never been with one before. Perhaps it was difficult for a man to know whether or not a woman...

Briggs shook his head, feeling the sharp sting of betrayal all over again. It wasn't that she'd done it before that bothered him; her past wasn't really any of his business. It was how she'd pretended to be the nervous virginal bride, and he couldn't help wondering why.

Out on the windy prairie where the grass whispered a thousand continuous secrets, Briggs pulled the wagon to a slow halt. The harness jingled lightly as the horses paused and shook the flies off their backs.

Sarah's insides reeled. Was he stopping to check a wheel or a hoof? she wondered. Or was this sick feeling in her stomach about to prove itself justified?

Briggs removed his hat, ran his hand through his hair, and donned the hat again. Squinting toward the west, he leaned back in his seat. "We need to talk about something."

Sarah felt as if a hand had closed around her throat.

"I think we need to know a bit more about each other," he continued, his tone frightfully thick with accusation.

"What is it you want to know?"

He looked up at the cloudless blue sky and frowned. "I know it ain't proper to talk about stuff like this, but I don't really enjoy brooding about things either—especially if they're just misunderstandings, and right now I can't seem to get something out of my mind."

"What is it?"

He looked directly at her. "I want to know why you looked so nervous last night when...you had me thinking you'd never..." He paused. "Not that it matters. Your past is your business, not mine, but why were you acting so nervous if you'd done it before? Were you trying to trick me?"

The calm, matter-of-fact tone of his voice did little to ease her nerves. "No, I wasn't trying to trick you."

"Then why all the nervous looks when I came to the bed?"

"I was afraid."

"Of what?"

Oh, she didn't want to talk about this. "I was afraid you'd know."

"Why? It wouldn't have mattered as much as being misled," he said, his voice empty of emotion.

"I didn't lie to you. I just didn't tell you. What was I supposed to say?"

He sat in silence a moment, as if contemplating that question. "Nothing. You weren't supposed to say anything. You came here, you married me, and now we're going home."

He made a move to flick the reins, but Sarah's hand came up to catch him, to rest on his soft buckskin sleeve. He lowered the reins and looked at her.

"I'm sorry you're upset," she said. "I never meant to mislead—"

"I'm not upset. Just a little disappointed, that's all."

Sarah withdrew her hand and clutched a white handkerchief in her lap. *Disappointed.* Somehow that was worse.

"Just tell me one thing." He slapped the reins lightly and set them in motion again. "Were there many?"

The question stung and she suspected he'd meant it to. "No, just one."

"One." He considered that a moment, then looked into her eyes. "Did you love him?"

His words came as a surprise. Sarah wanted to smooth things out between them, to set them back on track, and as unlikely as it seemed at this moment, she wanted Briggs to respect her. She swallowed nervously.

"Well?" he asked again. "Did you or didn't you?"

What was the correct answer? To tell her husband she'd loved another man didn't seem right, but to say she didn't…

"Yes," she replied, softly. "I did." In all her innocence, she had loved Garrison. Though now, she wasn't certain what that word truly meant.

Briggs slapped the reins again to hurry the team along the bumpy road. "How long has it been since you've seen him?"

She stared blankly at the horses' long manes, their heads bobbing up and down. "I suppose—" she paused, counting the days "—it must be two weeks now."

"Two weeks!" Briggs pulled the horses to a hard halt, wrapped the reins around the brake, and leaped out of the wagon. He stopped about twenty feet away, his back to her, his hands braced on his hips. He was shaking his head.

Oh, no. He's going to send me back. He's going to leave me in the streets of Dodge City with nothing but my bitter regrets and my traveling bag.

Squeezing her eyes shut, she tried to think positively. It wouldn't be so bad, she told herself. She could find work in a restaurant—she had experience—and start her own life. Alone. This dream of being married and living a simple life on a farm was just that—a dream.

She opened her eyes. Briggs was sitting in the grass, leaning on one arm stretched out behind him. She watched him fiddle with a long blade of grass. He was disappointed in her, to say the least, and his feelings were justified, but to see him like that, sitting alone on the wide-open plains…

She climbed out of the wagon and hopped to the ground, removing her hat pin and setting her hat on the wagon floor. The wind sailed through the rippling grasses, hissing like a snake, blowing loose tendrils of hair into her face. She owed Briggs a choice, a way out of this marriage if he wanted it. She knew why *she'd* been so quick to agree to be a mail order bride—she'd needed to get away from Garrison and start a new life—but maybe Briggs now regretted being so hasty. She would ask him to take her back to Dodge and she would agree to a divorce. How bad could that be? She'd been in worse situations.

When she reached him, she sat down. Staring at the distant horizon where the world met the sky with striking conviction, she waited a moment, steadied her voice, then spoke.

"I'm sorry I didn't tell you." Her heart felt like it was snapping in two. She was about to end her short-lived marriage, and she wanted to cry. "I'd been on my own for four years and—"

Briggs tossed the grass away. "You mean four months."

"I beg your pardon?"

"Four months. Since your folks died."

Sarah drew her eyebrows together. "No, four *years* ago."

Briggs shot her a glare. "You wrote in your letter that it was four months."

"No, I couldn't have. Perhaps my writing was a little—"

"Your writing was fine."

"Are you sure that—"

"I'm positive." His tone was so sharp, she knew he was telling the truth. As she remembered the haste in which she wrote and sent the letter, she began to wonder if she might have made a mistake. A horrible, horrible mistake. Oh, how could she have been so careless?

Then again, maybe it wasn't a mistake, she thought miserably. Maybe she'd known that marrying Briggs was wrong and she had purposefully tried to undermine her own desperate measures. It certainly seemed that way now.

"You've been living on your own in Boston for four years?" he asked.

Sarah nodded, not knowing what else to do.

Briggs plucked another blade of grass. He shoved the end into his mouth and pressed his lips together. His silence was more unnerving than any reprimand. All she could do was sit in the tangled growth and suffer, knowing what he must think of her—that she had purposefully lied about everything.

"What else did you tell me?" he asked. "Oh, yes. That you went to church. And I suppose you're about to tell me the church in your neighborhood burned down and you haven't seen a Sunday worship in what, four years?"

"No," Sarah said. "I do go to church. I wouldn't lie about *that*."

He continued to stare coldly at the distant, rolling hills. "But you'd lie about everything else."

Sarah looked away in frustration. It was futile to argue and it would be futile to trust him with the truth now. He was too angry. If she told him why she had needed to escape Garrison, Briggs might report her to the authorities and she might be blamed for Garrison's crime. Besides that, she *knew* what Garrison would do if he ever found out she'd told someone. He'd made that more than clear. She couldn't put herself or Briggs in that kind of danger.

Briggs brought his knee up and draped his wrist across it. "Do you still love this man?"

The question shook her. *Yes, I loved him two weeks ago, but I don't love him today.* Sarah knew Briggs would never believe that. No one would. But after what happened, it was the absolute truth.

Sarah shut her eyes, facing the wind. "I don't love him. I hope I never see him again."

"And what will you wish for two weeks from today? That you could be on your way again? Will you leave me and leap into another man's bed to drive the one you really love from your heart?"

His words stung her to the core. She deserved this, she knew, but it didn't make it any easier. Rising to her feet, she spoke with surprising confidence. "If you're sorry you brought me here, I'll understand. We can go back to town right now and get a divorce. I won't hold it against you. All I ask is that you find me a place to stay until I figure out where I'm going to go."

She turned to leave, angry at herself for getting into this mess and involving Briggs in it. It had all started when she'd met Garrison. She wished she had listened to her instincts then. Something about him had made her uncomfortable from the start, but his behavior had always been impeccable. Too impeccable. He'd said all the right things and looked the part of a gentleman. Handsome and wealthy, he had wooed her well and ruined her life in the process. Now Briggs thought the worst things about her and he deserved a way out.

She walked back to the wagon, realizing miserably that Briggs had every right to judge her the way he did. But what did it matter now? The marriage was over.

Chapter Five

Sarah marched back to the wagon, her long skirt gathered in her fists, her petticoats swishing through the tall, bristly grass. She could feel the wind at her back, pushing her away from Briggs and forward into this unfamiliar land. The sky seemed like nothing more than a huge suffocating circle all around her.

She reached the wagon and hoisted herself up with surprising swiftness. She bit down on her lip and forced herself not to think about the life she had thought only yesterday that she would be living. She would accept this fate and think positively about it. She was far from Boston. She was safe, and maybe the next town would welcome her in some way.

From the corner of her eye, she saw Briggs approach, but resisted the urge to acknowledge him. She sat with dignity, her backbone as straight as a steel skewer while he climbed into the wagon, making it bounce, squeak and wiggle.

He's going to turn us around and that will be the end of it, she thought with regret. She gripped the side of the wagon in preparation for its sudden lurch, but nothing happened. Briggs held the reins in his large, sun-darkened hands, as if thinking. Sarah waited, waited for him to click his tongue and turn this old wooden box toward town. But still, he said nothing, did nothing.

She'd been brave and strong a moment ago. Where did those feelings go? Now she was uncertain and more than a little intimidated. She could do nothing but wait for his decision.

After another agonizing moment, he slapped the reins and the horses plodded forward. They flicked their ears back and forth while Sarah held on to the wagon seat, waiting for them to shift direction and turn back toward town, but they did not alter their course. The horses lumbered along the straight and narrow road, lightly jingling their harness.

"We had an agreement," Briggs said cooly. "Whatever you did in Boston is your business and I'd rather not know about it. But you assured me you'd be a good worker and that much I hope is true. The rest doesn't concern me. Like I said, we had an agreement and I plan to stick to my end of it."

Surprised and hopeful, she sneaked a glance at Briggs, but was disappointed to find all traces of tenderness gone from his face. The word *agreement* held less allure than her dream of a real marriage, but at the moment it was something, however minuscule, to cling to.

It was late afternoon when they approached a homestead. Sarah saw a barn built of sod and roofed with hay, a noisy chicken coop, a vegetable garden, acres and acres of tall green corn to the west and golden wheat to the east, but no house. *Perhaps it's over the next hill,* she thought, then wondered why anyone would build a house so far from the animals.

The muffled sounds of moos and snorts from inside the barn interrupted the constant roar of wind as they drew closer. Sarah inhaled the scent of fresh manure and animals, and strangely, she found the smells agreeable. She realized she had become accustomed to the city smells of sewage and rotting garbage.

She sat forward in her seat, feeling like her behind had been battered with a washing board. Stiff and sore, she wanted to ask if this was to be her new home, but hesitated when she glanced at the scowling face beside her.

"Darn," he whispered.

Briggs pulled the wagon to a hard stop and hopped down. A wandering hen clucked and flapped its wings, scurrying out of the way.

"What are you doing out here?" he asked a pig. The swine was licking the cuff of a pair of work trousers hanging from a clothesline strung across the yard. "How'd this happen?"

Sarah waited in the wagon while Briggs strode toward the barn door. "Darn dog," he said, barely loud enough for Sarah to hear. He flipped the door latch with his finger, then called out, "Shadow! Come here!"

Sarah felt a nibble of concern as she imagined what he was going to do to this poor animal who had let the pig out of the pen. Just then, a flash of movement whisked past the wagon. It tore across the yard toward Briggs.

He knelt down to meet a golden retriever who bounded into him and nearly knocked him over. The

dog whimpered and licked Briggs's face and hands.
Sarah couldn't suppress a smile.

So this was his land. But where was the house? she
wondered, looking all around. She hopped down from
the wagon and splashed into a fresh, wet pile of manure that soiled the hem of her petticoat.

"Oh," she groaned, lifting her skirt and stepping
back to examine the sole of her boot.

"You gotta watch where you step around here,"
Briggs said. He disappeared into the barn, then returned a moment later towing a white goat. "Go
stretch your legs, Gertrude, but stay away from my
trousers on the line." He let her loose to wander the
yard.

Sarah, still scraping the bottom of her boot on the
hard ground, watched Briggs walk back into the barn.
She heard him apologizing to someone. "Sorry, Maddie. Didn't mean to be gone all night." He stayed in
the barn a while this time, and after a few minutes,
Sarah wondered what she should do. Should she get
her bag and find her own way to the house, or should
she wait for him to escort her? Most definitely, she
did not want to invade his home without his permission.

But she was his wife. It was her home, too.

Feeling an overall uneasiness, Sarah wandered
around the yard while a rhythmic squirting sound re-
verberated from inside the barn. She entered the
fenced pen that was attached to it, then peeked
through the door to see Briggs sitting on a small
wooden stool, milking a cow. He had removed his
coat and had draped it over the side of the stall, and
now sat with his loose white shirt stretched across his
back.

Leaning forward, he squeezed and pulled at the poor thing's feminine underparts while milk squirted out in thin, forceful streams. Sarah stood watching, entranced by the muscles in Briggs's back, tensing and relaxing in unison with the steady sound of milk striking the wooden bucket. She realized with some surprise that she'd never really watched anyone milk a cow before.

All of a sudden, a brown flash came bounding out of the barn and tackled her. Tired and less alert than she ought to have been, she toppled backward into the mud, only then realizing her face, sunburned and stinging from the long drive, was being licked clean with unbridled enthusiasm. The dog snorted, his long, wet tongue making its aggressive way up her nose. "Ugh!" she screamed, trying to cover her face with her white-gloved hands.

"Shadow!" Briggs hollered, emerging from the barn. "Get off her!"

The big dog skulked away with his ears pressed back and his tail between his legs, while the pig watched the entire spectacle with interest.

"Sorry about that," Biggs said, striding through the mud and wrapping his strong hand around Sarah's elbow. "Look what he did." He pulled her swiftly to her feet, but she lost her balance and fell forward on one knee into the mud before he scooped her up again.

Sarah fought to control her temper. She tried to catch her breath, but it seemed no use. All her troubles were catching up with her. She picked at her skirt with shaky, muddy fingers. "My Sunday dress. It's covered with mud." It was the least of her worries, but it seemed the only problem she could talk about.

"It ain't mud," Briggs said matter-of-factly.

"It's not mud," she repeated, refusing to accept what possibilities remained.

"Aw, hell," he said again. "You're gonna have to go down to the creek."

"The creek? Don't you have a tub?"

"A tub?"

Had he never heard the word before?

"Not out here, I'm afraid." He turned away from her, then pointed. "Creek's that way. You'll find soap on the big rock."

Sarah glanced hopelessly in the direction of his outstretched finger, and guessed the water was just over the hill. Struggling to mentally prepare herself to wash out of doors with the animals and insects, she staggered out of the pen alone. At least the dog had followed Briggs back into the barn and was no longer a threat.

She treaded across the yard, and with no shortage of grunts and groans, lifted her valise out of the wagon. She lugged it in the direction she hoped would bring her to water.

When she approached the top of a small hill, she saw the creek in the distance. It was at least a half a mile away. She certainly wasn't about to lug her bag all the way there.

Whispering an oath, she set it down and withdrew a clean skirt and bodice. She left the bag in the grass and hobbled wearily the rest of the way.

After stumbling down the creek bank, she found the soap in a battered tin bowl. How was she going to do this? she wondered, turning to check if anyone could see her. Of course not. There wasn't another soul for miles.

She unlaced her boots and kicked them off, then removed her dress and underclothing, feeling one level beyond nakedness. She was outdoors, stepping into a creek with God-knows-what kind of creatures swimming in it. She forced those thoughts from her muddled brain as she waded in, shivering at the sudden ice-cold shock upon her skin. Gooseflesh covered every part of her body that had a name, so she decided to bite the bullet and plunge in headfirst with a splash.

Her body soon adjusted to the cool temperature, and she began to swim around in circles, feeling uncommonly refreshed, but nevertheless wondering how she was ever going to live here. Surely Briggs would not expect her to crack the ice and bathe here in the winter. There must be some alternative plan.

Treading water and looking in all directions, she realized she had not once imagined it would be like this. She'd honestly believed there would be other farms nearby. She'd thought it would be a small community with charming country houses painted yellow, a church and a school within walking distance. Children playing games together. She'd fantasized about quilting bees and spelling bees and honey bees. There was none of that here or anywhere near here.

Nevertheless—and she was sure some would be surprised by this—she felt lucky and blessed. Maybe there weren't any quilting bees, but there was hope for a new beginning.

Feeling encouraged, she stepped out of the water and reached for the soap, bringing it to a cool lather between her palms. She washed her hair, her face, and her body, then dove into the water and swam beneath the surface to rinse herself clean. When she emerged, she took one look at her dung-covered dress, and groaned.

Briggs carried the bucket of milk around the back of the barn and into the house. When he walked through the door and descended the five steps, he saw, perhaps for the first time, the primitive conditions he'd been living in for the past year. A fly buzzed around his ear, and he swatted it away with his free hand, then set the bucket on the table.

What was Sarah going to say when she walked in here with her white gloves and her fancy purple hat? Briggs took one look at the narrow bed, felt his insides spin, then turned and walked toward the door.

She'd have to accept it, that was all. She didn't have much choice. He'd advertised for a farm wife, not some giddy, vain city girl who didn't know a harness from a grasshopper plow. If she didn't like his way of life, it was her own fault for answering his ad in the first place. Isabelle had been the same way, all desperate to get married no matter what, not thinking for a second about what she was getting herself into. When it finally hit her, off she went first chance she got, with that no-good, smooth-talking, randy gambler who had promised her the fine life.

And Briggs had let her go without a fight.

Not this time, he thought, climbing back up the steps and remembering Sarah out on the prairie in the middle of nowhere, suggesting a divorce. A divorce! First sign of trouble and, just like Isabelle, she wanted out. Well, *out* wouldn't come so easily this time.

Briggs stopped just outside the door. How would Sarah stand up to the challenges that faced her? He rubbed the back of his neck, stiff after the long drive

from town. Would she see his home as a damp, dark
hole in the ground and want to leave? How would he
stop her if she *demanded* he take her back to Dodge
for a divorce?

That was just what he didn't need—another scandal
setting more tongues flapping in the wind. The whole
town would probably think he was cursed.

He was beginning to think that himself.

Sweeping that notion away, he decided it was time
to show Sarah the house. For every moment he stood
stalling, he was wasting daylight hours that should be
spent preparing for the harvest.

He walked to the creek and strolled down the bank,
then spotted her and froze. She stood with her back
to him, fastening the back button on her pale-blue
floral skirt. Her shiny, wet hair flowed down her back
in a torrent of midnight waves, the tips of the dripping
curls grazing her tiny waist. He stood in bewildered
awe of this woman he had brought to this remote,
uncivilized place. She just did not fit. She stood out
like a red rose in a field of snow.

Just then, Sarah turned around. When her gentle
gaze lifted, her eyes narrowed. She folded her arms
in front of her. "You have the most inconvenient
habit of sneaking up on me when I'm half-dressed,
Mr. Brigman."

Briggs shifted his weight from one leg to the other.
"I just came down to remind you there's work to be
done. And you're more than half-dressed, *Mrs. Brigman.* You look fully dressed to me."

Sarah unfolded her arms. "What kind of work?"

"Chores. All day, every day. You didn't expect to
bathe and primp and brush that hair for hours on end
while I do everything around here, did you?"

"Why would you assume I'd want to do that?"

Briggs paused a moment, realizing he was being unreasonable, but knowing it was too late to take it back. All he could do was stand there and stumble over a dozen possible retorts.

Sarah raised her chin. "I did read your advertisement. I know what hard work is about, even though for some reason you think I don't."

Feeling a little guilty for being so hard on her, Briggs closed the distance between them and noticed the smell of lye soap in her hair and on her skin. "When you're done cleaning your dress, I'll show you the house."

"Thank you."

He cringed when he imagined what she would think when she saw it, then he chastised himself for caring, for being ashamed of his home.

Briggs started up the bank, but stopped. "By the way." He turned to point at her clothes. "Those are more practical out here."

She glanced down at her simple calico bodice and skirt.

"If I were you, I'd pack up that purple thing and save it for Sundays."

Sarah gathered her hair in her hands and wrung it out like a wet towel. "Fine. Now if you'll excuse me, I have some laundry to do."

Feeling as if he'd just been dismissed, Briggs resisted the petty urge to have the last word. When he saw Sarah pick up her dress and scrub hard enough to wear a hole in it, he knew she didn't want to hear anything he had to say anyway.

Chapter Six

Gathering her skirt in one hand, her heavy wet gown draped over the other arm, Sarah climbed the steep bank toward the yard. Finally she would see her new home. The place she would whip into shape. As soon as she got to work, Mr. Briggs Brigman wouldn't have one more thing to complain about.

And what a pity for him. Complaining seemed to be his favorite activity.

On her way back, however, she lost some time, unable to find her valise. She hadn't thought to mark the spot. Mentally kicking herself, she wandered in circles until she found an imprint in the grass about the size of her bag. Confused, she glanced toward the homestead and reasoned that Briggs must have picked it up and carried it back. At least, that was what she hoped. Otherwise, she'd have to return for it later, giving him one more excuse to criticize her.

Crossing the yard toward the barn where Briggs was leaning one shoulder against the door frame, his arms folded in front of him, Sarah felt her insides flutter with nervousness. She glanced down to see her valise on the ground at his feet, then resolved not to let this man intimidate her. She was ready to take on her role as prairie wife with all its challenges and hardships. He wasn't going to break her.

"It's about time," Briggs said, stepping out of the shady doorway and picking up her bag. "I thought you were waiting for your dress to dry, too."

Sarah smiled cooly. "Of course I wasn't. Let's not forget it was your rambunctious dog who did this."

Ignoring her, Briggs walked past. "The house is this way."

Sarah turned. That way? There was nothing *that way* but more prairie. Withholding her skepticism, Sarah followed her husband away from the barn.

"It's right here," Briggs said, climbing a knoll. He disappeared over the other side, and when Sarah reached the top, she realized with horror that she was standing on a roof.

This wasn't a house. It was a mound of dirt.

She stood dumbfounded, looking down at her husband.

"It's called a dugout," he explained, "because it's—"

"Because it's dug out of a hill," Sarah finished for him. Gulping back her astonishment, she ambled across the roof and down the side. "Do many people live in dugouts?" She struggled to appear unruffled.

"At first. Until they earn enough to buy timber for a real place. As you can see, there's nothing out here for building material except sod."

"Yes," she replied, gazing across the obstinate ocean of grass. "I see that."

"The door is here." He wrapped his hand around her elbow and hurried her along.

Sarah looked more closely at the outside walls. She

was amazed by the construction and the resourcefulness of a man determined to build a house in a land without wood. They reached the door and had to walk down five steps carved out of dirt. The inside, about four feet below ground level, seemed dark at first until Sarah's eyes adjusted. Coolness swept over her skin as she breathed in the damp scent of earth and grass. Still doing her best to appear calm and composed, she smiled at Briggs, who walked into the one-room house, dropped her valise by the table, and spread his arms wide.

"This is it," he said proudly, but it was a pride Sarah suspected was less than genuine. He expected her disapproval. In fact, he seemed to want it!

"It's very...solid," she commented, determined to prove his infuriating expectations wrong. She tapped her foot three times on the dirt floor.

"The dirt was like putty when I dug the hole. It dried nicely though, don't you think?"

"Oh, yes. Yes, indeed. Very nicely."

They stood in silence a moment while Sarah glanced around at the furniture. A nail keg and soap box stood against the wall, and two mismatched chairs accompanied a weathered plank table. A rude bed with shaved tree trunks as bedposts stood in the corner.

She walked to the table and set her dress down next to the bucket of milk. At least there was an iron stove, she noticed, her gaze following the steel chimney to the ceiling. She scanned the back wall, carved out of the side of the hill, then the front and side walls which were made of chunks of sod, each block laid with the grass side down, staggered like brickwork.

Briggs stepped into her line of vision, as if he had

been watching her reactions, waiting expectantly for the first teardrop to fall. "The constant wind may rattle the window and door," he said, "but not the walls. They're about thirty-six inches thick."

"Thirty-six inches," Sarah repeated. "My, my." She looked up at the roof, wondering if she should worry about it caving in. "What's that made of?"

"A lattice of willow poles. Then there's brush, long grass, a layer of clay from the creek bank, and a final dressing of sod. Strong enough for you to stand on."

"How reassuring," she said, fearing her composure was reaching its last limit.

But she would not let him know.

She turned and looked at the bed. "Is that, uh…?"

"The bed. It's too small, I know. I was planning to build another one before you got here, but things got behind in the haying and I just didn't get the chance."

Sarah swallowed the throbbing lump in her throat, wondering with concern when he intended to find the time, and what they were going to do until then.

"Don't worry. The bedbugs are minimal."

"Bedbugs?" she echoed, feeling her skin prickle all over.

Briggs walked toward the door. "Now that you're settled in, I gotta get to work. You'll find all the food I got in that box over there and in the garden. You can expect me back around dusk." He walked up the dirt steps without looking back, then disappeared into the daylight.

Sarah stood wearily, wondering if he realized his house was a dark dungeon. She felt a sudden tickling at her neck and slapped at it, inspecting her palm for some foreign creature, but finding nothing, assured herself she had imagined the sensation. It was probably just a loose sprig of hair.

Sarah looked around with uncertainty. Briggs had given her no direction as to her duties, but had said there was plenty to do. The obvious chore at the moment was to unpack her bag, then prepare dinner before he returned from the field. That couldn't be too difficult, could it?

She carried her bag to the bed, but when she found nothing that resembled a chest of drawers, she had little choice but to leave everything packed for the time being.

Next, she went to the cupboard—an open wooden box by the stove—and knelt down to see what it contained. She found a sack of cornmeal, a small jar of sorghum molasses and another one of fat, coffee, flour and some salt pork. A bag of potatoes sat next to the box, and beside that was a barrel of salt, half-full.

How had Briggs survived before she'd arrived? No wonder he'd advertised for a wife.

From this moment on, she decided, meals would improve around here. Tonight, he would bite into the best biscuits he'd ever tasted in his life. Sarah would find a way to make that salt pork into something mouthwatering, and her surly, stubborn husband wouldn't be able to deny it.

All she had to do now was light a fire and start working on the biscuits. She went to the stove and pulled open the door. Ashes. She sighed. Wondering when Briggs had last cleaned them out, she looked around for a shovel. Unable to find one, she scooped the residue out with a soup ladle and filled a bucket.

When the stove was empty, she proudly swiped her palms together and looked around for some kindling.

A careful inventory of the so-called kitchen left her with nothing flammable to speak of, so she went outside and searched the yard and the barn. Still nothing. What did he use to light fires? Grass, perhaps? It seemed he used it for everything else, but how could anyone keep a fire going with only grass?

All of a sudden, she didn't feel so clever. The simple task of cooking supper was now a daunting assignment. Her insides reeled with frustration. Briggs was probably crouching out in his field, spying on her and waiting for her to fail, even if it meant coming home hungrier than a lion to a wife in tears, hunched over an empty table.

What was she going to do now? She couldn't face him with a cold slab of salt pork when he came home, but she wasn't about to waste time experimenting with the art of burning grass, either. Heaven forbid her husband should return and discover her doing something wrong. She'd never hear the end of it.

She walked onto the roof, raising a hand to shade her eyes from the sun while she looked all around for Briggs. Strangely, her stomach flipped when she spotted him, far off across the field. At least he wasn't spying on her, she thought with a wee snippet of inopportune humor. He was piercing hay with a pitchfork and tossing it into his wagon. Standing shirtless in the tall grass, he was visible only from the waist up, his golden hair and golden skin blending into the prairie. At that moment, Sarah remembered how wonderfully promising she had thought this land when she'd looked out the train window only yesterday.

It seemed a hundred years ago.

She flopped down onto the grassy roof. Why had Briggs left her so soon without explaining how things were done here? She could feel that irksome lump forming in her throat again, but she would not cry. She'd managed to survive the day so far and she would manage to survive the rest of it. All she had to do was venture out there and ask a few simple questions.

May a thorn prick her pride for making it so difficult.

Hiking along the wagon tracks, carrying a bucket of cold water and a tin cup, Sarah rehearsed her questions. She had to ask them in a way that made her seem confident and comfortable in her new surroundings. In order to truly feel that way, she had to learn a hundred-and-one new ways to be a wife, and fast.

The bucket grew heavier with each labored stride she took into the hot summer wind, until her arm felt like it was being wrenched from its socket. Water sloshed and splashed into the grass but she didn't mind, if it lightened her load a bit. All she had to do was ignore her own thirst and forget the idea of taking a drink herself before she reached her grumpy husband.

Huffing and puffing, she tramped onward with forced confidence until Briggs looked up from his work. An unwelcome tremor of exhilaration pulsed within her as she tried not to stare at his muscular chest with the sun raining down upon him, reflecting off the droplets of perspiration like tiny diamonds. He paused for a brief second or two and watched her, then leaned to the task again, spearing hay with the

pitchfork and tossing it over his shoulder into the
wagon.

"Hello, there," she said shakily, reaching him.

He pitched one last mound of hay, then stopped
and leaned the fork against the wagon. "What are you
doing out here?"

"I brought you something to drink." She set the
bucket in the grass, scooped out a cup of water and
held it out to him.

He glared at it suspiciously, as if he thought it
might contain arsenic. A trickle of sweat made a trail
from his temple along his hairline, and he wiped it
with his forearm before raising the cup to his lips. He
closed his eyes and tipped back his head while Sarah
watched his Adam's apple move as he swallowed.
The skin on his neck shone with perspiration, and she
found herself taking shallow breaths at the awesome
sight of him.

Despite his determination to dislike her, and despite
his wild, ungroomed appearance, she found herself
noticing how ruggedly masculine he was. He was
nothing like Garrison, who enjoyed dressing fashion-
ably and styling his mustache and hair each evening
before going out.

No, Briggs was significantly manly in a style she'd
never encountered before. She'd be surprised if he ran
a comb through that thick hair each day. Yet it fell
naturally onto his shoulders without the slightest dis-
agreement. His trousers were stained with ground-in
dust and dirt, which for some reason did not disgust
her. In fact, it had the opposite effect.

He drank the water then bent forward and filled
another cup. Resting a muscled arm along the side of

the wagon and crossing one ankle over the other, he met her gaze. "Not enough to keep you busy today?"

"There's plenty," she responded, trying to come up with a dignified way to ask how to light a fire.

"I appreciate the drink, but it wasn't necessary."

Sarah wet her parched lips. "I thought you might be thirsty. And why do you have to make me feel irresponsible for trying to do you a favor?"

"I'm not trying to make you feel anything at all, Sarah. If you feel irresponsible, don't blame me." He flicked the cup, tossing the last shimmering diamonds of water into the wind.

"I don't feel irresponsible! I—" She stopped herself, realizing with stunning presence of mind that she was reacting just as he wanted her to. He wanted to frustrate her, to punish her for the secret she'd kept from him last night. Well, she wasn't going to break. She wasn't.

"In all honesty, I would like nothing more than to get to work, but you left me behind with little idea as to how you like things done in your home, so I had to come all the way out here to ask what you use for firewood. Now, whose fault is that?"

A sly, subtle grin crossed his lips. He wiped his forearm across his mouth while Sarah resisted the thrill of staring into eyes that twinkled like emeralds.

He set the cup on the wagon seat behind him. "You don't know much about prairie living, do you?"

Sarah clenched her jaw. "Why do I get the impression you're happy about that?"

"Happy? Me? I'll be happy when I get this hay in. As for your difficulties, I haven't given them much thought."

She found that hard to believe.

He walked to the horses to tug at a harness buckle. "Ask me anything and I'll tell you. I'm not trying to keep any secrets."

Sarah looked down at the bucket at her feet. "I just want to know what you use for firewood."

He came around to stand before her, only inches away. Her gaze fell to his hard, rippled stomach.

"Oh, yes. Firewood. You won't find much of that out here."

Sarah managed to make eye contact. "What do you burn, then?"

"We burn cow chips."

She stared blankly at him, trying to interpret his meaning. "Cow chips? Do you mean…?"

"Yep."

She wondered for a moment if this was a cruel joke, but decided her husband couldn't possibly be that inventive. She could feel her insides beginning to whirl at the thought of collecting this so-called fuel and stoking the stove all day long. "Isn't there anything else you can—"

"Nope."

She swallowed uncomfortably. "Do you have a store of these chips in your barn?"

Briggs shook his head. "No, but you should start one. Take the wheelbarrow and head out that way." He stretched his long arm and pointed. "A herd drove by not long ago. The chips will be scattered everywhere, nice and dry."

Sarah gazed despondently at the horizon.

"Careful not to get lost," Briggs added, bending forward at the waist. He lifted the bucket and dumped the remaining water over his head. It cascaded down his smooth hair and onto his shoulders, then he shook his head like a wet dog and splattered Sarah's dress.

She raised both hands protectively and jumped back. "Do you mind? I've already had my bath today."

"Thought it might cool you off."

With the hot sun burning her face, Sarah stared for a stifling moment at the rivulets of water blazing silver trails down his chest, then she dutifully tore her gaze away and flicked her hand over the front of her bodice. Trying to recapture some of her dignity, she brushed a tendril of hair away from her perspiring forehead. "I'll see you at dusk," she announced curtly, pivoting on her heel and stomping away.

She'd gone at least twenty paces before he called after her. "You forgot your bucket!"

Sarah stopped and squeezed her eyes shut. She'd been so happy with that dramatic exit, too.

Taking a deep, frustrated breath, she considered ignoring him and continuing on her way, but that was the only bucket in the house that wasn't filled with ashes, and she'd likely need it to cook supper. Raising her chin, she turned and marched back with no shortage of theatrics. Sarah scooped up the empty bucket, glared at his insufferable, grinning face, then pivoted on her heels again. Ten more paces, and he called out one more time. "And your cup!"

Sarah stopped. If she returned and met that self-satisfied expression one more time, she would likely swing her bucket by the handle and bat him over the head with it. After considering that option for a second or two and receiving some satisfaction from the image in her mind, she forced herself to forget it. She would persevere. Sarah leaned into the wind and strode forward. Even if she was shriveling with dehydration, she would do without that cup until supper.

Chapter Seven

This is comical, Sarah convinced herself, as she dropped her weary body into a chair, trying to translate her devastated dreams into something worth laughing about.

In the past hour, she had stoked the stove with cow chips, carried the heavy cornmeal sack to the table, added more chips to the fire, washed her hands, measured the flour, added more chips, washed her hands, measured the fat, mixed the biscuit dough, added more chips, washed her hands....

Now, as she wiped perspiration from her brow and waited for the biscuits to cook, she wondered in a panic if she'd washed her hands again before dropping the biscuits onto the pan that last time....

Maybe she'd pass on the biscuits tonight.

Without warning, a dark silhouette appeared in the doorway. Sarah gasped and jumped to her feet. Briggs strode down the stairs, and she wished she'd heard him approach so she could have freshened up. She'd wanted so badly to appear in control, but her hair was a wild mess sticking to the back of her neck, and when she swept two fingers across her cheek, she discovered her face was damp with perspiration.

"You got grease on your nose," Briggs pointed out, reaching the bottom step and removing his hat, then stroking Shadow who had risen to greet him.

Sarah turned away and frantically rubbed both hands over her face. When she faced Briggs again, he was sitting down at the table. Shadow returned to his spot on the floor by the bed.

"Supper will be ready in one minute," she said quickly, opening the squeaky oven door. The smell of golden, cooked biscuits floated out and filled the sod house. Sarah smiled triumphantly, hoping Briggs possessed a keen sense of smell.

She reached into the hot oven and grasped the pan, using her apron to protect her hand, but exclaimed when the heat sneaked through to her fingers. "Ouch!" She dropped the pan with a clatter onto the table, directly in front of Briggs.

He leaned back in the chair, raising the front legs off the floor. She was sucking her stinging fingers. "Do I get a plate, or do you want me to eat out of the pan?"

Sarah pulled her fingers out of her mouth with a *pop,* then balled her hands into fists. The man was enjoying himself too much for her present mood. She turned on her heels, picked up two plates from a shelf by the stove, and set them onto the table. "There, how's that? Would you like some fresh oysters and wine? Perhaps some strawberries and cream? It shouldn't be a problem."

Briggs stared up at her for a long second, then leaned forward and dropped the chair legs onto the dirt floor. "Difficult day was it, Mrs. Brigman?"

''My name is Sarah, and you…'' She clicked her
teeth shut. *Control yourself,* she thought, closing her
eyes to shut him out for a second or two. When she
opened them, she forced a smile as sweet as candy,
then took a deep, calming breath. ''No, it wasn't difficult at all. In fact, I found it quite pleasant. Would
you like a beverage? I was just waiting for the biscuits
to come out of the oven before I skipped down to the
creek to fill a bucket of water.''

A tremor of fatigue shook her as she stared spell-
bound into his lush, green gaze. Whatever emotion
lurked beyond those eyes was a mystery to her, and
she wondered dismally if a day would come when
she would understand her husband's mind.

Briggs leaned forward and rested an arm on the
table. ''The biscuits are out of the oven.''

''I beg your pardon?''

''I said the biscuits are out of the oven. What are
you waiting for? Time to go skipping down to the
creek.''

Sarah took a step back, exasperated, resisting the
desire to fling the hot pan of biscuits into his lap.
Instead, she picked it up using her bunched apron,
and with a measure of poise, scooped the biscuits into
a bowl. ''I'll be right back,'' she said, wishing she'd
had the forethought to carry the water up before she
put the biscuits in the oven. But having to stoke the
stove so often, she didn't dare leave it alone.

Wiping her hands on her skirt, she headed for the
door, adding with a sharp bite, ''Why don't you relax
for a minute? Put your feet up. I'll be right back.''

Fuming, she picked up the bucket of water she'd
used to wash her hands a hundred times that afternoon, climbed the steps, and emerged out of the stuffy

sod house into the evening. The western horizon beyond the cornfield glowed a radiant pink, and a cool
breeze blew by, lifting the hair off the sticky skin at
her neck. The walk to the creek would do her good,
she decided, staring at the magnificent magenta sky
and struggling to appreciate it.

When she returned to the house with a half-full
bucket of water, she slowed when she discovered
Briggs lounging in a chair outside the front door with
his back to her, one foot raised and resting on a barrel,
Shadow sitting beside him. They were both facing the
sunset. Sarah stopped and gently set the bucket in the
grass, realizing he hadn't heard her footsteps beneath
the hissing whisper of the wind across the grass and
wheat.

Odd, she thought, how the first day of this marriage
seemed more like a contest than a relationship. She'd
revealed nothing of herself since they arrived here,
and she considered for a moment that she was as
much to blame as he was for the state of things at
this moment. She was determined to hide her emotions. How long could she continue being this person
who would not give him an inch of what she truly
was?

Staring at his broad shoulders beneath the loose-
fitting white shirt, she remembered his gentle reas-
surances of the previous night, before he had made
love to her and put the finishing touch on their so-
called agreement. It had turned out to be surprisingly
enjoyable. Trying to understand it, she decided that it
must have been his hands. They'd been warm and
gentle and somehow more knowledgeable about certain parts of her body than she was. How did he know

where to touch her to make her feel the way he had made her feel?

It had been nothing like her night with Garrison. Yet it had ended more disastrously.

Pity, that the marriage act could twice ruin her life. She wished there were no such thing!

Her battle instincts somewhat deflated, Sarah picked up the bucket and walked toward her husband. She understood where his hostility was coming from—they'd gotten off to a bad start, to be sure—and she realized she wanted things to be better. She was tired of being angry. It was time to stop perpetuating the friction. Perhaps if she warmed up to him, he would let it go.

When she paused in front of him, he dropped his leg to the ground and squinted up at her. "Did you have a nice *skip* down to the creek?"

Putting it behind them, it seemed, was going to prove a challenge. "Yes, I did, thank you." Her shadow fell across his face, and she waited for his next attempt to rile her, but oddly, he leaned forward and placed his large hand on her hip.

Sarah's blood burst into hot embers, speeding through her veins. What in heaven's name was he doing, and why couldn't she relax about it? They were married, after all.

"You're blocking my view of the sunset." He gently pushed her to the side. The dog whimpered at his feet.

Sarah stood like a fool, her heart racing while she had to remind herself to breathe. She wished she could just live here without reacting so strongly to this man's every move! She simply had to give it more time, she decided. This was only their first day.

Once she got used to things, she'd barely notice his presence.

He crossed his ankle over his knee, then glanced up at her again. "Don't you have something to do?"

Unable to understand how a man could be so attractive in one way and so utterly contemptible in another, Sarah hoped a hearty supper might warm his nature a bit. She turned to go inside, clinging to that hope. "Come in anytime. Food will be on the table waiting for you."

Briggs rubbed Shadow's ears, then stretched his arms over his head, wishing he hadn't sent Sarah all the way to the creek for fresh water when she was obviously exhausted. He sure did overdo it with her today, but he reckoned the things she told him about her lover bothered him more than he realized.

He rose from the chair and pulled it back against the front wall of the house, glanced once more at the scarlet-streaked sky, then retreated with Shadow into the dark little soddie.

"I'll light a lantern," he said, reaching the bottom step, then his gaze fell upon Sarah whose head was resting in her arms on the table, her eyes closed.

Briggs crossed the room to the lamp by the bed and struck a match, breathing in the scent of sulphur as he lowered the flame to the wick. He expected Sarah to wake, startled upon seeing him in the sudden light, but the poor exhausted woman continued to sleep. His stomach roared with a reminder that he had not eaten since breakfast, and his eyes searched the stove for food.

When he looked at the golden biscuits arranged with care on a plate, the table set with an unlit candle in the center and some fresh wildflowers in a cup, a stone of regret weighed heavily in his gut. Sarah was trying hard to make a cheerful adjustment. Why couldn't he?

Briggs moved to the stove and uncovered the pot to find a thick stew simmering with salt pork and potatoes. Just the smell was enough to buckle his knees. Still holding the lid, he turned to check on Sarah, who was still sleeping quietly. He looked around for a couple of tin bowls, served stew for the both of them and set Sarah's down first.

"Sarah," he whispered, gently shaking her shoulder. "Are you hungry?"

She did not respond, so he knelt beside her chair to study her face. Her chin was cradled in her arms, her full lips puckered, her long lashes swept down. She looked innocent. Childlike. The sight of her reminded him of happier days when June, his youngest sister, would fall asleep where she sat, usually in the middle of some game after a valiant battle to stay awake. He closed his eyes, trying to see her again. His heart at first warmed with the memory, then it flooded with sadness and longing. June would have had her fifth birthday this Christmas.

He pushed those thoughts away and looked again at Sarah. When was *her* birthday? he wondered.

She whimpered sweetly, and he found himself wondering what in the world she was dreaming about that she would not awaken at his touch. He wondered if she was dreaming of her lover.

He felt a sudden jolt of irritation.

He rose to his feet and shook Sarah again. "Sarah, wake up. You're dreaming. Wake up."

She stirred, finally, and raised her chin as if in a

daze. "Oh," she murmured. "I must have fallen asleep. It's time for supper."

She made a move to push her chair back, but stopped when Briggs said, "I've already taken it up."

She leaned back, blinking. Then she noticed the bowl in front of her. "Thank you, but I could have gotten it."

He gathered his bowl of stew from the stove and sat across from her. "I know."

Sarah cupped her hands together, pausing before lifting her spoon. Feeling ill at ease, Briggs realized that prayer was something he'd forgotten over the past three months, ever since he'd stopped being thankful.

He cleared his throat. "Would you like to say a few words?"

"I thought you might like to." She stared at him silently until he had no choice but to comply.

Closing his eyes, he thanked the Good Lord for the meal, the sunny day and the roof over their heads. He quickly said "Amen," then opened his eyes to find Sarah still staring at him. "Pass the biscuits," he said gruffly, even though he could easily reach them himself.

She handed the plate across the small table, then jumped as if something bit her. "Water!" She rose from her chair and filled two cups from the pail next to the stove. "I walked all the way to the creek for this and forgot to serve it up." She set the tin cup in front of him and sat down.

"You know," he said, "if you knew how to drive the wagon, you could fill the barrels. I'd help you set them down outside, and the rain would top them up every once in a while. It would save you walking to the creek ten times a day.''

Sarah paused with her spoon in midair. ''That would be very kind of you.''

They dug into their meals, but a second later, Briggs couldn't help adding, ''In fact, maybe I'll do it for you in the morning before I head out to the field.''

Why was he offering to do that? he asked himself. He had work to do and he was behind as it was. The harvester would arrive in only a week.

''Thank you,'' she said quietly, then continued eating her stew.

Chairs squeaked, the lantern hissed, but neither of them spoke a word. Briggs leaned into his plate, savoring each bite, believing this had to be the best meal this little house had ever seen. The only decent meals he'd eaten were over at his neighbor's place. Martha, Howard's wife, could make a meal out of sod if she had to.

When he emptied his bowl, Sarah stood immediately, as if she'd been measuring his progress. ''Can I refill that for you?''

''Please.'' She set another helping of steaming stew in front of him.

He ate his supper quietly, thinking. Maybe one day of anger was enough. Not that he'd forgiven her for lying to him and for being fixed on some other man, but he'd brought her here for a reason and there was work to be done before winter. She had a lot to learn, and in all honesty, he couldn't teach her. How Martha managed to run that household with the few resources available out here had always astounded him.

He swallowed another bite and looked up. ''It

might be a good idea for you to visit the Whitikers tomorrow.''

Sarah's eyebrows lifted. ''The Whitikers? You mean we have neighbors?''

''About a mile past the creek.''

''But I thought we were the only settlers around. I didn't see any homes on the way out here.''

''That's because most of them are living in dugouts. Unless you know where they are, they're easy to miss. The Whitikers live in a sod house, above the ground. You shouldn't have a problem finding them. You might want to talk to Martha about surviving out here.''

He could feel Sarah's steady gaze upon him and suspected she was a little surprised he'd bothered to suggest it, but there was no time for ignorance during harvest season. ''I told her about you. I reckon she's expecting you to come by tomorrow.''

''Tomorrow? That sounds wonderful.'' He could hear the excitement in her voice, even though she had tried to hide it.

''Don't expect me to come with you for a formal introduction, though. I'm too busy. Quite frankly, things out here won't always be as proper as you're used to. Necessity and survival come first. In a bad storm, whole families will share their house with the chickens if it means saving the flock. So be prepared for a different kind of—''

''I get your point,'' she interrupted, shoving her chair back. She began to clear the table and abruptly changed the subject. ''I was thinking that butter might be nice, but I didn't see a churn.''

''There's one in the barn. I'll get it after supper.''

''That would be kind of you. Shall I make coffee?''

"Sure."

Sarah walked toward the door.

"Where are you going?" he asked.

"To get some more…I have to light the fire again. It went out when I fell asleep."

He saw the look of failure in her eyes and realized how desperately she wanted everything to be perfect. "You know," he said, rising and moving toward her. "I didn't really want coffee. It's usually a morning beverage for me. Keeps me up at night, otherwise. I was just being polite."

They stood face-to-face, perhaps a little too close, staring curiously at one another. "I see."

At that moment, Briggs realized with some discomfort they were about to spend their first night together. In their home. Alone.

He glanced at the narrow bed, imagining how crowded it would be. Their bodies would be pressed together all night long, whether or not he wanted it that way. And despite her pretty face, despite her alluring figure, the thought of touching her made something inside him squirm. How could he lay his hands on a woman who was probably dreaming about someone else? How could he make love to her, knowing another man had possessed her heart—and her body—only weeks before?

Briggs felt his cheeks flush with fiery irritation. None of this should matter to him, he knew, but he could not fight the irrational urge to find this man, wherever he was, and show him what the muddy ground looked like up close. What had he been up to, robbing a woman of her innocence, then leaving her so desperate she had to answer an ad to become another man's wife?

Angry at himself for becoming so troubled by this—he did not even know what truly happened between Sarah and this man—Briggs needed to leave the house.

''I'll go get that butter churn.'' He breezed by Sarah and made a dash for the door.

As he walked across the yard feeling the coolness of evening touch his skin, he thought of her, only seconds ago, standing uncomfortably at the bottom of the steps, dreading the necessity of lighting another fire, but doing her best to hide it. If he had wanted coffee, he reckoned she would have prepared it with a smile, and something about that made him wish she could be a little less conscientious. At least then, it would be easier to tell her that he intended to sleep in the barn tonight.

Chapter Eight

The next morning when Sarah woke, it seemed as if the sun had taken a holiday. The tiny house was as black as a preacher's Sunday cloak. She sat up and looked around, relieved to see some sign of the world—a narrow ribbon of light sneaking in through a clean patch on the dust-covered window and illuminating a single sod in the far corner just above the toppling mound of cow chips.

What time was it? she wondered sleepily, stretching her arms over her head. She glanced over the one-room house, wishing there was a clock ticking somewhere. Anything to disturb the perpetual silence.

Sluggishly, she tossed the blanket aside, swung her legs off the edge of the bed, and laid her bare feet on the cold dirt floor. She yawned and touched the pearls around her neck, wondering why in the world she was still wearing them, and to bed, no less. As she considered it further, she knew she wore them because they were a piece of her old life. The life before Garrison.

Forcing that unpleasantness from her mind, she reached for her gold timepiece. Holding it up to the dim light and focusing on the fine black hands against the white background, she felt her insides twist like a corkscrew. Ten o'clock!

She leaped to her feet and ripped off her nightgown, then quickly donned the same dress she'd worn yesterday. While she hurriedly laced her boots, she prayed that Briggs had not come in here expecting breakfast before tending to his crops. Surely he would have awakened her. Oh, heaven forbid he should find out how late she had slept!

She splashed some cold water onto her face and pinched her cheeks. She reached for a biscuit, took it with her and ran up the stairs into the daylight. The sun was shining, the sky was blue, and the wheat field was flapping and hissing beneath the incessant breeze. Briggs was nowhere to be seen, so she started off for the Whitikers' place, thinking a visit there would be a good excuse to explain her lack of productivity that morning.

As soon as she rounded the corner of the house, she stopped, noticing two barrels standing at attention, both filled to the brim with fresh water. ''Oh, dear,'' she said aloud, fully aware she was talking to herself. He *had* been there.

There was still a chance he had not gone into the house, she told herself, trying to be optimistic. Surely, he would have awakened her.

When she passed the barrels, she found herself feeling a flicker of encouragement. It was kind of him to haul the water for her even though he had his own work to do in the field. Perhaps there was a chance for civility, if nothing more. It had been clear to her last night, when he'd announced he would sleep in the barn, that he couldn't endure the idea of touching her.

Well, maybe that wasn't such a bad thing, she thought, picking her way through the barnyard and past the snorting pig in the pen. Touching her would only remind him of the thing that had scarred their marriage on the very first day.

A few minutes later, Sarah reached the creek. Looking in both directions and knowing enough not to expect a bridge anywhere close by, she decided there was no other option but to wade across. She removed her boots and hoisted her skirts up to her waist, then waded through the cool, resistant water, carrying her boots in one hand over her head. She climbed the creek bank on the other side, and while she sat in the grass retying her boots, she saw chimney smoke against the blue sky in the distance. With her drawers wet and sticking to her legs beneath her skirts, she started off in that direction, soon discovering that the mile Briggs had described was an understatement. By the time she walked into the Whitikers' yard, Sarah was certain she'd walked three or four miles at least.

Looking around, she found the Whitikers' homestead far more established than her own. A large vegetable garden grew just beyond the wood fence—a wood fence!—and the sturdy sod house stood square and straight, topped with a plank roof. Ah, what a luxury, she thought, recalling how she'd had to keep the stew covered last night while it was cooking, just to prevent dirt from dropping into the pot.

Warm and perspiring from the long walk in the sun, Sarah approached the front door. She noticed with interest a birdcage hanging by the front window, the songbird making cheerful music. Below the window, potted flowers turned their pink and purple faces to the sky and seemed to giggle in the wind. Sarah wished she'd had the forethought to bring along some of her biscuits. Too late now, she said to herself, as she raised her fist to knock.

Almost immediately, a plump, brown-haired woman opened the door. Her face beamed with a smile. "Why, hello there! You must be Sarah. Come in, come in."

Right away, Sarah felt more welcome and thankful than she could ever have expected. She hadn't realized how the idea of being isolated had gnawed at her since she and Briggs had left Dodge City. "How do you do?" she greeted.

"I'm Martha Whitiker." The woman ushered Sarah into the kitchen. "I've been waiting every day for you to come. Ever since Briggy placed that ad."

Briggy? "You knew, then?"

"Oh, yes. He's like a brother to both Howard and me. In fact, it was our idea. Though I don't know how we'll get along without his company so often. But as Howard says, we're not losing a friend, we're gaining one, and poor Briggy was in desperate need of your arrival."

Overwhelmed by this news she found hard to believe, Sarah accepted the chair Martha offered and sat at the table, admiring the bright red-checkered tablecloth.

"Would you like a cup of coffee?" Martha asked.

"I wouldn't want to trouble you."

"Not at all! I slipped the bread into the oven only five minutes ago and I started a pot then."

How easy Martha made it seem. Sarah watched her

fill two china cups full of rich-smelling coffee. Compared to Sarah's new home, this place was decidedly lavish.

Just then, the door flew open and a little girl blew into the house, her blond curls frazzled and windstrewn. "Mama!" she shouted, overflowing with excitement. "Papa caught a prairie chicken! It walked right past him and he threw the hammer at it, struck it stiff!"

Martha scooped the child into her arms. "That's wonderful. What a feast we'll have tonight." She set the girl down but held her hand. "Mollie, this is our new neighbor, Sarah Brigman." The little girl shyly stepped forward.

Sarah leaned down to greet the child at eye level. "Hello, Mollie. What a pretty dress you have on."

"Mama made it. She made my other one, too."

"You're a very lucky girl. How old are you?"

Mollie held up three fingers, then buried her face in her mother's skirt.

"She's pretending to be bashful today," Martha whispered. "We don't get many visitors."

Sarah smiled warmly, then heard footsteps tapping over the ground outside. Mollie suddenly forgot her shyness and darted to the door. "Look! Frank's got the chicken!"

Sarah swiveled in her chair to see a young boy step into the doorway. Blond like Mollie, he stood barefoot, proudly displaying a dead chicken he held upside down by its spindly legs. He couldn't have been more than nine or ten years old. "You got some pluckin' to do, Ma."

Martha smiled, her hands resting on her wide hips.

"I can see that. Come in and meet our new neighbor, Mrs. Brigman."

He lowered the lifeless chicken to his side, wiped one hand on his trousers and held it out. "Pleased to meet you, Mrs. Brigman. I'm Frank." Sarah shook his proffered hand. "Will you tell Briggs *I* saw the chicken first?"

Sarah looked up at Martha, questioningly.

Martha said, "Frank thinks very highly of Briggs."

"He's going to let me help him dig his well."

"A well?" Sarah repeated, hoping she'd heard him correctly.

"Yes, ma'am. I was too little to help Pa when he dug ours. And Briggs said I oughta know how to do it if I'm gonna be a farmer like him someday."

Martha stepped forward and ushered the children toward the door. "All right, all right. Back to your chores. Thank you for bringing the chicken."

Frank dropped the dead hen with a *plop* onto the table in front of Sarah, who quickly leaned back in her chair. The feathers shivered, then went still. Frank and Mollie bolted out the door.

Martha picked the bird up by its claws and plopped it on the counter, much to Sarah's relief. "Our children..." she remarked, smiling. "I don't know how we'd get along without them. It would be dreadfully quiet around here." She sat across from Sarah and sipped her coffee. "So, how are you making out?"

Sarah raised her cup to her lips, considering that question. A part of her wanted nothing more than to spill all her woes onto the table in front of this woman, but wasn't it enough that Briggs thought she couldn't manage out here? She didn't want Martha to agree with him. "Well, I..."

Martha began nodding before Sarah could finish. "I felt the same way when I first came. In fact, I burst into tears the moment Howard stopped the wagon in front of the dugout."

Sarah raised her eyebrows. "You lived in a dugout, too?"

"Oh, yes. What a time that was. I thought I'd go out of my mind. I was used to life in town with the mercantile down the street. You can't imagine how I suffered that first year."

Sarah glanced with hope around the tidy, well-stocked kitchen. "It seems like you have everything you need now."

"Yes, we put a lot into this place. Most of the big improvements came when Briggs arrived, though."

Sarah set down her cup, suddenly more curious than she cared to admit. "Really? How's that?"

"He was all alone. Life out here isn't easy for a loner. In fact, it's darn near impossible. He traded work for a meal or a loaf of bread and came by often. That's why he was so desperate for a wife. He'd get behind in his own work, coming here to help us. He didn't have time to do what a woman would have done for him. Make no mistake about it, you'll work just as hard as he does. But you'll make a good life, I know you will."

Sarah felt her optimism returning. It wasn't like her to give up, yet last night, when her husband had walked out the door, she'd come close. "It just seems like there's so much to learn. I thought I was all alone until Briggs suggested I come here and talk to you."

"I told him to send you over the moment you arrived. I said, 'Don't let her lift a finger before she talks to me.'"

"Well, he did let me lift a finger. In fact, he enjoyed watching me agonize over every little thing from lighting the fire to hauling water from the creek."

Martha reached across the table and touched Sarah's hand. "Don't be too hard on him. He's had a rough time of it."

She drew her eyebrows together in confusion.

"You don't know?" Martha asked, sitting back. "Perhaps I shouldn't have said anything."

"Please, tell me," Sarah implored, wishing she had known more about her husband before their wedding night. She might have handled things differently.

"It really isn't my place to say."

"Martha, please, it might help if I knew. Otherwise, this marriage is going to last about as long as a snowman in July."

Sarah watched her neighbor shift uncomfortably in her chair. "We can't have that, now. Briggs couldn't handle another heartbreak like the first one."

Sarah tensed. "Heartbreak?"

"Worst thing I've ever seen."

Astonished, Sarah couldn't imagine Briggs feeling so deeply for anyone, much less admitting to it.

"Oh, dear," Martha remarked. "I knew I shouldn't have said anything. Howard told me not to."

"Of course you should have. I need to know. It will help me understand what's going on. What happened? Who was she?"

"It was a terrible thing." Martha stood and refilled Sarah's cup with more hot coffee. "Briggs came here last year from Nebraska after his family died—"

"His family died?" Why hadn't he said anything?

"Consumption. Every last one of them except for

George, who had moved to Dodge to open his law office the year before. Briggs lost his parents, his younger brother, his three young sisters. After all that, he just couldn't stay there. He wanted to start fresh somewhere else. So he sold everything and came to Dodge to be near George and buy some land. Then he met Isabelle in town. Her father is the reverend. Very friendly fellow.''

''Isabelle...''

Martha nodded. ''Yes, she's the one.''

The one. So, Briggs wasn't so innocent himself.

''But Isabelle wasn't exactly suited to the plains,'' Martha went on. ''She was a beauty though, and that made Briggs a little foolish in the head, I think. He spent most of his savings on an engagement gift—a necklace. I suppose he wanted to make sure she didn't change her mind.''

Martha paused. ''So Briggs built his little dugout and brought her out to see it, promising he'd build her a real house the following year. She took one look at that place and said she'd have to rethink their engagement. Not a week later, she ran off with another man—a rich one. It was the betrayal that broke Briggy's heart. He said nothing was more important than trust, and that he'd never fall for a beautiful woman again because other men would always be trying to woo her away.''

Martha seemed to jolt back to the present, then squirmed in her chair as she looked into Sarah's eyes. Sarah had the distinct feeling Martha suddenly wanted to eat her words. ''I'm sure he's over that now, though,'' she added.

But when Sarah remembered the expression on Briggs's face when he first saw her, she doubted it.

She understood now that he had wanted someone plain. "How long ago did this happen?"

"It's been about three months."

Sarah stood and crossed to the window, wishing she had known about this sooner. Because of what happened to Briggs, keeping quiet about her past was a worse mistake than confessing would have been.

"Are you all right, my dear? Was I wrong to tell you?"

Sarah faced her neighbor. "No, you were right. I think I understand now, why he's been so cold."

"I hope I haven't interfered. But you should know that it's nothing *you've* done. He'll warm up soon, I know he will."

Sarah looked out the window. *Nothing I've done.* If only it could be so.

When Sarah turned around again, Martha was folding the tablecloth. She set it on a shelf and carried the chicken to the table. "You don't mind if I pluck while we talk, do you? If I can get this into the oven as soon as the bread comes out, I'll be able to send you home with some fresh cooked meat for that hungry man of yours. That'll help him forget about Isabelle."

Sarah smiled, thinking Martha was going to be a good friend.

"Now, sit down," she said, "and I'll tell you everything there is to know about being a prairie wife. Briggs will think he's struck gold when he sees how useful you'll be to him."

Sarah had to admit she wanted nothing more.

Chapter Nine

Briggs watched the pink sun sink into the horizon as he unhitched the team in the barnyard. He glanced at his little house, saw smoke rising from the narrow chimney poking out of the grass roof, and felt a confusing wave of emotions wash over him. Part of him saw that smoke as a dream come true. What he'd always wanted had finally become a reality. He had a companion now, a partner, the beginnings of a family.

A family.

Something inside him shook. It hadn't occurred to him before, but what if Sarah had been desperate to get married because she was already with child?

He dropped the leather harness strap he'd been holding and rubbed a hand over Gem's warm muzzle. There was so much about Sarah that he did not know. Was this why she had been so quick to answer his ad?

That was probably not the case, he told himself, taking his time unhitching the team and getting the horses into the barn. He was simply overreacting to everything he'd learned about her yesterday.

A few minutes later, he closed the barn door and secured the latch. He sauntered across the yard toward the door, his heartbeat quickening with every slow step. Why was he feeling this way? It didn't matter if Sarah loved someone else, he told himself. She'd get over this man in time, and if she was expecting, that was okay, too, just as long as she stayed. Part of the reason he wanted a wife was to have children. It just might be sooner than he'd expected, that's all. But another man's child? How would he feel about that?

He reached the house and went inside. A delicious aroma hit him like a prairie wind. It was hard to believe a simple scent could soothe his concerns and make him feel so calm, considering what he'd just been thinking about.

How long had it been since he'd smelled anything like that? What was it? Cookies? A cake?

He walked down the steps to find the house warm and flickering with golden light from the kerosene lamp. He petted Shadow who had come to greet him.

Something was different. Everything was different. A red blanket had been fashioned as a wall, hung from the ceiling and dividing the sleep area from the eating area. The table was covered by a white cloth, but as he looked closer, he realized it was an old flour sack cut to fit. Again, fresh wildflowers stood in a cup in the center.

He removed his coat and turned to hang it on the hook by the door, but noticed a yellow calico sun bonnet hanging there. Where had she found that? The only thing he'd seen her wear on her head was that ridiculous purple thing.

Just then, the blanket shuddered and Sarah stepped

out from behind it. He found himself staring at her. Wondering…

"You're back," she said, her tone cheerful. "How was your day?"

Even if the cheeriness was an act, it was welcoming, just the same. "Fine. I'm catching up." He glanced around again. "You've been busy."

Sarah crossed to the stove and Shadow settled down next to her feet. "I went to the Whitikers' place today."

"I figured as much. You weren't here when I came back midday."

She whirled around. "You came back?"

"A man's gotta eat."

Her face grew pale. "I'm sorry…I should have prepared something for you before I left."

Briggs wondered why she was so apologetic all of a sudden, like she thought he was going to blow a gasket. "Forget it. I've been getting by on my own for the past year. What's one more day?"

She stared at him for a moment, squeezing the fabric of her skirt, then seemed relieved and turned back to the stove.

"What smells so good?" Briggs asked, all too aware of her tiny waist and curvy backside. She certainly didn't look like she was in the family way, though it may be too soon to tell, he knew.

"I baked a cake. I collected the eggs today and Martha gave me a little sugar. She said it was a welcoming gift. She also gave me a bonnet and that blanket over there."

"That was mighty neighborly."

"She's a lovely person."

Sarah flitted around the stove a little longer while

Briggs sat back in his chair and watched her. Her graceful movements, mixed with the velvety texture of her voice as she hummed a sweet melody, were enchanting. Almost enough to make him forget the things he'd been thinking. She lifted the pot's lid with a towel wrapped in one hand and tipped her face over the rising steam to take a whiff.

A few minutes later, she turned around with a steaming plate of food and set it down in front of him. Briggs found himself wondering where his thoughts had been the past few seconds—in some other heavenly world, he guessed, a place where nothing but the present mattered.

"Is this chicken?" he asked, unable to mask his surprise. She hadn't gone out and shot herself a bird, too, had she?

"Yes. Courtesy of the Whitikers."

His new wife must have made quite an impression on them, he thought, his mouth watering.

When Sarah finally sat down, they said a quick prayer, then began the meal. They ate in silence, partly because Briggs didn't know what to say and partly because he was too hungry to talk between mouthfuls.

When they finished eating, Sarah began to clear the table. "I learned a lot today. I think I'm going to manage just fine when I settle in and start a routine."

She planned on staying....

"I'm going to try my hand at making soap before winter," she continued. "I've started saving ashes from the stove. Martha said we can do it together after the pigs are slaughtered."

Briggs stared at the back of her slender, pale neck as she rinsed the plates in a bucket. She actually seemed to be enjoying herself. "Watch your eyes around the lye when you make that soap," he told her. "The fumes can sting."

"I'll be careful."

She bent forward to open the stove. Her behind jutted out close enough for him to lay his hand on—if he was so inclined—but he fought the urge and concentrated on the wonderful smell of baked cake.

Sarah removed it from the oven and set it on an upturned barrel. "That should cool a few minutes before I cut you a slice. Can you wait?"

"Sure."

"Are you certain you don't want some coffee?" she asked, pouring herself a steaming cup.

The pleasant aroma floated to his nostrils and he found himself liking the idea of sitting at the table after dinner sipping coffee with his wife, who suddenly seemed comfortable and confident in her surroundings. A wife who was making plans for the future, even if they were just plans about soap.

Would it really matter if a cup of coffee kept him up late? "Maybe I will have some," he answered. She set a cup in front of him. "You ever milk a cow before?"

Sarah cleared her throat. "No. But Martha explained—"

"Did she show you?"

"Not exactly." Sarah rose and touched the cake with her finger. She sliced a few pieces and set them down on the table. "I suppose you want to teach me."

"You won't learn if I don't, and you're gonna have to do it sooner or later."

"I'm ready to learn as soon as you find the time to show me."

"I'll wake you in the morning and show you how it's done. At least that way you'll be up at a decent hour."

Sarah choked on her coffee. Her cheeks blushed like a couple of ripe tomatoes, and for the first time since he'd met her, Briggs laughed.

For a moment, Sarah looked mortified, her eyes wide, her eyebrows perking up toward the ceiling. Then, as if she couldn't fight it any longer, she burst into an infectious, cheek-splitting grin. "All right, so I slept late this morning. It won't happen again."

Briggs nodded, smiling at her, wondering how it was possible that simple laughter could sweep so much joy through a room.

Briggs rolled over in his bed of hay, scratching at his chest and arms and wondering in the darkness what time it was. Slowly, groggily, he sat up, unable to sleep with Maddie stomping in her stall next to him. She seemed restless. Must be morning.

He stood and stretched, tossed the blanket over the side of the stall, then picked some hay out of his hair and brushed some more off his shoulders. Was his wife up yet? he wondered. He remembered his promise to teach her how to milk Maddie and supposed he should go into the house and wake her.

Faint traces of light brightened the sky as he crossed the yard and entered the dark house. He moved directly to the lantern to light it, but for some reason he winced when he struck the match. He was trying to be quiet, which made no sense considering he'd come here to wake Sarah. The silence of the dawn and the peaceful little house seemed too special to disturb.

When the room brightened, Briggs turned his gaze toward the red blanket hung as a curtain. He could hear Sarah's steady breathing behind it. Slowly, lightly, he made his way toward the curtain, remembering her sweet smile at the dinner table the night before. All night long, it had stuck in his mind like honey, and now, here he was, confused by the thrill of anticipation sneaking up his spine. Waking her seemed such an intimate thing to do. He found himself simply wanting to watch her slumber for a while.

Fighting that notion, he steeled himself and pushed the curtain aside.

There she was, lying on her side with the covers pulled up to her ear. He paused for a moment to admire what he could see: her coal-black hair, her eyelids and long lashes, the curves of her hips and the trail of her legs beneath the blanket. As he watched her sleep, his body awakened in the most surprising way. He wanted to forget about the chores and crawl under the covers with her, wrap his arms around her and feel her warmth against his bare skin.

Letting that thought rest only briefly in his mind, he leaned forward to lay his hand on her shoulder to wake her, before his body convinced him to do what his heart was not ready for.

Still in a dreamy state, Sarah began to awaken in time with the gentle swaying of her body. A hand was resting on her shoulder. She sighed, then gazed sleepily into a pair of green eyes. As she recovered consciousness, she realized it was her husband kneeling in front of her, waiting for her to say something.

"Is it morning already?" she asked, her voice breathy.

"Yes. Maddie's waiting."

"Maddie," she repeated, trying to make sense of the word while she sat up. Her blanket fell away to reveal the top of her nightdress, which was unbuttoned at the neck, and she noticed Briggs avert his gaze.

Her heart lurched and she wondered if he'd ever forgive her enough to look at her again—to see her as a woman, to desire her. She had hoped it would not matter, but strangely, this morning, it mattered more than she cared to admit.

"I'll wait for you in the barn," he said, rising to go.

"What about breakfast?"

"After we get the milk and collect the eggs."

Sarah listened to his boots tap up the steps, then lowered her bare feet to the cold floor. She tried to cling to a hope that one day, things would be different. They would have to be, if he ever wanted children, assuming, of course, she wasn't already with child. But Garrison had told her there was only a short time each month when a woman could conceive, and he'd assured her it didn't happen as easily as most women thought.

If there was any truth to that, she may never find herself in the family way. Not with a husband who insisted on sleeping in the barn.

She dressed quickly, pulled her shawl around her shoulders, and hurried outside. Cool air struck her cheeks as she crossed the yard, her footsteps light over the dewy ground. She stepped through the barn door to the now familiar smells of horse and hay. By the light of a lantern, Briggs was shoveling dung out from under Maddie, dropping it into a wheelbarrow. The fringe on his leather coat swung back and forth with each toss. Sarah stood in the doorway, pulling her shawl tighter around her shoulders, waiting for some instruction.

"You might want to shovel out some of the mess before you start each morning," he told her. "You can add it to your fuel store." He pushed the wheelbarrow past her. "I see you started one outside."

A few moments later, he returned and pulled a small stool up beside the cow. He reached for a bucket and set it down with a *clunk*. Sarah, still standing by the door and feeling rather daft, swallowed when he leaned out of the stall and looked at her, his golden hair falling forward onto his face. "Coming?"

She nodded, then moved toward him. "Where do you want me?"

He placed his large hand at the small of her back, guiding her to the stool. "Have a seat right there. Maddie, be still."

Sarah sat down, now at eye level with the cow's broad side.

Briggs knelt down beside her. "You're going to have to spread your knees apart to lean forward."

Sarah tried to suppress her blush as she slowly spread her legs. "All right."

"Now grab hold of her teats and squeeze."

Sarah reached forward, but as soon as her fingers wrapped around the warm teats, Maddie took an anxious step sideways and knocked Sarah off the stool and onto her behind. Her head hit the wall and immediately began to throb.

"Maddie!" Briggs called out. "Be still!" He set

the stool on its legs again. "You okay?" he asked, as he helped Sarah up. She nodded, trying to hide her shakiness, trying not to melt into the warmth of his strong hand. "She knows you're a stranger. She'll be better this time. Try again."

Sarah nervously reached forward, steadying herself for another fall, her heart thumping away inside her chest. Why did she have to do this? Couldn't Briggs continue with it? Obviously, Maddie preferred him. But when she wrapped her hands around the warm teats, she discovered Briggs was right. Maddie stood still long enough for her to get a tight grip.

"That's it. Now squeeze the milk out."

Sarah squeezed with all the strength she possessed, but nothing happened. She'd never felt so incompetent in all her life.

"Keep trying," Briggs told her. "You have to get the feel of it."

Sarah squeezed and squeezed until her knuckles turned white, but still, no milk. "It's not working. What's wrong?"

Briggs stared down at Maddie's full udder. "She won't let the milk down. Stand up. Let me try."

Sarah moved aside and Briggs sat down. He wrapped his hands around Maddie's teats and without any effort at all, he drew milk into the pail like a song. "You have to pull and squeeze at the same time," he said. "See?"

And Sarah did see. She saw a pair of sun-bronzed hands, capable and strong, yet gentle at the same time, massaging the milk out of Maddie. Coaxing it with a natural rhythm. She wondered ridiculously if Maddie was enjoying herself. When Sarah remembered how

Briggs had caressed her on their wedding night, she wasn't surprised Maddie kicked her aside.

"Now, you try," he suggested.

Sarah squatted down on the stool again, this time trying to imitate her husband's style. Nothing happened at first. Then a drip fell. "There! It's working!" It wasn't long before Sarah, too, was coaxing the milk into the bucket in steady, forceful streams. She was doing it!

"Good job," Briggs said.

She looked up to find him smiling. That smile was so rare, it was paralyzing. It made her skin tingle and her bones turn to jelly.

The milk stopped coming and the barn went quiet. Sarah tried clumsily to fix her grip, wishing she could understand these feelings that kept rising within her. She was so desperate to please a man who clearly did not want her to please him. If only she hadn't made such a critical mistake on their wedding day. If only they could go back to those moments just before he'd discovered her secret—when he was touching her and wanting her.

Sarah dropped her hands onto her lap. Looking up at Briggs, she pleaded with her eyes for some return of affection. He stared down at her briefly, then looked away as if he had something else to do directly.

Feeling rejected, Sarah looked at the floor. She knew he had seen the emotion in her eyes, felt her desperation, but for his own reasons, he had chosen to ignore it.

He gave Maddie a pat on the back. "It shouldn't take you much longer. Just keep going till there's no more milk." Then Briggs quickly turned away from her and walked out of the barn.

Chapter Ten

Two days later, Sarah was leaning over the butter churn, pumping vigorously and massaging her sore back, when she heard the wagon jingle and creak into the yard. She quickly abandoned her work to prepare the fried salt pork with gravy, corn bread and coffee, Briggs's usual midday meal.

She was slicing the bread when his shadow filled the open door. "How was your morning?" she asked, realizing she asked the same question every time he entered the house for dinner.

He always gave the same answer. "Fine."

When he reached the bottom step and went for the coffeepot, Sarah noticed a tear in his sleeve. "What happened to your shirt?" She served up his plate of food and set it on the table.

He tipped the coffeepot over a cup. "Gem tried to nip me."

She walked toward him to examine the rip. "The horse did this?"

"Yes, but I deserved it. I nearly knocked her tooth out setting the bridle in place. Clumsy, I guess."

The torn fabric hung down to reveal his bare, muscled arm. Sarah folded the sleeve back in place to see if it was a clean rip. "I can fix this while you eat. Why don't you take it off?"

He paused with the coffeepot still in one hand, the battered tin cup in the other. Their gazes met and locked, and Sarah was suddenly aware that she still held the torn fabric in place to cover his skin.

"It can wait till tonight," Briggs said.

Sarah steeled herself, fighting the oncoming blush. "But what if you hook it on something? I'll have twice as much sewing to do. Take it off and I'll be done before you finish your dinner."

He hesitated, then set down his cup and turned away from her. The muscles in his back tensed and relaxed as his arms came back to shrug out of the sleeves. Sarah stood behind him as the shirt fell into her waiting hands. It still held heat from his body and moisture from his hard work. She had to fight the urge to raise it to her face and smell the outdoors mixed with his male scent.

"I'll be quick," she assured him, turning to find her needle and thread. Her hands trembled as she dug through her belongings, all too aware of his shirtless presence at the table. When she finally found what she was looking for, she headed for the door without looking up.

"Where are you going?" he asked, his mouth full.

She stopped on the bottom step. "It's too dark in here. I need better light to thread the needle. I won't be long."

She hurried up the stairs with the shirt draped over her arm. Why did he have the power to reduce her to this? She was melting like butter at the sight of him.

With a huff, she flopped into the chair outside and began to stitch the seam.

When she was nearly finished, she heard his boots tapping slowly up the steps. She quickened her stitching, wanting to be done before he reached her, and in the panic, pricked her middle finger. "Ouch!"

She immediately slipped it into her mouth but only for a second, then returned all her attention to the task of mending his shirt. Before she could complete it, his shadow fell across her lap.

"Stick yourself?" he asked.

Sarah nodded.

"Don't hurry. I'm not ready to face the haying just yet. I think I ate too much." He moved past her and sat down in the grass.

All was silent as she stitched his shirt at record speed, refusing to look up for even the space of a heartbeat. Yet she knew exactly where—and how—he was sitting. He was leaning back on one elbow, one leg bent and a bare arm draped across his knee.

She was beginning to perspire.

When she tied the thread into a knot, he sat up. "All done?"

"Yes. Good as new." She examined her work then flapped the shirt into the wind.

They both stood. With the pretext of smoothing her skirt, Sarah handed the shirt to him with her gaze lowered. But she was more than mindful of the haste in which he pulled it on, fastened the buttons and tucked the tails into his trousers.

He cleared his throat. "Back to work, I guess."

Sarah smiled nervously. "Yes, back to work."

He walked toward the wagon, examining where the tear in his shirt used to be. When he hoisted himself up into the seat and gathered the reins, he paused there, staring straight ahead. Sarah raised her hand to her forehead, shading her eyes, watching and waiting for him to slap the reins and be off. Instead, he glanced down at her.

"Thanks for mending my shirt."

Sarah gazed up at his perfectly angled face, his jaw shadowed with stubble. For the first time, she felt as if she'd been rewarded. Joy swelled within her. He *did* appreciate her. Whether he would admit it or not.

"You're very welcome."

With elbows to knees, he flicked the reins. The harness jingled as the wagon ambled forward and out onto the vast prairie. Sarah wanted to leap up and down and squeal with delight. Instead, she returned to the house, skipping once on her way to the door.

Later that day, with a shiver of disgust, Sarah flicked a grasshopper off the tablecloth. Before she could blink twice, another one leaped into its place. "Get away!" she cried, swiping him with the back of her hand. Gooseflesh erupted on her back and arms like a thousand wriggling spiders.

Rubbing her palms on her skirt, she collected herself and turned back to the hot stove. Earlier that afternoon, she'd collected some wild greens Martha had told her to look for, mixed them with some salt pork, onions and potatoes, chopped everything up, and made a stew. She bent forward and removed it from the oven, breathing in the aromatic tendrils of steam. She wondered what Briggs would think of it.

Sarah looked up at the open door when she heard the wagon roll in. It seemed a little early for Briggs to return. She went to see what had brought him home. As she emerged from the tiny dugout and into the sunny afternoon, a hot and drowsy stillness enveloped her. It seeped uncomfortably into her skin.

"What are you doing home so early?" she asked, trying to shake away the uneasy feeling.

Briggs hopped down from the wagon and landed with a thud. "There were too many grasshoppers." He walked toward her, his brow furrowed.

"I noticed a couple of them, myself."

He removed his hat and stared at the darkening horizon.

"Would you like some supper?" Sarah asked. "It's just about done."

"No, not yet."

He stared at the sky for another few minutes, pacing back and forth, then donned his hat and moved past her toward the house where Shadow was dozing. Briggs stopped outside the door. Shadow stood up, his long ears tilting back. Whimpering, he padded toward Briggs, who squatted down to scratch behind his ears. "What's the matter, boy? Do you smell something?"

The dog looked around and began to bark. Sarah walked to the edge of the house to see if someone was coming, but nothing moved, not even the grass. Nothing chirped or sang or squawked.

A single nervous breeze lifted Briggs's hair, then quickly disappeared as if it had hurried to take shelter. Feeling anxious, Sarah hugged her arms around herself.

"Darn," Briggs grunted, then marched angrily toward the geranium plant Sarah had set outside the front door. "What's going on?"

He removed his hat and used it to slap at the petals,

shaking his head the whole time. Only then did Sarah notice the grasshoppers falling from the shivering leaves, flitting about in a panic.

"Do you usually get this many insects?" she asked.

"No, never." His tone was laden with concern.

Sarah stood in silence, not knowing what else to do.

Briggs replaced his hat again and looked at the dusty window. Grasshoppers were beating against it as if trying to gain entry to the house. "I think you better close the door."

Briggs picked up the broken geranium plant to give to Sarah to take inside. They stared at each other, both of them pale with worry. "The vegetable garden," Sarah said.

He nodded once, as if that exact thing had been registering in his mind, then gave over the potted plant. He turned to run around the house. "Go inside and get some blankets!"

Without another thought, powered by fright and courage combined, Sarah bolted into the house and down the steps. She dropped the plant onto the table and ripped the red blanket from the tacks in the ceiling. Quickly, she tore the quilt and sheets from the bed and the flour sack from the tabletop. Snatching a fistful of her skirt and yanking it up to her knees, she ran up the stairs with the pile of blankets in her other arm, slamming the door behind her.

Grasshoppers were flitting about, banging into the wagon and tormenting the horses, who swung their long tails and shook their heads in a feeble retaliation. Her chest tight with fear, Sarah darted around the house. She felt a sting on her cheek as she collided with one and then another of the vexing insects.

Keeping her head down, she rounded the house and reached the little garden where Briggs was slapping his hat over the defenceless tomato plants. Shadow was pacing back and forth, growling.

Briggs looked up and gestured with his arm. "Bring the blankets. Cover what you can."

Sarah dropped the pile onto the ground. Without a second's hesitation, four or five grasshoppers leaped onto the mound of bedding. "Shoo!" Sarah hollered, as she picked up the top blanket and flapped it hard into the air. The bugs were flung heedlessly about, disoriented, then they righted their course toward the garden.

She covered the plants, knowing she was trapping dozens of the hungry insects beneath. Briggs continued to wave his hat over the green leaves, slapping and fanning the trembling plants.

"Maybe we should cut what we can and take it inside," Sarah suggested, blanketing the last corner of the garden.

"Go get a knife. I'll stay here and fight them off."

Sarah ran, waving her arms around to scare them away, but bumping regardless into the hard, winged creatures. Frightened calls came from the barnyard— the cow bawling, the pigs squealing. The horses snuffled and whinnied and shook their harnesses.

Sarah dashed into the house, her shoes tapping quickly down the dirt steps. It was dark—where was the knife? Her gaze darted to the table. The stove. There. Her fingers closed around the wood handle and in a flash, she was scurrying back up the stairs and outside. Sarah slammed the door behind her.

She dashed around the side of the house to the garden. Then she found herself frozen in space, staring in confusion at her husband. He stood in the center of the garden, ignoring the grasshoppers on his shoulders and sleeves.

What was wrong? Why was he just standing there?

She lifted her skirts and approached. The yellow sunshine of only moments ago was turning gray. There was a loud ringing in her ears, a violent pounding against her rib cage. Briggs looked pale.

Sarah gazed into his empty eyes, then found herself turning slowly, without conscious thought, toward the horizon that had captured her husband's attention.

"Oh, no," she whispered.

A peculiar cloud moved from the west, too light in color to be a rain or dust storm, too dark to be fog. It advanced all too quickly, as if powered by some unearthly energy, floating higher until it blocked the sun. Sarah moved closer to Briggs, who protectively closed his hand around her forearm. "This can't be happening," he said, his voice flat with disbelief.

"What is it?"

Seemingly calm, he escorted her out of the garden. "I think you better go inside."

Sarah stopped and pulled her arm out of his grasp. "Why? Tell me what it is."

Without taking his eyes off the darkening sky, he answered. "It's a swarm of locusts."

Chapter Eleven

Briggs watched the grasshoppers pass like a dense shadow over the wheat field. The stalks hushed, as if they were too frightened to even breathe. The dark cloud whirled about like snowflakes in the chaos of a winter storm.

Shadow barked while Sarah and Briggs stood astonished, hypnotized as they watched the seething, fluttering mass. It roared like a prairie fire, rasping and ringing and crackling.

After a few moments, Briggs snapped out of his daze and began dragging Sarah toward the house. "What about the crops?" she cried, the full meaning of this invasion settling into her brain.

"I'm going to cut what I can."

Sarah pulled him to a stop. "You're going to fight them?"

"As best I can. Give me the knife."

"You have to let me help you."

He stared at her for a second, then took her by the arm. "No. You stay inside. Seal up the house."

"I will seal up the house. Then I'll come and help you."

The pests suddenly came upon them, flying into their faces and lodging in their clothing. Sarah screeched, waving her arms.

"Sarah, I don't think you—"

"You need my help!"

Surprised at her willingness, he looked around the yard. The horses, frightened and restless, were still hitched to the wagon, the pigs scrambling inside the pen. Briggs shot his gaze back to Sarah. "Okay. Cut what you can from the vegetable garden. Get the animals into the barn and close the doors. I'm going to get my corn knife. We'll start there."

"What about the wheat?"

"We can only be in one place at a time. Go!" He touched the small of her back and sent her off.

Crunching grasshoppers under her feet with every step, Sarah ran first to the barn to seal it before it became infested. She screamed at the pigs—"Yah! Yah!"—and herded them, squealing and snorting, inside. Sarah slammed and latched the door.

Next, she ran to the edge of the yard where Maddie stood at the water trough, lowing and stomping about.

"Everything's going to be okay, Maddie."

Sarah led the cow to the barn and slapped her rump. *Slam,* the door was shut—*click,* it was latched. She swung around. What next?

A grasshopper hit her in the eye. "Ouch!" she cried, rubbing it. Sarah gazed across the yard and saw Shadow. "Come, boy! Come!"

The dog ran toward her, but stopped a few feet away. His ears rose and fell as if he knew she meant to lock him up and keep him from his duty as guard dog. He sat down.

"Shadow!" Sarah yelled, her patience snapping. "Get in here!" She clapped her hands and opened the door for him. "Hurry up! There's no time for this!"

After a moment's deliberation, he ran into the barn. "Good boy," Sarah said, stepping outside and closing the door behind her. She heard Shadow barking his protest as she looked past the house.

The garden.

Feet drumming over the wiggling, crunchy ground, she ran into the house to fetch a knife and buckets. Up the stairs she dashed, pausing at the top. Briggs had tried to convince her to stay inside and the temptation was all too great. Sarah took a deep breath, searching deep inside herself for courage. He needed her help. This was her farm, too. They owned a crop that needed everything they both could give.

She strengthened her will and pushed the door open. A warm wind of winged creatures blew into the house.

"No!" Sarah yelled, forcing herself to dash at the swarm and slam the door behind her. Insects beat against her bonnet and clothing. She clutched the knife and ran to the vegetable garden.

The blankets, she discovered in horror, were almost invisible, covered with locusts. Sarah ripped the blankets from the ground, sending a flurry of creatures into the air. Soon, she had filled two buckets with whatever vegetables were left, leaving the potatoes, which she hoped would be safe underground.

She carried the buckets into the house, then ran outside again to help Briggs in the cornfield. He looked exhausted. His face was damp with perspiration, his hat literally being eaten off his head.

"Did you save the vegetables?" he asked, wiping a sleeve across his forehead.

"They're in the house and all the animals are in the barn."

"Why don't you tie up the stalks I've cut and pile them on top of each other?"

"But we can't leave them out here."

"It's too far to haul them back and forth, even with the wagon. If the stalks are bunched, some will be safe."

Nodding, Sarah gathered what fell behind Briggs. The green stalks were fast disappearing, impossible as it was to keep up with the grasshoppers' greedy jaws.

Before they had stacked a tenth of the crop, the sun was setting. "It's getting dark. What should we do?" Sarah called out, trying to see through the cloud of insects between them.

Briggs stopped working and approached her. He was covered with sweat and dust. "You're exhausted. Look at you."

Sarah gazed down at her feet. She wanted to be strong.

"Why don't we go inside?" he suggested.

"We don't have to stop on my account."

"No?"

"I can keep going."

"I'm sure you can. But, my dear, I can't."

My dear.

"Let's go," he said, holding out his hand. "We need a break and I'm hungry."

Sarah placed her hand in his and let him lead her through the field toward home. When they walked into the yard, Shadow began to bark inside the barn.

"It's only us!" Sarah called out. "Maybe we could bring him into the house for the night. He'll go crazy sleeping in there with the grasshoppers."

She realized, all of a sudden, that she was making an assumption: Briggs would be sleeping in the house, too.

A tremor of distress ran through her. Where exactly would Briggs sleep? In the bed with her? Or on the floor with Shadow? It was ridiculous to think of such things at a time like this, but she couldn't help wondering if he was contemplating the same thing.

"I'll get him," he said. "Why don't you go inside and get the food ready?" The look in his eye told her he wasn't thinking about sleeping arrangements at all. He was thinking about the crop. And he was losing hope.

Sarah nodded and ran into the house, anxious to escape the locusts.

By the time Briggs came in with Shadow, Sarah had managed to get her salt pork stew onto the table while killing a few dozen grasshoppers in the process. She wiped a damp cloth over her forehead and tried to pat down her messy hair.

Shadow sat down next to the stove. Briggs removed his hat. He looked solemn.

"How long do you think this will last?" Sarah asked.

"I don't know." He sat down at the table and rubbed his eyes.

The house was all too quiet. "Do you think they'll get the wheat?"

"Looks that way."

Serving up the stew, Sarah sensed Briggs's discouragement, his need to sit and eat without talking.

He probably didn't know how to tell her that the profits from the wheat harvest were supposed to be their sustenance for the winter. She wasn't sure she wanted to hear it, either.

Troubled, she scooped some water out of the bucket for each of them and gave Briggs a cup. He quickly downed it, his face contorting sourly after he'd swallowed. "Agggh!"

Sarah cringed, examining her own cup of water. "Oh, no," she said. "I scooped them out of the bucket as best I could—the ones that were floating. There must have been some at the bottom."

He set down his cup. "It's not your fault."

"I could make coffee. That might mask the flavor a bit. The stove's already lit." She prepared a pot and while it was heating, she sat down to eat.

"I'm inclined to skip the prayer tonight," Briggs said. "I don't see much to be thankful for. The timing couldn't have been worse. If that swarm had just waited another week, the harvester would have arrived and cut all twenty acres in a couple of days."

Sarah looked across the table, hearing the gloom in her husband's voice. Even so, he seemed all too calm, and it worried her. Maybe he thought this would be the final thing to send her running and screaming back to Boston. Well, not so. Not so...

"We mustn't fret over what we can't change," she replied, closing her eyes and clasping her hands together. "We need prayer now, more than ever. *Thank you, Lord, for giving us the strength to save some of the corn and the vegetables. Thank you for keeping Briggs and I safe through all of this. And thank you for this supper. Amen.*"

She opened her eyes to see Briggs staring dazedly

at her, his mouth slightly open. *"Amen,"* he said, finally.

"Go ahead, dig in," Sarah prompted.

They began to eat, both of them famished. Occasionally, a stray locust would spring onto the table, only to meet a sudden death under Briggs's heavy hand.

"I wonder how the Whitikers are managing," Sarah said. "Do you think they were invaded, too?"

"I hope not. Howard has a bigger crop, more to lose."

"But they have the children. Frank would be a help, I think."

"Yes, he likely would be. Mollie wouldn't like it much, though. I hate to think of it."

Sarah felt her heart throb for the little girl. "I hope she's all right."

Briggs finished his first helping. "Is there any more?"

"Yes, I'll get you some." Sarah rose to fill her husband's plate.

When she sat down again, Briggs rubbed his forehead. "I have bad news. Before I came in, I went to the vegetable garden to get the blankets we'd left there. I'm afraid there wasn't much left."

"Much left of the garden?"

"No," he answered, his voice tired. "There wasn't much left of the blankets."

Sarah covered her mouth with her hand and looked toward the bare mattress on the bed.

"The darn things chewed right through them," Briggs added. "They were in shreds."

"That was all we had."

Shadow perked up, whimpering at her.

"I know," Briggs said. "You'll have to cover yourself with some clothing, at least until we can get something else."

But without the wheat harvest, how could they buy blankets, much less the bare necessities for the winter?

Briggs slid his chair back. "I should go milk Maddie and water the horses."

"What about the coffee?"

"When I come back," he answered, donning his hat. "Can you keep it hot for me?"

"Of course."

Briggs left, taking Shadow with him, and Sarah set to work clearing away the supper dishes. Milking Maddie was supposed to be Sarah's job. Truth be told, she couldn't face stepping outside again, where it was dark and she wouldn't be able to *see* the locusts. She'd only *hear* them crunching under her boots and *feel* them beating into her face.

A short time later, Briggs returned with a bucket of milk in his hand. Shadow followed, tail wagging. Life from inside the house seemed almost normal until Briggs set the bucket down. Sarah looked inside and saw a tidy layer of insects squirming about in a panic, trying to crawl over each other to save themselves from drowning. "Ugh!" she groaned, as gooseflesh tingled down her back.

Briggs appeared beside her and scooped them out with a cup.

She felt tears coming, tears she'd fought against all day. As she considered it more, she realized they were the same tears she'd been fighting every day since she'd stepped off the train. Every time her husband looked at her with that disappointed expression, she'd wanted to weep. But she hadn't. And she wouldn't now. *Things could be worse,* she told herself. Though how much worse, she could not imagine.

Feeling Briggs's gaze upon her, she looked up. He stared at her, his eyes full of apologies. Apologies for what? she wondered. For the grasshoppers? For the lost crop? For the coming winter? Or was it for all that had passed between them?

"I can't believe this is happening," he said. "When I brought you here, I didn't mean for it to be this bad."

As she digested his words, all her efforts to keep tears away failed her. All she'd wanted for so long was a kind word from her husband, anything to say he cared for her, even just a little. She'd wanted to see the gentle man she had seen in the courthouse on their wedding day, the man who had cared enough to sit her down and fan a cool breeze into her face....

And here, now...there he was....

"It's not so bad," she managed to say, her voice shaky.

"I have to go back out. I have to try to save whatever's left. You don't have to come. You can stay here. Get some rest."

She thought of him out there in the darkness alone, cutting cornstalks and fighting off the insects. He would be discouraged and he would lose hope with each passing hour. No, she decided. She would not let him down. Not now. She would go out there, frightened or not, and carry the cornstalks or what was left of them to safety.

"I'll come with you."

"You don't have to." But she saw the look of

gratefulness in his weary eyes. She saw, for the first time, that he was not disappointed in her.

His appreciation breathed new life into her exhausted body. Sarah picked up her bonnet, tied it tightly under her chin, and gazed with a driving purpose at her husband. "Just try to stop me."

Chapter Twelve

Briggs and Sarah worked until midnight in the cornfield, cutting what was left of the stalks and tying them into secure bundles. Neither of them said it, but they both knew there was little chance much of the crop would survive the night.

Worn-out and thirsty, they returned to the dark little sod house. Briggs could never have imagined any place on earth more warm and welcoming. While Sarah lit the lantern, he went outside to fill a bucket with water from one of the barrels. He had to scoop the grasshoppers out with his hand, and he knew it would taste bitter, but his mouth was so dry, he could have devoured a gallon of sour milk.

When he entered the house, he and Sarah both filled their cups and gulped down the water. "Ugh," she groaned, her delicate features twisting into something unrecognizable. "Do you think the creek water will taste like this, too?"

"Probably."

"Will it ever taste good again?"

"I reckon sooner or later."

A locust fell from the grass ceiling and dropped

discreetly onto Sarah's head without her noticing. Briggs set down his cup and moved toward her to brush the insect away. As he approached, a glimmer of surprise danced across her face. The closer he came, the wider her brown eyes grew, and he could not help but wonder with an odd sense of regret if she feared him in some way....

He reached out and flicked the insect into the air.

She did not flinch. Most women, he thought, would cry or shriek or do worse, but he supposed Sarah had toughened considerably somewhere between the nibbled geranium plant and the ingested cornfield.

He lowered his hand and noticed her eyes were still as round as two harvest moons. "Something wrong?"

"I'm just tired."

He stood close enough to brush his nose lightly across the top of her head. He could smell her—not the rosewater this time. It was just her. He shut his eyes, wanting to enjoy it for a few seconds. "I couldn't have done this without you," he said.

Her soft hand cupped his cheek.

Without a conscious thought, he turned his lips into her warm palm and kissed it. He wanted to cocoon into her warmth and stay there forever. He didn't want to face the grasshoppers, the field, the certain devastation that would greet him in the morning. To his complete surprise, he only wanted Sarah.

Startled by his feelings, he forced himself to let go of her hand and take a step back. He was just searching for solace because of what was happening outside. Tomorrow, the crop would be gone. Making love to Sarah tonight would not bring it back. It would only plunge him into that black sea of heartache if she decided to leave him.

After this ordeal, that was a very real possibility.

Sarah kept her features composed, but he saw in her eyes that she'd been wounded by his withdrawal. "Are you all right?" she asked.

He nodded, feeling badly, but at the same time trying to remember that he had a duty to himself to maintain an emotional distance between them—at least until he felt more sure of her.

"We'll get by," she said.

He stared into her dark eyes and for the first time saw the enormity of her strength, and against his better judgment, he saw his partner. His companion. His mate. How could he stop himself from feeling what was growing inside his heart? He took a step forward again and gathered her into his arms. Her body melted into his. She was small and warm and refreshing. The day's trials had emptied him, but as he held his wife, he felt hope returning.

"Sarah," he whispered. "There won't be anything left in the morning. The wheat crop will be gone."

She nodded, pressing her face into his chest.

Instead of the deafening hiss and crackle of locusts, Briggs heard only the sound of his own breathing, light and slow, and knew he was feeling everything he'd vowed never to feel again.

"We should get some sleep," Briggs said, leaning back in his chair as they sat across from each other at the table. "There's no point staying up all night worrying. We're going to have a lot to do tomorrow."

Sarah couldn't bear to face the idea of tomorrow. But when she turned her exhausted mind toward sleep, she realized uncomfortably they were both inside the house together, both staring at the single, narrow bed.

Uncertain as to what to do, she glanced at Briggs and fought the tightening in her chest. They had not shared a bed since their wedding night, and that had turned out to be a disaster. In fact, both times she'd given her body to a man, it had caused nothing but despair.

Wouldn't it be better to wait until Briggs had forgiven her and gotten over his anger completely? she wondered, biting her thumbnail. She and Briggs had come so far, she did not want to remind him of their painful beginning and spoil things again.

She realized uneasily that her hands were shaking. She dropped them to her lap to hide them under the table.

Briggs stood and scratched his head. "I guess I'll sleep on the floor. The bed's not really big enough for two."

Sarah's shoulders slumped. All her nervous reasonings seemed silly, now. Briggs didn't even *want* to sleep with her.

She rose from the table and sat on the edge of the bed, wishing she had a blanket to cover herself. She removed the pins from her hair and set them on the rough bedpost while Briggs lay down on the dirt floor beside the table. Within seconds, Shadow curled up beside him and Sarah could not help but envy the body heat they were sharing.

Resigning herself to her empty bed, she reached into her bag for her nightdress and made her own blanket, forcing her mind to stumble backward into a restless sleep.

* * *

The next morning, Sarah awakened to the sound of Shadow shaking himself, his ears flapping noisily like a startled pigeon. Briggs had risen and was dipping his tin cup into the bucket of water. He gulped it down, and his eyes clamped shut at the sharp taste.

"I could make coffee," Sarah offered.

Briggs set down his cup. "I didn't know you were awake."

"I wasn't. Until a moment ago." Still wearing her clothes from yesterday, she threw off the nightdress she'd used as a cover and stood. She tried to ignore Briggs, who stared at her while she filled the stove with cow chips. Feeling self-conscious, she struck a match, which thankfully whisked and flared on the first try.

"Your hair," he said, squatting to pat Shadow.

Sarah froze with uncertainty, then realized she was still holding the burning match. She tossed it quickly into the chips, feeling like her cheeks were catching fire as well.

"I'm used to you wearing it up," he added.

She turned around. "I'll be putting it up in a minute or two."

Still stroking Shadow, Briggs glanced briefly at her, then away. "Whatever suits you."

"Have you been outside yet?" Sarah asked, changing the subject.

"No, and I can't see anything out the window. It's too dark. Maybe I'll go milk Maddie while the coffee's brewing."

"I'll do it. It'll take a while for the stove to heat up, anyway."

Briggs pulled on his hat and studied her a moment. "We'll both go." He gestured for her to follow. They

climbed the steps and reached the door. Briggs lifted
the latch, but before he pushed the door open, he
turned and looked down at Sarah. "I hope you said
a prayer last night."

She felt her pulse quicken as she answered, "I
did."

Slowly, he pushed the door open. It was not the
sight, but the eerie sound that crushed all hope—a
monotonous, deafening buzz that hurt Sarah's ears.

Briggs quickly stepped back and slammed the door.
He said nothing. He stood there, head bowed, clutching the latch.

Sarah touched his shoulder. "I'm sorry."

His body moved with a sigh. "I didn't expect them
to be gone. I'd hoped, of course, but I didn't expect
it." He gazed down at her, his eyes strained with
worry. "Do you still want to come out to the barn?"

"Yes," she answered, needing to be with him,
needing to see what was left of their farm.

Ushering Sarah by the elbow, Briggs pulled the
door open and hurried outside. He raised his arm to
shield their faces from the pesky creatures. A pink
haze colored the horizon but barely lit the sky as their
feet crunched over the ground. Millions of grasshoppers surrounded them, flitting about and feeding hun-
grily on anything they could find.

Sarah and Briggs reached the barn and rushed inside. The animals were restless, crying and complaining. Grasshoppers had infested the tiny structure.

Briggs lit the lantern and the room brightened.
"Good God," he said, his voice a pale whisper.
Sarah's mouth dropped open in shock.

The locusts had been everywhere, devouring, con-
suming. The wooden handle of a hoe that stood by

the door had been chewed where the sweat had soaked in. The worn parts of the harness were badly eaten, and the creatures were still feasting on it. Ropes were cut through and in pieces. An old straw hat which had been left hanging on a post by Maddie's stall was in shreds.

Two insects simultaneously beat against Sarah's face. She waved them away while Briggs stood staring at the stalls, astonished. The pests had eaten the hay. They were crawling around on the horses' backs and scooting through their long manes.

He went to the harness to examine it more closely. Sarah followed. "Can we save it?"

"I think so, but you better take it inside the house." He placed it in her arms. "Is it too heavy?"

It was heavier than she expected, but not unmanageable. "I'll be fine."

"Why don't you go inside?" He looked around the barn, the frustration evident in his green eyes. "I'm going to milk Maddie, then check the crops, but it doesn't look good."

Sarah nodded in anguish and left the barn. She walked back to the house with the harness, squinting through the swarm and feeling her hopes sinking quickly. She had come here with a dream of farm life, but it seemed that dream would not be granted so easily.

She only hoped, that after all this devastation, Briggs wouldn't decide to pack it in. And pack her off at the same time.

Chapter Thirteen

The unwelcome visitors stayed two more days, feasting on the helpless homestead. Each night, Briggs slept on the floor with Shadow, and Sarah slept uneasily in the bed. Several times she started from her pillow, dreaming that the locusts had invaded her bed. Then she would discover that the little sod house had kept its promise of shelter. It had forbidden entry to almost all the enemy insects.

On the third day, Sarah and Briggs awakened with little hope the grasshoppers would ever leave, but as soon as the sun rose in the sky, the wind shifted. By noon, the swarm departed as quickly as it had come, leaving nothing but shredded cornstalks and bare fields where wheat had once been.

Nothing survived in the vegetable garden either, the dry soil strewn with dead grasshoppers. The water in the barrels looked like grasshopper soup and probably tasted worse. Briggs hauled the barrels to the garden and tipped them over, watering the soil and assuring Sarah that the locusts would make good fertilizer for the new crop he'd plant.

That evening, they sat in silence over a dinner of

cornmeal pancakes and sorghum molasses, trying not to think about how they would survive the winter without the profits from the harvest. Sarah just wanted to forget everything for the night and pray that she would someday feel happy again.

"What do you think the creek looks like?" she asked, trying to keep her hopes from fading completely.

Briggs sipped his coffee, the only thing fit to drink that didn't taste like grasshoppers. They needed to keep the milk for making butter to sell, though they wouldn't get much for it. "I don't know. I haven't gone down yet. Why?"

She sighed. "I'd love to take a bath."

"I was just thinking the same thing."

"You were?"

"Yes. Why don't we walk over after supper?"

Sarah nodded, too tired to even speak.

They finished eating within minutes, and Sarah cleaned off the table. She untied her apron and draped it over the chair. "Are you ready?"

"I've been ready for three days."

Sharing a much needed chuckle, they climbed the steps and opened the door. Magenta light struck Sarah in the face as she turned toward the sunset.

"Ah," Briggs sighed, stopping just outside the house. "Do you feel that?" Eyes closed, he breathed in the warm evening breeze.

Sarah gazed at his subtle smile, admiring the angular shape of his face. He had a perfect nose and an attractive dimple on his squared chin. "It's wonderful."

"It's so quiet and peaceful."

"It's like heaven." She took in another breath of

air like a thirst-quenching drink. Then she noticed Briggs staring toward what had once been the wheat field.

She reached out and closed her hand around his. His warmth traveled to her fingers and up her arm, all the way to her heart. She felt his grip tighten ever so gently. For an instant they were connected in some intangible way, communicating, feeling the same disconcerted emotions and knowing it.

Sarah felt a brief joy in the shared moment, then led Briggs forward. They'd come out here to celebrate their freedom from the locusts, not to mourn what they'd lost. "Let's go see how the creek looks."

They walked across the fields, through the dead grass and the leafless stubs of corn, saying nothing. By the time they reached the creek, the rolling plains had swallowed the sun. The sky was a deep shade of royal blue—that rare color that remains only a few moments before the day surrenders to night.

"It looks pretty clear," Briggs said, his voice fringed with surprise as he looked down at the water. It was flowing slowly downstream, gurgling in shallow places, swirling silently in deeper ones.

"Thank goodness."

Sarah barely had a chance to blink before Briggs tossed his jacket over a leafless shrub. He pulled his loose white shirt over his head, then hopped to keep his balance while he pulled off a boot. "Look away if you have to, 'cause I'm in no mood to worry about your delicate sensibilities. That water looks too tempting."

He dropped both boots onto the ground and reached hurriedly to unfasten his trousers. Stunned and wide-eyed, Sarah watched him step out of his pants. The darkness dulled any image of him, and she wasn't certain if the knots in her belly were tightening because she was thankful or disappointed.

The next instant, a tremendous splash cut through the quiet dusk.

"Aah!" he called out, poking a hole in the water as he resurfaced. Brisk waves splashed onto the bank and forced Sarah back.

Briggs flicked his wet hair, shooting bullets of water upward to the sky. "Come on in. It feels great."

He was treading water, watching and waiting for her to undress. A passionate fluttering arose within her. It was both thrilling and frightening at the same time.

Stalling, she began to pull out her hairpins, one by one. She shook her head so her thick, wavy hair swung down her back. It wasn't late enough to be completely cloaked by darkness, but Briggs didn't seem concerned. He continued to tread water, looking up at her.

She unbuttoned her bodice, but then hesitated, holding it closed. Hot nerves knotted tightly in her stomach. She'd never undressed like this in front of a man before.

He did a backstroke away from her, but kept his eyes fixed.

Good heavens, this was too much! Her heart skittered within her, causing her whole body to tremble. He would simply have to turn away.

Embarrassed at having to ask, but even more afraid of what would happen if she didn't, she met his gaze. "Would you mind looking away?" She felt her cheeks suddenly flame red and hated them for it.

Briggs stopped swimming. For a moment, he

seemed to hold back a response, his lips dipping into the dark water. Then, came the reply. "Yeah, I would mind."

Stunned, Sarah clutched her unbuttoned bodice. All thoughts skidded to a halt inside her muddled brain.

"Don't look so shocked. We're married, aren't we?"

His tone was playful, which relaxed her a bit, but not entirely. Oh, why had she suggested this? She hadn't thought about this part at all. She only wanted to feel clean again.

"Fine," she said, trying not to sound apprehensive. She pulled her bodice off her shoulders, deciding then and there that she would swim in her chemise and drawers. They needed laundering anyway and wash day wasn't until Friday.

Feeling her husband's stare, she stepped out of her skirt and draped it neatly atop his coat. Next she unhooked her corset, tossed it onto the ground, and unlaced and removed her boots.

In a hurry to hide within the water's dark shelter, she waded in to her waist, then gently dove under. Cool freshness enveloped her. The muffled din of water in her ears blocked out everything else. She felt all her problems rinsing away....

Upward she came, in a speedy flight. Shattering the silence, she broke through the surface and sucked the clean air into her lungs. Satin droplets tickled her face and neck.

"Feels great, doesn't it?"

"It's wonderful."

"I wish we could stay in here forever."

Sarah smiled, understanding. "But we can't."

"I know."

They swam around each other a while, enjoying the silence.

"What are we going to do?" Sarah asked, after they'd had a chance to enjoy the moment.

Briggs pushed his wet hair back from his face. "I can plant fall wheat, but that won't do us any good until we harvest it in November, and it won't be enough to keep us in provisions for the winter."

"Is there nothing else we could do?"

He swam closer. "I've been thinking about that...."

His hesitation raised Sarah's doubts.

"I could find work in Nebraska for harvest season, if they haven't been hit by the locusts. I could wire my pay back here and—"

"And leave me behind?" Sarah interrupted sharply.

"It would only be for a few months."

"A few months! No. Absolutely not."

She would have thought her outburst would displease him. After all, who was she to decide what should be done? Oddly enough, a twinkle of moonlight reflected in his eyes and revealed a trace of delight.

Delight?

Watching him, Sarah dropped deeper into the water until it touched her ears.

"We'll need the money for winter supplies and food," he said. "We don't even have any blankets and it gets plumb frigid around here in February."

Sarah wanted to sink beneath the surface and drift aimlessly through the water's blackness. She didn't want to think about Briggs leaving her alone.

"Sarah?" He swam a little closer.

"Couldn't I go with you?"

He tilted his head to the side, his expression apologetic. "No, that wouldn't be possible. I'd be sleeping in a bunkhouse, most likely. Besides, you'd have to take care of things here."

The thought had barely settled in her mind before she realized what it meant. She would miss him. She would long for him.

She watched him dive below, then almost immediately resurface and throw his hair back. "I don't want you to go," she said, matter-of-factly.

He paused, his green eyes brimming with wonder. "I don't see any other solution."

Perhaps it was affection, perhaps it was desperation, but whatever it was, it found an answer. "I know one. I'll sell my pearls."

For a moment, he simply stared at her.

"Did you hear me?"

"Yes. But I can't let you do that."

She had expected that response, but she had to convince him. "Why not? I don't need them out here. I'd rather do without them, than do without you."

He swam closer. "You surprise me."

"Will you think about it?"

"You won't be selling them. I won't let you. You deserve to have something fine."

I do have something fine.

They gazed into each other's eyes for a few seconds, until Sarah felt suddenly shy and couldn't look at him anymore. She swam in a circle, dunking her head and leaving the discussion behind. The sky blackened, the moon grew brighter.

"Have you noticed yet," Briggs asked, "that the

stars are more brilliant out here than they are in town?''

Sarah looked up, and as cool water caressed the back of her head, she saw that he was right.

A sudden splash broke the silence as Briggs dove under. Smoothly and unexpectedly, he came up before her and rested his hands on her hips. She tried to remain calm, but her blood was racing.

He touched her cheek, then let his fingers wander to her earlobe. Gooseflesh moved down her body as he played with the hair above her ear. ''You look very pretty.''

His strong arms came around her, and she felt the evidence of his arousal. Something tingled in the pit of her stomach. She remembered the ways he had touched her on their wedding night and realized she desperately wanted to feel him loving her that way again. To feel him holding her, caring for her. Had he forgiven her? she wondered hopefully, shivering when his lips touched her cheek.

Her feet, rooted to the soft, muddy creek bottom, suddenly lifted. She squeezed his broad shoulders while he guided her legs to straddle him.

In his arms, she felt as light as a leaf floating in the water. She wasn't sure what to do next, so she followed her instincts and locked her ankles together around his waist.

There in his embrace, she felt secure and safe from everything. She let her cheek rest upon his shoulder. Droplets of water tickled her skin, sending waves of commotion through her veins. A delicate thread of intimacy was taking shape between them, and she feared if she let him go, it would snap and transport them back to the beginning.

And more than anything, she wanted to go forward....

"Sarah," he whispered, leaving a trail of kisses across her face. He kissed her nose, her eyelids, then opened his mouth and covered hers. She squeezed her legs around him as their lips met. Was this truly happening?

He spun them slowly through the water, his hands grazing up and down her back. Sarah cupped his stubbled cheeks and deepened their kiss, not knowing how long this would last, but wanting to enjoy it for as long as it did.

His breathing intensified as his hand moved quickly to unfasten the tiny buttons of her chemise. The soft contact made her gasp—it was all happening so fast.

He pulled back. "Do you want this or not?"

"I—I do."

"Are you certain?"

Briggs aroused her senses in a way she'd never known, yet she was frightened at the same time. The last time they'd come together this way, it had been disastrous.

"I'm sure. I'm just nervous."

"Why? You've done this before."

Her arousal skidded to an abrupt halt. She knew it was the truth, but he had used it to hurt her. To make her remember what she'd done. He wanted her to know he'd not forgotten that she had lied to him.

She felt ashamed all over again, and a painful lump clogged her throat.

"Sarah, I didn't mean that like it sounded."

"Maybe not, but you said it just the same."

"I'm sorry."

She didn't want to talk about this. She just wanted to go home.

"It's been a rough few days," he said, backing away through the water. "We're both tired. I didn't mean that."

She nodded, but couldn't look at him knowing how he still felt about her. She had so wanted his respect and had thought she'd earned some over the past few difficult days.

Swallowing, she watched him wade out of the water, his naked body barely visible in the darkness. "We'll go home. Why don't you come out of there before you catch cold?"

Sarah waded out of the creek hugging herself, her teeth chattering. She picked up her corset and put it on over her wet chemise. Briggs held her bodice up for her, and while she buttoned it, he retrieved her skirt. After they were both dressed, he took her arm and helped her up the creek bank, but all his gentlemanly courtesies could not mask how he truly saw her, and how wretched it made Sarah feel.

Chapter Fourteen

Leading his wife across the prickly, ravaged field, Briggs wondered in the darkness if this marriage would ever work. He reckoned she'd told it like it was, down at the creek. He had said what he said to hurt her. A part of him still thought she must care for the man who had loved her first. Why wouldn't she? It had only been a few weeks.

Briggs tightened his grip on Sarah's slender arm, leading her around a pile of shredded cornstalks. They walked in a cloud of uneasy silence, the moon lighting their way.

When they walked into the barnyard, he finally relaxed his grip on her arm and let her go. Head down, she quickened her pace to the house and went inside. Briggs stopped and watched the tiny window brighten with a warm, flickering glow. He turned toward the barn—his bed until the locusts had come. He turned back to the little dugout.

What should he do? Where should he sleep tonight?

He remembered holding Sarah in his arms only minutes ago, the way she had curved into his body.

He remembered her by his side two nights ago, on her hands and knees cutting cornstalks. She'd been fearless. Everything he could have wanted in a wife.

He gazed up at the dark sky, breathed in the clean night scent of the prairie, and felt an evening chill. His hair was still wet. Autumn would soon be here.

Burying his hands deep in his pockets, he wanted to kick himself for saying what he'd said.

He stood outside a while longer, kicking at the dirt, then walked to the dugout. If he could find the courage, he would ask Sarah if she would let him sleep indoors tonight.

Sarah sat on the edge of the bed, pinning her hair up after donning dry underclothes and a fresh bodice. The golden lantern light flickered, but the dugout seemed empty and cold. She wondered miserably if Briggs would ever forgive her. Then the door creaked open and he walked in. She stared up at him in dismay. She had expected him to stay in the barn tonight.

"Hello," he said, hesitating on the top step.

"Come in." She hadn't realized how tense she was until that instant when her shoulders loosened and she exhaled lightly. "I'm glad you're here."

"Really? After what I said at the creek, I hadn't figured on that."

She gave him a melancholy smile. "I doubt it's very comfortable out in the barn."

He slowly descended the steps. "It's not."

"Would you like something to eat? I could get a—"

He stopped her with a raised hand. "Please. Don't bother. I'd rather talk."

Sarah's nerves wrenched beneath her skin. Talk. He wanted to talk. About what?

"All right," she replied, trying to hide any apprehension.

He sauntered toward her. "You had every right to be angry earlier. What I said was wrong."

Sarah blinked in surprise. "Please, you don't have to—"

"Yes, I do. You didn't deserve that. I just said it to hurt you."

A part of her was thankful they were finally communicating, but another more fragile part of her ached as she took in his full meaning. He was still angry with her and he wanted to cause her pain.

Briggs removed his coat and draped it on the chair. His loose shirt clung to his still damp skin.

"I just want to be a good wife," Sarah told him, her voice shaky. "*Your* wife. I wish I could rewrite everything that happened to me before I met you."

"I guess I've made you feel that way, haven't I? Ashamed, I mean." Briggs took her hand, led her to the bed, and they both sat down. "I want all that to stop. You can't rewrite the past and neither can I." He looked down at their joined hands and ran his thumb over hers for a moment, as if thinking about something. Sarah's whole body tingled at the sensation.

Without looking up, he added, "Even if I could rewrite the past, I wouldn't. It might change what I've got now."

Sarah stared wordlessly at him, barely able to comprehend all this.

"I know we had a rough start, Sarah, but we need to put it behind us."

She lowered her lashes, unable to look at him without crying. How she'd dreamed of hearing those words. "I wish you'd found me sooner."

He turned her small hand over in his strong one, lacing his fingers through hers. "It's true, neither of us got what we expected. I know you wanted someone more...polished. I saw it in your eyes the first time you looked at me."

Sarah wet her lips, surprised and saddened that he'd noticed.

"And I wanted someone plain," he added. "Instead, I got you."

"You also wanted someone who wouldn't lie to you."

He paused, then nodded. "That's over and done with. We have a life here now. We need each other. I don't know what I would have done the past few days without you. You may not have been what I expected in some ways, but in other ways, you've been the best wife I could have imagined."

Feeling her eyes flood with joy and fear at the same time, Sarah touched his cheek. There was still so much he did not know about her.

Briggs kissed her hand—a kiss filled with affection and respect. *Respect.*

His eyes bathed her in admiration. His hands moved sensually along the inside of her forearm. "You've been trying to be a wife to me," he said, his voice deep and smooth like velvet. "But I haven't been a husband to you. Tonight, let me be your husband. Let me make love to you." He slowly leaned in, and she could smell the magnificent outdoors in his hair as his lips brushed gracefully over hers. It seemed her dreams, one by one, were all coming true. All that she had ever wanted…

His kiss deepened and he laid her onto the bed. Butterflies danced within her as his tongue explored her mouth. Gently, he rolled on top of her and their bodies melted together. With moist lips, he seared a path down her neck, over her shoulders and across to the top button on her bodice.

"Can I take this off you?" he asked, his eyes burning with desire.

She tried to control the pulsing knot in her stomach, but gave up the effort, nodding her permission. Briggs unbuttoned her bodice and pressed it open to reveal her corset and chemise. He dropped tender kisses along the line of her collarbone. His breath was warm and moist against her chest, and her blood blazed with fire.

"There are so many ways I want to touch you," he whispered. "Things are going to be different from now on, I promise you that."

Sarah inhaled sharply.

Reclaiming her lips, he smothered all talk. His hand slid down to her thigh and rested there a moment. "Can you be patient, love, while I light a fire?"

Nodding, she relaxed while he rose from the bed and walked to the stove. She watched his broad back as he crouched on one knee, built the fire, then struck a match. The room took on an exquisite golden glow that seemed to warm all her senses.

Briggs rose to face her and began to unbutton his shirt. "I don't want you to be cold."

Sarah leaned up on both elbows while Briggs stripped off his shirt and draped it over the chair, revealing his muscled, sun-bronzed chest and powerful arms. He sat on the edge of the bed and slid her bodice off her shoulders, then proceeded to remove her corset, leaving her in only her chemise and skirts.

"Why don't you roll onto your front?" he suggested. "Let me rub your back."

When warm fingers touched the small of her back, she quivered. "Relax," Briggs whispered, his hands rubbing the muscles on either side of her spine. "You worked hard the last few days." With smooth strokes, he massaged her back and shoulders. She had not realized until now how sore and tired her body was. She closed her eyes and sighed.

Time slowed to a surreal pace as his graceful hands worked over her body. Minutes passed, or maybe hours, for all she knew. Then he pulled the hairpins from her hair and moved the long locks aside and kissed the back of her neck.

With an exploding affection she could barely contain, Sarah turned over to face him. She wrapped her arms around his neck and pulled him down for a kiss. He lowered his weight fully upon her, and she reveled wondrously beneath him. She hadn't known it could be like this, that she could want so badly to be held.

"Wrap your legs around me, Sarah." His voice shook with need.

Trembling, she clung to him as he explored her body with his tender hands. "Please," she whispered, not even sure what she was pleading for as the word escaped her.

He rose and stood before her. Gazing up at him in bewildered awe, Sarah heard his clothing drop to the floor, then he came down upon her. His lips were moist as he kissed her and her heart raced with hungry expectation as he shifted. He removed the rest of her clothing, then slowly, gently, he entered her.

"You feel so good," he whispered, and they moved together in the dim light until, a few moments later, the sensations surged to a peak and Sarah's body tensed with unexpected spasms.

Briggs squeezed her and kissed her, then laid his palms on either side of her shoulders and rose up to look at her. His golden hair fell forward, and Sarah reached out to push it back, then met his tender gaze.

Soon, he bowed his head and she lost sight of his eyes behind his hair and he shuddered. A few seconds later, he relaxed upon her.

"I feel so close to you," he whispered in her ear. "On our wedding night, I didn't know you." He looked into her eyes. "But now I do, and everything will be different. I promise I'll be a better husband."

But as his lips came down to brush over hers, Sarah realized miserably that he still did not know her. Not at all. If he did, the feeling that had grown between them would surely die.

Her heart wrenched. She could not let that happen. Even if it meant lying to him for the rest of their lives.

His mouth closed over hers, and she decided with staunch determination that he would never know the truth. She would carry it to her grave. Garrison had been more than her lover and she knew that if he ever found out she'd told someone—much less married someone—he would come after her. Both she and Briggs would be in terrible danger. The whole wicked truth would come out and the world would know that she had more than one husband.

Chapter Fifteen

The next morning, Sarah awakened beneath Briggs's buckskin coat, the fringe tickling her nose. She stretched her arms over her head and yawned, noticing that her long skirt was draped over her legs like a blanket. Sometime during the night, Briggs must have covered her. His kindness caused her a twinge of guilt.

She remembered the day she answered his advertisement for a wife and how she had not revealed her true situation. She had not wanted to admit to herself back then that she was being dishonest. Her marriage to Garrison was irrelevant, she'd told herself. Legally, it did not exist.

But she doubted Briggs would be much interested in the legalities. He'd only care that she had kept something else from him.

She covered her face with a hand and squeezed her eyes shut. She had not known Garrison at all when she'd agreed to marry him. She had been so naive, so lonely after her parents died, she'd only wanted to be loved by someone again. If only she'd been stronger, like she was now.

She hoped she was strong enough to live with this dishonesty.

Sarah buried her face in the pillow and smothered a sob. She hadn't counted on falling in love with a man who valued honesty and trust more than her pretty face. She would never forgive herself for lying to him, but she'd had no choice from the beginning. Garrison was a dangerous man. There's no telling what he might do if he found out someone knew the truth. She couldn't put Briggs's life at risk. If anything ever happened to him…

Somehow, she would have to find the strength to continue this lie, no matter how much it killed her inside.

A little later, Sarah rose from bed, pulled on her clothes and lit the stove. As soon as the fire crackled to life, she climbed the steps to go outside and fill the coffeepot with water. A warm shiver passed through her. Despite everything, she could still feel the pleasure of being held last night, of being kissed. As she dipped the pot into the barrel, the cool liquid touched her fingers and she was acutely aware of physical sensations—the bright sunlight on her cheeks, the smell of cows and horses and pigs, the cold wetness on her hand.

Life was full of miracles, she realized, admiring the sunrise as she returned to the house. Even for those who did not deserve them.

She was just preparing to go out and milk the cow when Briggs walked in carrying a bucket. Her heart quickened at the sight of him—hair disheveled around his shoulders, face shadowed with whiskers, and a smile moving across his seductive lips. She couldn't prevent an awakening arousal when she remembered how those lips had kissed her the night before....

"Good morning," he said, setting the bucket down, the rope handle silently dropping. With two long strides, he backed Sarah up against the sod wall and swept her weightlessly into his arms. His mouth covered hers and she responded with parted lips, sliding her hands up under the thick hair at his nape and into a delectable warmth there. His kiss fired through her veins and thawed the morning chill still lingering in her bones. By the time he came away, she felt overheated.

"Good morning," she sputtered, trying to keep her balance.

"I brought you some milk." He walked to the bed and examined it. "You know, I think what's left of the cornstalks would be perfect for a bigger mattress."

The idea of a bigger bed breathed new life into Sarah's tired spirit, knowing that Briggs intended to share the bed with her from now on. Dreams could come true, she thought, but realized with some disappointment that she did not feel completely happy. Perhaps someday she would be able to forget.

They moved to the table and Briggs sat down. "Corn bread?" she asked, snatching her thoughts back to where they were supposed to be. "Or I could make cornmeal griddle cakes if you feel like waiting for me to gather some eggs."

"That sounds good."

She dug into the bag of meal but turned when Shadow barked outside. She looked questioningly at Briggs, who rose and climbed the steps.

"Howard!" he called from the door. "Good to see you!"

Thrilled to be receiving her first guest since she'd arrived, Sarah wiped her hands on a towel and hurried up the steps to greet their neighbor. Howard sat high up in the wagon, rubbing his dark beard. Although happy to see him, Sarah felt mildly disappointed that Martha hadn't accompanied him.

"Hello, Sarah," he said, touching the brim of his straw hat. He set the brake and hopped down, giving Shadow a quick pat on the head.

"Have you had breakfast, Howard? I'm just about to cook up some griddle cakes if you'd like some."

"Appreciate the offer but I just finished a big meal and can't stay long. I'm on my way into Dodge." He turned to Briggs. "I see you didn't escape the swarm."

Sarah stood and listened for a moment, but retreated into the house when the men decided to walk into the field to survey the damage. She worried about Martha, unable to imagine how it would feel to be a mother without food for her children. Sarah decided to go and visit as soon as she could.

About a half hour later, Briggs came into the house and walked to the far corner. "Howard's heading into town now," he said, pulling the bed out from the wall.

"What are you doing?" Sarah asked.

He crouched down and lifted a small tin box out of a hole in the floor. "I'm giving him some money to buy seed for fall wheat."

Sarah watched him riffle through the box, then set it back in the hole and pull the bed over it.

"I didn't think we had any money," she mentioned.

He stopped and looked at her. "We don't. I mean, this is it and it's going with Howard." Briggs approached her. "What's wrong?"

She dropped her gaze to the floor. "Nothing. I just hope everything will be okay. What if something happens to this crop, too?"

"Please, don't worry."

"But if something does happen, what will we do?"

He touched her arm. "We'll get by."

"But I don't want you to go away."

He touched her shoulder. "I won't go. I promise. Everything will be all right."

Despite her fears, he was her husband and she had to trust him. As he walked out the door to give Howard their only savings—at least the only savings she knew about—she wondered with an aching heart how much money they would get for her mother's fine pearls.

The match whisked and flared between Briggs's finger and thumb. Slowly, watching it burn, he touched it to the chips in the stove. Within seconds, the fire caught and he was closing the door.

He turned to look at Sarah lying back on the bed, the lantern light reflecting off the buttons on her calico dress.

"My God, you are beautiful," he whispered, wondering how he could ever have wished Sarah to be plain. She was perfect just the way she was—her black hair splayed out on the pillow, her full lips moist and parted, her sweet cheeks flushed. He sauntered toward her, grinning, a ripple of anticipation moving through him. He would undress her again, piece by piece, and enjoy every minute of it.

He would enjoy every minute of the rest of their lives.

Good God, did he care for her that much?

He stopped and paused, pulse thrumming in his head. He wasn't ready to feel so much, so fast.

"Is something wrong?" Sarah asked, leaning up on one elbow.

Startled, he buried his fears and walked to the bed. "No, nothing at all. I just wanted to look at you. Why don't I remove your boots?" He sat at the foot of the bed and untied the laces, then pulled each one off and set it lightly on the floor. "And your stockings..."

In a few seconds, he was rubbing her calves and massaging her delicate feet.

"That feels nice," she said, leaning up on her elbows again. "But why are you being so good to me?"

He grinned. "What makes you think I'm not enjoying this?" Pressing his thumbs into the silky arch of her foot, he traced tiny circles. "Pleasure for you is pleasure for me."

She tilted her pretty head to the side, considering his answer. "I didn't think it was like that for a man."

"Well, maybe you learned from the wrong man."

Sarah paled and he froze, realizing he'd once again said the wrong thing. Several moments of torturous silence filtered between them.

"I suppose I did," Sarah finally said, lying back. "But I believe the *right* man is going to teach me what I missed."

Her words reassured him, and he felt a strange, soft comfort. They'd come a long way since their first day on the prairie. There was forgiveness between them now. He set his hands back to work, massaging her beautiful feet.

Later that night as they were making love, their bodies moving together in exquisite harmony, Briggs felt a tension mount as his body arched in a burning release. He was loving her so much more than he'd ever intended. He felt a sudden urge to resist it, to fight it. How long would it be before he gave in to it and let go of his fears?

Exhausted and confused, he collapsed on top of Sarah. She squeezed him tightly, nibbling on his earlobe. "Was that enjoyable for you?" she asked innocently.

"Yes, my dear wife."

He told himself to enjoy her, to let himself fall in love with her. She was his wife, after all. He smiled and buried his face into her thick, black hair. "But satisfied only for a short time, I think. Then I might need your assistance again."

"It would be my pleasure, Mr. Brigman," she answered, and he held her closer than he'd ever held anyone.

Chapter Sixteen

A week later, pale-gray clouds settled over the prairie, their cottony textures seeming near enough to touch. The air was heavy and uncommonly still, the distant horizon shrouded in mist.

Sarah walked back from the barn carrying a bucket of fresh milk and feeling the prickly rope handle dig into her palm. Breathing fast, she struggled not to spill any of her valuable cargo. She would set the bucket out overnight to let the cream rise to the top, then wear herself out making yet another batch of butter to trade for wool blankets.

"Come, Shadow!" she called over her shoulder when she reached the door to the dugout. "Looks like rain."

The dog trotted out of the chicken coop, creating a flurry of feathery commotion and clucking, and his cheerful wagging tail swept Sarah's skirt as he went by.

Inside and down the steps, the house seemed darker than usual for this time of day, the clouds stealing what precious light could normally sneak into the tiny dwelling. Sarah set down her bucket and rubbed her reddened palm. She looked around the empty house and decided to light the lantern to avoid straining her eyes. Shadow yawned and stretched out next to the unlit stove.

As she struck the match and touched the flame to the lantern wick, she reminded herself to purchase matches before winter came. And more lamp oil.

Oh, how would her meager butter collection pay for everything if something happened to the fall wheat? There was no chance she'd be able to churn enough to save her from selling her mother's pearls.

She glanced curiously at the bed made of narrow tree stumps, wondering if the box beneath it contained any money besides what Briggs had given to Howard. Strange, that her husband had not mentioned the box before, but she supposed he had never mentioned much of anything at all.

Until very recently, that is.

Thanks to a swarm of locusts.

She sat on the chair, still staring at the bed, trying to decide if she could move it herself. But would that be snooping? Would that be a breach of trust? Not that there was a heavy load of trust to breach in the first place, but there was something growing, no matter how small or fragile.

Shadow whimpered and Sarah jumped. She turned to see him staring at her, his dark eyes wide, his head tilting.

"What are you looking at?" she asked, feeling ridiculously guilty over something she hadn't even done.

Thunder rumbled outside and Sarah rose from her chair, absentmindedly smoothing the creases on her skirt. Thinking not a moment longer about trust and guilt, she moved toward the bed and closed her palms around the rough tree bark that covered her bedframe. Her back strained when she lifted it, inching it out from the sod wall. She felt Shadow's judgmental glare and reminded herself that he was just a dog.

When she pulled the bed out far enough, she saw the tin box sitting unobtrusively in the square hole. Odd, that she had not known of its existence before a week ago, having slept above it all this time.

Her stomach did a quick flip and she found herself glancing nervously at the door. If it had begun to rain, Briggs may have decided to return early from plowing the field.

Not that it would matter, she told herself. She wasn't doing anything wrong. She only wanted to know how much money they had so she could plan their trip to town and prepare a list of supplies.

Forcing herself to ignore the nervous tightening in her belly, she crouched down on her knees between the bed and the wall, lifted the cold tin box, and set it on the mattress. She stared briefly at the tarnished tin, back at the door, then back at the box again. Slowly, tentatively, she raised the lid.

The small, rusty hinges squeaked, and Shadow trotted over to sniff what was inside. Sarah looked down at a few buttons sitting on top of some papers. Reaching in and unfolding them, she discovered the deed to the property and a few old grocery bills marked Paid.

Feeling a little foolish for having been so curious about nothing, she moved to replace the papers. It was then she noticed a small blue velvet bag with a drawstring tucked into the corner of the box.

Shadow dropped his furry chin to rest on her outstretched arm, watching closely as she withdrew the bag and inserted two fingers to open it and feel inside. She touched something cold and hard, and pulled it out.

Eyes wide in disbelief, she stared at the sparkling discovery—a jewel necklace—undoubtedly worth far more than her mother's pearls. A large oval diamond surrounded by smaller sapphires was set into a teardrop-shaped setting of gold, suspended on a shiny gold chain.

Sarah held the exquisite object between her fingers, feeling her pulse soar at the sheer beauty of it as it reflected the golden flame from the lantern.

Shadow whimpered again and she patted the soft fur on his head. "What's the matter, boy?" she asked, knowing he sensed her uneasiness and wanting to convince him everything was all right.

But in all honesty, it wasn't. What was this necklace doing here and why hadn't Briggs mentioned it? They were literally sleeping on a fortune—a fortune that could see them through the winter and probably the following winter, too.

She squeezed her eyes shut, wanting to believe there was a good reason he hadn't mentioned it or offered to sell it instead of her pearls. Perhaps it was made of paste and worth nothing. No. Most likely it was a treasured family heirloom.

She opened her eyes and looked down at it, deciding immediately that it had to be genuine. Only true gemstones could sparkle so beautifully, so brilliantly.

Then something clicked in her mind.

With a growing sense of dread, she turned the necklace over in her hand. The inscription made her body go numb: *To Isabelle. Love forever, Briggs.*

Briggs had told Martha and Howard that he'd sold the necklace, but really, he had kept it. Why? To hold on to the memory of his first love?

Sarah shuddered. He had loved this other woman. She would have been his first choice—if he'd had one.

Sarah sat back on her heels. Shadow lay down beside her, resting his chin on his paws and staring up at her. She ran her fingertip over the diamond. How had Briggs given this to Isabelle? Had he knelt down on one knee and proposed at that moment, or had he held her in his arms and kissed her and felt like he would never love anyone else that way again?

She stared blankly across the room and thought of the day her mother gave her the pearls. It was Sarah's thirteenth birthday. She had felt like a woman that day. For the first time.

She gazed once more at the inscription. *Love forever...* Did Briggs think his memories were worth more than hers?

The pettiness in her wanted to throw the necklace straight at him as soon as he stepped through the door. But no, that would not do, she decided. She was not a hysterical person and neither was he. He had not thrown anything at her on their wedding night when he'd made a similar discovery about her past experiences. He'd just walked out. Maybe there was a simple explanation for this and for why he hadn't told her about it when she'd offered her pearls. She could not very well be judgmental, given her own circumstances.

Carefully, she dropped the necklace into the tiny velvet bag, pulled the drawstring closed, and returned everything to its proper hiding place. As she pushed the bed back against the wall, she knew she must let this unreasonable jealousy settle a bit, and like a sensible adult, she would simply ask Briggs about it when he returned.

Sarah leaned over the butter churn and forcefully—too forcefully perhaps—pumped the smooth wooden handle in and out. Her back was going to pay for this tomorrow, she thought, feeling her muscles strain. But she couldn't help it. She needed to work off some tension somehow.

Her arms soon felt like they were going to fall off. Straightening to rest a second or two, she glanced down at Shadow, stretched out on the floor at her feet. She remembered the hectic days in her old life back in the restaurant in Boston, when another server would quit or walk out—most of them had after a short while—leaving Sarah to tend all the tables by herself.

At least here, Garrison couldn't wander in any time he pleased, sit at her kitchen table, and expect her to wait on him.

She tightened her clammy grip on the churn handle and pumped it again. If she could handle Garrison and get herself out of that mess, she could confront a husband about a simple necklace.

Shadow raised his head and perked his ears, drawing Sarah's attention away from that prospect. Hearing a wagon, she glanced out the dust-covered window and saw Howard, Martha and their children. Though she was happy to see them, a part of her wished they had chosen another day.

Shadow barked and darted out the door. Sarah pushed fallen tendrils of hair away from her forehead and wiped the perspiration from her nose and cheeks. She would try to forget her problems for now.

She gathered her skirt and walked up the steps and outside into the sunny afternoon. "Martha. Howard. How wonderful to see you."

Howard helped his wife down from the wagon, and as soon as her feet touched ground, she strode to Sarah and clasped her hands. "I've been after Howard to let me come calling. It's dreadful what happened to our farms, but we will survive. You'll see."

Sarah nodded politely, hoping it was true.

"Shadow!" Mollie shouted.

Tail wagging, the dog paced back and forth in front of the wagon. Howard lifted Mollie out while Frank hopped down on his own. Sarah smiled as she watched them stroke Shadow's golden fur and nearly crush him with hugs.

"Please, come in. I'll put on a pot of coffee," she said, hoping her first time as hostess would go well. "I hope you'll all stay for supper."

Martha smiled and followed, but Howard stayed behind. "That sounds mighty neighborly," he said. "If you ladies will excuse me, though, I think I'll head out to the field to see how Briggy's doing." He climbed back into the wagon and drove away. The children took off with Shadow, laughing and chasing him around the yard in circles.

"They'll tire out soon enough," Martha mentioned, her arm looped through Sarah's. "But until then, let's enjoy the silence indoors."

They went into the dark little house. "Oh, my," Martha commented. "You've made quite a difference here. I knew you would, but I see you've given up on your window."

Sarah looked sheepishly toward the dirty panes. With all her work, she'd forgotten to wipe them these last few days. "With the wind, it gets dirty so fast, and I just haven't had time to—"

Martha held up a hand to hush her. "Please, don't apologize. I know what it's like." She picked up a wet cloth from the table, went outside and scrubbed off the dust. Welcome sunlight beamed into the house. "What you need is a little helper or two," she said, returning. "Things will get easier when you have children old enough to take over some of your chores."

Still thinking about Isabelle's necklace beneath the bed, Sarah replied, "I'm sure you're right. Why don't we sit down?"

Martha sat and dug into her bag. "I have something for you. Howard returned from town this morning and it's our habit to pick up the mail for the entire vicinity." She pulled out a letter and handed it over.

A warning voice whispered in Sarah's head as she reached for it. Who would write to her? No one knew she was here. There must be some mistake. But when she accepted the tattered envelope, she saw it was addressed to Sarah MacFarland. Her maiden name.

Cold fingers of fear slowly crept up her neck. She'd sneaked away from her old life without even informing her employer. This letter could be from only one person.

She ran her finger over the tidy, familiar penmanship. All it said was, "Sarah MacFarland, Dodge City, Kansas." How could she open this in front of Martha? What would she tell her?

Sarah walked toward the window, keeping her back to her neighbor, fighting the panic that came at her.

She hesitated, then gently tore open the seal and began to read.

My dearest Sarah,

I don't know if you'll ever receive this. All I do know is that your ticket took you as far as Dodge City. The train master was kind enough to help me.

My heart forces me to write to you, regardless of where you may have traveled since Dodge. Why, my dear? Why did you go? And why so far away? What are you hoping to find in such untried country? Who there could give you the things you deserve? Fine things, for a fine woman. That's what you were meant for.

Please, love, come home. Couldn't we put that misunderstanding behind us? I know you love me. You said so in your vows. And surely I don't need to remind you what will happen if you've betrayed me. Come home, Sarah. Come home to me before I am forced to fetch you.

Your truest love,
Garrison

Numb with shock, Sarah folded the letter. She stared unblinking out the window at the frolicking children, hearing their muffled laughter as if it came from a distant world.

A hand on her shoulder startled her.

"Sarah, my dear. Is it bad news?"

She was breaking out in a sweat. Her head was throbbing as she tried to find an answer to Martha's question. "No, no everything's fine. I—I was churning butter before you arrived and I must have worked a little too hard.''

Martha led her to a chair. ''Perhaps you should sit.''

Sarah knew her friend was right. If she didn't get off her feet, she might swoon, but when she sat down, the tension in her neck and shoulders failed to leave her. The pulsing of rushing blood continued to pound inside her head.

''Is that better?'' Martha asked.

Sarah could barely respond. She didn't know what to do. Her hand trembled as she stuffed the letter back into the envelope. She wanted to burn it now, but she couldn't. Not in front of Martha.

''Tell me, Sarah, what is it?''

''It's nothing. Just a note from my old employer. It seems he wants me back.'' She laughed nervously and slid the letter under the cup of flowers on the table.

''The patrons must have liked you.''

Feeling flustered, Sarah stood up again, but realized immediately that Martha noticed her sudden restlessness. Searching for something to do, Sarah stoked the stove.

''Do you need some help?'' Martha asked.

''No, I'm fine.'' She wiped her hands together. ''Would you like some coffee?''

''That would be lovely.''

While Sarah moved around the kitchen, she couldn't help sensing that Martha knew something was wrong. After sitting in silence for a moment or two, Martha began to talk about the locusts. Sarah nodded and tried to respond accordingly, hoping she hadn't driven a sharp wedge into this blossoming friendship.

Sarah finally served the coffee and sat down again, finding it difficult to ignore the letter that was screaming at her from under the cup.

She couldn't let Briggs find out. She couldn't drag him into this. He would try to do something about it, with no idea who he was up against. Garrison would kill him. She had to figure out a way to solve this problem on her own. In the meantime, she would have to burn that letter.

Chapter Seventeen

Holding the soft leather reins in his hands and resting his elbows on his knees, Briggs steered his creaky wagon into the yard. Behind him, he could hear Howard's team rolling in, the horses nickering and jingling their harness as they came to a stop. With Howard's help, Briggs had plowed more field than he'd expected. He decided just this once to quit early. Besides, Howard had brought his fiddle.

Mollie and Frank came darting out of the house shouting, "They're back! They're back!"

"Hello there!" Briggs called out.

Little Mollie ran straight into her pa's arms while Frank ran toward Briggs and grasped Gem's bridle, eager as usual to help in some way.

"How about unhitching the team, Frank?"

As he hopped down from the wagon and landed with a *thud* in the dirt, Briggs couldn't mistake the pride and excitement in the boy's face.

Just then, the ladies' melodic voices emerged from the house. He turned. Something happened inside him—a sudden burst of joy, a contentment. He couldn't take his eyes off Sarah, who bent forward to pick up little golden-haired Mollie, then approached him with the wee girl straddling her narrow waist. One day, Sarah would be the mother of his children. He wondered if that time would come sooner than he thought. He'd just have to wait and see....

"How was your day?" she asked.

"Fine, thanks."

For some reason, she wouldn't look at him. Instead, she watched Martha speak to Howard.

Briggs took Mollie into his arms. "What do we have here? A little mermaid?" Mollie giggled and planted a wet, smacking kiss on his cheek. "Why thank you, Miss Mollie," he replied, chivalrously. "I was waiting for that."

"You need to shave!" she blurted out, rubbing her tiny soft hand over his stubbly chin.

Martha marched over. "Mollie! You shouldn't say such things!" Martha smiled playfully at Briggs as she took the child from his arms. "Hello, Briggy," she greeted, touching her cheek to his. "It's nice to see you. Did Sarah tell you we brought a letter?"

Briggs looked at Sarah. Her face went pale. "No, she didn't. Not yet, I mean."

"My old employer," Sarah said, too quickly. "The restaurant is very busy and..." She stopped talking and her smile quivered.

A sick feeling crept into Briggs's stomach. "He wrote to you?"

"Yes," Martha answered for Sarah. "He wants her to come back, but we shouldn't be surprised. Who *wouldn't* want her back?"

Briggs barely heard what Martha was saying. All he could do was stare at Sarah, whose gaze was shifting about.

"Thank you for delivering the letter," he said to Martha, never taking his eyes off his wife.

"My pleasure." Martha stood with them for a moment, but when nothing was said, she smiled awkwardly and walked back to her husband.

Without looking Briggs in the eye, Sarah turned toward the house. "Coffee's on if you all want to come inside."

"Where do you want the horses?" Frank asked. "In the stalls or the pen?"

Briggs had to search his mind for an answer. "In the stalls, I guess." The boy began leading them one at a time into the barn. When Briggs turned around, Sarah was going into the house. He wanted to trust her about who had written the letter, but at the same time he wanted to take a look at it for himself.

Martha hurried in behind Sarah. He would have to wait.

He hated himself for assuming that Sarah was keeping something from him, but how could he help it? She'd been so vague about her past, and even now she seemed nervous about something. He hoped the letter wasn't from who he thought, and he hoped this wasn't the beginning of the end.

With her heart racing like a runaway wagon, Sarah pulled open the door to the dugout and hurried down the steps. She fixed her gaze on the letter on the table. Was the stove still burning?

Just before she could reach for the envelope, the door squeaked open. Sarah whirled around, expecting to see Briggs, but it was Martha with Mollie in her arms. "Shall we set the table?" Martha asked.

Sarah tried to breathe normally. "Yes. I was just going to do that."

Martha set Mollie down. "Why don't you play with your doll? I have to help Mrs. Brigman."

Sarah glanced at the letter. She had to hide it.

With the pretext of clearing away the flowers, she picked up the cup, set it on the windowsill, and stuffed the letter into her pocket. First chance she got, she would toss it into the stove.

Briggs and Frank swung the barn door closed. They walked together to the little dugout, Shadow at their heels. Once inside, Briggs paused on the bottom step, inhaling the delectable scent of freshly baked bread mixed with coffee and spices.

Sarah stood at the stove stirring the supper in the cast-iron pot and humming quietly. He stared at the back of her head with its loose bun of raven-colored hair, and noticed his palms had become clammy. What if her lover had asked her to come back? How would she feel about that?

He cleared his throat and pulled his gaze away to see Howard lighting his pipe in the far corner. Mollie was sitting on the floor playing with a ragged old doll. It was the scene of his dreams—a house full of loved ones.

Briggs took the last step down and tried not to think about the letter and what it might mean. It might not even be what he thought. Maybe the letter was as she said—from her employer.

"Smells good," he said, removing his hat and setting it on the nail keg by the door. "What is it?"

"Rabbit stew," Martha replied. "Howard caught it special for tonight."

"Much obliged, Howard."

Howard held his pipe in one hand, looping the other hand through a suspender. "Well, that fool rabbit leaped right in front of my wagon on the way back from town. Stopped and stared at me like he wanted to treat me to dinner."

Everyone laughed. "Howard has always been rather lucky that way," Martha said to Sarah. "Animals seem to fall over themselves trying to get in line to be his next meal."

Sarah laughed, but Briggs noticed that the usual sparkle in her eye was missing.

Frank proceeded to tell every last yarn about his pa's good fortune with a rifle while the ladies served up the meal. They all ate the delicious stew, laughing and going on about Briggs's comparatively poor luck when it came to hunting.

After supper, the ladies cleaned the kitchen, while Howard, Briggs and Frank sat outside watching the sun streak the sky with pinks and purples. They listened to the clanging of dishes inside while talking about their plowing, and when the sky finally grew dark, they started a small fire in the center of the yard to warm their hands against the evening chill.

"What's this?" Martha asked, appearing unexpectedly behind them. "We clean the dugout until it sparkles, and you want to sit out here with the snakes?"

Howard reached for his wife's skirt and pulled her onto his lap. "I picked out a star for you, my dear. We've been waiting for you to come out so we could show you."

"No, we haven't!" Frank piped up. "We were talking about butchering the pig!"

They all broke into fits of laughter, except for Frank who didn't see anything funny about it. The hysterics were just dying down when Sarah came out of the house holding Mollie's hand. When she reached their little gathering, Briggs stood and offered his chair to her. She nodded politely and sat down, lifting Mollie onto her lap. Briggs sat on the ground beside her.

"How 'bout some music?" Howard asked.

Frank sat up on his heels. "Yeah, Pa! Play something good!"

Martha rose from her husband's lap to let him stand, then took the chair for herself. "He's been itching to play that thing ever since we got here."

Frank fetched the fiddle from the case, handed it to his father who cupped it under his chin. "Any requests?"

"Play 'Buffalo Gals'!" Frank hollered.

"'Buffalo Gals' it is." He touched the bow to the strings and filled the night with music. The children leaped to their feet to dance, hooking arms and skipping in circles.

Briggs laughed as he watched their faces light up like a hundred candles burning at once. He glanced up at Sarah. He wanted to be alone with her. How could he enjoy all this when he needed to ease his mind?

"Play 'Jimmy Crack Corn'!" Frank suggested, when the first tune came to an end. Howard quickly drew bow to strings again and started up anew. Mollie giggled and leaped onto Briggs's lap, and he promptly squeezed her in a bear hug, growling at the same time.

Frank reached for Sarah's hand. "Come dance with me, Mrs. Brigman!"

Without waiting for an answer, he pulled her out of her chair and looped his arm through hers. Briggs watched his wife skip around in circles with young Frank, her face alight with joy, her skirts flapping as her feet came off the ground. Despite everything, how could Briggs help but smile, too?

When the song finally ended, Sarah flopped into her chair, panting and laughing at the same time. "That was wonderful!" she said to Frank, who stood in front of her, still holding her hand, waiting for the next song to begin.

"Come and sit with me, Frank," Martha said. "Give Mrs. Brigman a chance to catch her breath." Frank went obediently to his mother and climbed onto her knee.

"How 'bout I play something for the newlyweds?" Howard suggested, rubbing his chin.

"Oh, you don't have to do that," Sarah said, but her protest went unheard. Howard played "Lorena," a haunting ballad, and Martha began to sing, her voice as deep and rich as the dark sky above. The sounds floated upward with the crackling sparks from the fire.

Briggs whispered into Mollie's ear and gently set her onto the ground.

He stood and held his hand out to his wife. She looked up at him, hesitated briefly, then let him guide her to her feet. Briggs led her away from the fire, placed his hand on her waist, and stepped into a fluid waltz. The night closed around them, drowning out the fears locked in his heart, while only the sad sound of the fiddle and Martha's voice remained. Briggs squeezed Sarah's hand gently while he led her through the dance, admiring her lightness as she followed without falter.

When the last note floated up to the stars, Briggs reluctantly stepped back. He still held Sarah's hand, however, and they stood facing each other, staring into each other's eyes.

"Play something good now, Pa!" Frank called out.

Briggs let go of Sarah's hand. She lowered her gaze to the ground and sat down.

Within seconds, lively fiddle music struck a new mood and the children leaped up to dance. Briggs, all too aware of the melancholy place he'd just been, sought to yank himself out of it by pulling Martha out of her chair. Sarah clapped her hands while the rest of them danced around the fire.

They laughed and hooted, but for the remainder of the evening, Briggs never quite recovered from the affection he'd felt while dancing with his wife.

When midnight came, Mollie fell asleep in Martha's arms. "It's time to go," she whispered to Howard, touching his hand, preventing him from lowering the fiddle bow for another song.

Howard rubbed his chin. "I suppose you're right. My arm's about to fall off."

Everyone giggled. "Thank you so much for calling on us," Sarah said, rising. "I can't remember ever having so much fun. We must do it again soon."

"We will." They exchanged hugs and goodbyes. After loading their family and belongings into the wagon, the Whitikers left Sarah and Briggs standing side by side outside their door, waving as their neighbors drove off into the night.

Soon all was quiet. Briggs was finally alone with his wife.

"Shall we go in?" he suggested, letting his hand rest on the small of her back.

She glanced up at him, all smiles gone. "You go ahead. I'll put out the fire."

"I'll do it."

"Don't be silly. You worked hard today. I'll make sure it's out completely." She reached forward and brushed his hair away from his forehead.

They stared into each other's eyes in the dark until Sarah swept her lashes downward, then she walked toward the roaring bonfire. Briggs watched her go. He had the most uneasy feeling, but wanted more than anything to trust his wife.

After hesitating for a moment, he turned and went inside.

Chapter Eighteen

Sarah sat down in front of the bonfire and felt inside her pocket. The letter was still there, and she reconsidered what she was about to do. If she burned it, wouldn't Briggs wonder why? Paper was a valuable commodity on the prairie, and for her to be so wasteful...

Oh, if only Martha hadn't mentioned it!

She sat in the chair, staring at the yellow flames, wondering if it would be better to simply tell Briggs the letter was from Garrison. Then she could rip it up in front of him to prove she didn't want to go back.

But what if he asked to read it? *I know you love me. You said so in your vows.*

Dear Lord, she would have to confess everything.

She looked at the house with growing dread. She hated keeping all these secrets from Briggs, but she couldn't put him in danger, either.

Besides that, what would it do to him if he knew? Their relationship had come a long way in the past little while, but not far enough to handle anything like this. He would be angry and probably devastated. She couldn't bear to think of it.

Oh, if only they had been married longer. Surely, in time, when their rocky beginning was a distant memory, Briggs would be more forgiving. She would tell him one day, when Garrison was no longer a threat. By then, the marriage would grow stronger and it would be able to bear the weight of this news.

But not now. Not until Garrison was in jail.

Sarah looked up at the black sky and made up her mind. She would burn the letter. Now. If Briggs asked to see it, she would tell him she used it to light the stove and foolishly hadn't considered keeping the paper for future use.

Sitting at the table and fiddling with a spoon, Briggs didn't like what he was thinking. He just couldn't stop being suspicious, could he? Why had Sarah been so bent on putting out that fire, and why had he let her do it alone?

Growing more and more impatient, he went to the dark window and cupped his hands to the cool, clean pane. Sarah was sitting in one of the chairs, staring up at the sky.

It shamed him not to trust her, but he had to know what she was doing. He crossed the room, climbed the steps and pushed open the door. Its creaky hinges drew Sarah's attention. The fire illuminated her face, and he saw a flash of panic. She quickly dropped what must have been the letter into the fire. It sparked and crackled, then disappeared.

Sarah stared at Briggs from across the yard. Seconds passed. They felt like hours. All she could do was wait for the other shoe to drop.

He walked toward her, his face tense with anger. Or was it disappointment?

"What did you burn? The letter Martha brought?"

Sarah nodded, her heart sinking.

"It wasn't from your employer. Was it?"

"No."

She saw his jaw clench. "Why did you burn it? Weren't you going to tell me who it was from?"

"I thought you'd be angry."

"Should I be? You didn't encourage him to write, did you?"

"No."

He glanced at the fire, still crackling loudly, the flames quivering in the wind. "What did it say?"

"It said he wanted me back. That's why I burned it."

Briggs glared uncertainly at her.

"I was going to tell you…."

"Why should I believe that?"

She stood and moved toward him, but he stepped back. She halted, then took a deep breath and breached the space he'd tried to keep as his own. "I had to wait for Howard and Martha to leave before I could talk about it."

He considered her answer, then kicked dirt over the fire and smothered it. "You say he wants you back. Doesn't he care that you're another man's wife?"

Sarah shrugged her shoulders, panicking, not sure how to answer that.

Briggs's expression hardened. "Does he even know you're married?"

The truth was, Garrison did not know, but Sarah was afraid to say anything more.

Briggs grabbed hold of her arms and squeezed. "Does he?"

Fear was rioting within her. Briggs had never been rough with her, not even on their wedding night, but she'd seen enough in her recent life to know where a man's anger could lead. She frantically shook her head.

"Why not? You just ran off without an explanation?"

"I didn't see any need to give one."

Briggs let go of her and turned away. He kicked more dirt onto the dying fire. "Well, I hope if you decide to vacate our *arrangement*, you'll at least tell me when you're leaving."

"I won't be leaving you, Briggs."

"You haven't given me much reason to believe you."

Briggs turned away from her and walked toward the house. Desperate to make things right, Sarah picked up her skirt and followed. Once inside, Briggs sat down at the table and cupped his forehead in his hand. The little house was silent.

"What are you going to do?" she asked, her voice quivering.

"The question is, what are *you* going to do?"

"I hardly think the choice should be mine."

"Why not? You're the one with the lover back in Boston. If you want to go to him, I'll survive. I only wanted help around here. I can find someone else."

Sarah felt as if she'd been punched in the stomach. "You have to believe me. I was going to tell you about the letter eventually. I hadn't meant for you to find out like this."

"I'll never know for sure, will I?"

Sarah knelt before his chair. "Please, Briggs, you have to believe me. I don't want to go back to him. I know it's hard for you to believe, after what happened with…" She stopped herself.

"After what happened with what?" he asked, his tone accusing.

"After what happened with Isabelle."

Briggs sat staring at her as if she had slapped him.

"Just because she left doesn't mean I'm going to leave, too."

"Who told you about that? Martha?"

Sarah nodded. "She had to tell me. I needed to know why you were so angry with me."

"I thought you knew why. Because you married me while you already had a man in Boston. Did you tell her *that?* Did you tell her how you'd kept that from me?"

"No."

Briggs pinched the bridge of his nose. "I wouldn't have thought so."

Sarah sat back on her heels, feeling suddenly defensive. "I'm not the only one keeping secrets, Briggs."

"What are you talking about?"

"I'm talking about the trinket under our bed."

"What trinket?"

She could tell by his eyes that he knew exactly what she was referring to. "I found the necklace you said you sold."

The color drained from his face. He glanced at the bed, as if he were trying to imagine her moving it aside to look through his private things. "When?"

"Today."

"Sarah, that necklace doesn't mean anything."

"Then why did you lie to Martha about selling it?"

It seemed as if he didn't have an answer.

"The worst part of it all," Sarah continued, "is that you were going to let me sell my mother's pearls to get us through the winter while you didn't even mention you had something worth even more. You were going to find work somewhere else and leave me here alone. Why?"

He reached out and touched her hand. "I wasn't going to let you sell those pearls." He was silent for a long moment. "I didn't know you knew about Isabelle."

"Well, I do."

"Sarah, I was going to *marry* her. I never took the way I felt about her lightly. That's why I couldn't sell the necklace right away. Then you came, and things got busy, and..." He looked at her, his eyes accusing. "Maybe *you* could stop loving someone on a whim, but I couldn't. My heart doesn't work like yours."

Sarah folded her arms. "You have no idea how my heart works. You seem to think that because you can't let go of Isabelle, I shouldn't be able to let go of Garrison. Yes—that's his name. Garrison. And you don't know what happened before I came to you. You have no idea."

Briggs sat forward. "Then tell me."

Chapter Nineteen

Sarah stared at the black window, wondering how much of the truth she could reveal without ruining everything.

"I don't love him, Briggs. I might as well tell you that now. I thought I did at the time, but I was very naive and very alone." She shook her head solemnly. "He wasn't what I thought he was."

"And what was that?"

She had to consider it a moment. "Decent."

Briggs shifted in his chair but his expression remained untouched. She wondered if he was believing any of what she was saying. "What are you trying to tell me?" he asked.

"I'm trying to tell you I made a mistake. After my parents died I was suddenly on my own. I was very close to them and I don't think I'll ever get over that loss."

"Wasn't there anyone you could go to? Any other family?"

"No. There was no one else and I wasn't a child anymore."

"How did they die?"

"Their carriage turned over and went down a sharp incline. They died instantly."

Sarah walked to the window. She heard Briggs's chair slide back and felt his strong hands rest on her shoulders. "I'm sorry."

She nodded, unable to speak without her voice breaking, but thankful for his small kindness.

"Garrison was nice to me at first," she said, needing to change the subject and to explain something to her husband who knew so little. So little...

"He was handsome and polite," she continued. "I had taken a number of jobs since my parents died. I worked in a shoe factory, then a clothing factory. When I met Garrison, I was working in a hotel restaurant. He came in every day for supper. He seemed like such a fine gentleman, always charming. When he began bringing me a flower each day, I have to admit, I was flattered." She faced Briggs. "I enjoyed his attentions. I was alone and missing my parents and I wanted a family. I wanted marriage and children. I saw no reason to turn him away. He seemed so genuinely interested in me."

Briggs took a step back, as if he didn't want to hear this, but she had to tell him. She had to explain and make him understand she had not been as shallow-hearted as he thought.

"He took me driving every day and was always so attentive to my welfare and happiness. After only a few weeks, he..." She stopped, uncertain she'd be able to tell the rest.

"He what, Sarah?"

"He proposed to me." She moved past Briggs and sat at the table, resting her chin in her hand.

"He proposed?"

Sarah heard the surprise in his tone, the subtle jealousy. "Yes."

"Did you accept?"

She forced herself to meet his questioning gaze. "I did. But—"

"You did?" Briggs sat down again, his face drawn and pale. Sarah could see how shocked he was at this bit of news, and she couldn't imagine what he would do when he learned all of it.

She couldn't look at him. She was too angry with herself. She had been so fanciful, so trusting and so foolish. She had been raised by ethical parents and she had not seen what other kinds of people lived and operated in this world. She had wrongly assumed Garrison would be decent, too.

Oh, if only she had known about his other marriage. She would never have become involved with him.

"Sarah."

She jumped, her gaze flicking through the dim light to her husband. She continued, her voice shaking. "As soon as I accepted, he insisted I never go back to the boardinghouse where I lived. No wife of his would ever have to live in a place like that, he had said. He booked me into a fine hotel."

She stumbled around words, trying to continue her story. "That was when…"

"He stayed with you in the hotel?" Briggs leaned forward in his chair, his brow creasing. "I would very much like to get on a train bound for Boston tomorrow and wring his scrawny neck."

Sarah froze with panic. Briggs couldn't go to Boston. He simply couldn't meet Garrison. She had been right to think that when Briggs found out about the unlawful marriage, he would try to turn Garrison in to the authorities. There was no telling what Garrison might do. She left him because she feared for her safety and the marriage was void anyway. Why go back there?

But to keep it from Briggs when she wanted so desperately to trust him with this…

What was worse? To lie or to risk both their lives?

"So, why did you leave him?" Briggs asked directly.

"Because…because after we…"

"After you spent the night together…" he said for her.

She nodded. "Yes, after that, he showed a side of himself he'd not shown before. I think because he had taken my innocence, he felt he *owned* me in some twisted way. He tied me to a chair in the room while he went out to take care of some business—"

Briggs shoved his chair back and stood. "He did what?"

She couldn't look up. Tears were coming. Her hands were trembling. "He tied me to a chair."

"For how long?"

She searched for strength to continue, to remember it all. "Not long. As soon as he closed the door behind him he turned around and came right back because I was making too much noise screaming for help."

Briggs covered his face with a hand and paced back and forth. "I want to meet this man in person. I want to—"

"No, Briggs, please. Just leave it be. I want to forget it. I just want to stay here with you and forget any of it ever happened."

Briggs was dangerously angry. He would insist on finding Garrison. She couldn't let that happen....

He paced toward the bed. "He should rot in prison for what he did to you."

"I wish that could be so, but I have no proof of any of it. No one would believe it. He was powerful and well-respected. I just wanted to get away from him."

He looked at her. "That's why you answered my advertisement."

"Yes. He told me he would never let me go and I knew if I wanted to be free of him, I would have to go very far away, where he wouldn't find me. I slipped out of the room when he was indisposed, and I was wandering the streets trying to decide what to do when I found the newspaper."

Briggs rose and paced the dirt floor, shaking his head. His eyes had gone from green to icy gray.

Sarah stood. "I told you I loved Garrison before because I didn't want you to think I'd give myself to a man I did not love."

Briggs sat down on the edge of the bed and said nothing for a long time. Sarah hoped this would be the end of it.

His eyes narrowed when he finally looked up. "Sarah, the fact that you weren't a virgin—that didn't matter to me. What mattered was that I believed you continued to love this man. Why couldn't you have just told me the truth? I would have understood."

"Would you? If I had written about all of it in my letter, you never would have accepted me. You would have taken someone else with a prettier past."

He raked his fingers through his hair. "You don't know that."

"Yes, I do. After Isabelle, you wanted calm waters. No unexpected difficulties that might require you to *feel* something."

He glared icily at her.

"Maybe it didn't matter to you that I wasn't a virgin, but it mattered to *me*. I will always regret giving myself to a man I didn't know or truly love."

"But you gave yourself to me on our wedding night. We barely knew each other."

She lowered her gaze. "That was different."

"Why? Because we were married? Or because you were no longer innocent. The first one mattered? The second one *didn't?*"

"Of course it mattered!" she cried, unable to control her desperation. "Can't you see? It's not the first time that matters so much as the last. *The last!* There will never be anyone else after you. Doesn't that count for anything?"

An unrecognizable emotion flickered across his face. She wished she knew what it was. "Do you intend to keep your vows?" he asked.

"Yes."

"Then write to Garrison and tell him. Tell him you are married, and that if he ever contacts you again, your husband will hunt him down and make him regret the day he met you."

Sarah saw the rage in Briggs's eyes and realized he meant every word.

"We'll post it tomorrow. We'll go to town for some supplies." He brushed by her to leave but stopped and turned. "And if this man knows what's good for him, he'll put you out of his mind for good."

Briggs stormed out of the house, leaving Sarah

standing in the middle of the room, feeling doubtful and afraid, and fully aware that Garrison McPhee, unfortunately, did not know what was good for him.

He only knew what he wanted.

Chapter Twenty

Sarah swayed, rocked and bounced in the wagon seat, holding her white woolen shawl closed with fingers that were beginning to feel numb with cold. The temperature had barely warmed since she and Briggs left the dugout. The sky was pure white, the morning colorless. The prairie grass quivered beneath the steady wind. Without the sun, the summer heat seemed to be relinquishing itself to autumn too early.

A chilly breeze blew over her cheeks as she sat quietly with the letter to Garrison in her pocket, feeling its presence like a lead weight. She knew its contents by heart. She'd worked hard to find just the right words.

Dear Garrison,

I received your letter. Please do not write to me again or try to contact me. It's over between us. I do not love you. I love someone else.

Sarah

She'd been torn over the last line, but in the end, she'd left it.

Briggs cleared his throat beside her. She wished he would say something. Anything. All he did was flick the reins and hurry the horses on. She guessed he wanted this mess over with as much as she did.

All of a sudden, the wagon rose and fell, then jerked to a halt. "Tarnation," Briggs cursed quietly beside her. "Yah! Yah!"

The horses labored, but the wagon would not budge. "We're stuck," he said, throwing down the reins and hopping over the side.

Sarah felt like this was all her fault.

Briggs leaned into the left front wheel. "Take the reins and get the horses to pull."

Sarah slid across the seat. The horses strained to walk, their large hooves thumping against the ground. Briggs grunted and groaned.

"Okay! Stop, stop!" he yelled, breathing hard. He went around to the front and tried to lead the horses backward, but the wheel was wedged in a deep hole.

"Maybe I should get off," Sarah suggested. "Maybe the wagon's too heavy."

Briggs glanced up at her, his expression clouded with frustration. He nodded.

Sarah hopped down into the grass, seeing for herself the depth of the hole. From the ground, the wagon looked tilted at an impossible angle.

Briggs moved to the wedged wheel again. "Go in front and lead them forward."

Sarah did as she was told, and for ten long minutes she and Briggs pushed and prodded and grunted, but to no avail. Sarah walked back to examine the situation. "How long have we been traveling?"

"It must be almost noon. Four hours at least."

She felt uncomfortable making a suggestion, but at

the moment, things didn't look very promising and she couldn't bear any more of her husband's angry looks.

"Why don't we have lunch?" she suggested. "You're tired, the horses are tired, and maybe if we just take our minds off it for a bit, we'll come up with a way out."

He ignored her suggestion and pushed the wheel one more time. After a worthy effort, he cursed and backed away. "We're going to be late. The post office will be closed."

Sarah wet her lips, understanding why he was so angry. They'd have to stay over and wait until tomorrow which would mean another day of plowing lost. All because of that wretched letter.

Well, they were stuck and they were hungry. It wouldn't hurt to eat something and then start fresh. She went to the wagon and withdrew the box she'd filled with corn bread and a jug of water. "Let's sit down and eat and think about how we're going to get the wagon out."

After sitting down and spreading her skirt around her, she sliced a piece of bread for herself. Sarah was biting into her second helping when Briggs finally came and sat down.

"Corn bread?"

He nodded and helped himself. They ate the whole loaf without saying another word.

When they finished, Briggs leaned back, bent one knee and covered his face with an arm. Sarah watched his lips and his stubbly jaw. The rest of his face was covered by that fringed sleeve. "We'll get on the road as soon as we can," he said, "then we could either camp on the outskirts of town or stay with George. But I reckon he'll string me up if we don't come by.''

''That sounds like a fine idea. We can run our errands first thing in the morning.''

He didn't say anything for a few minutes, then asked, ''Did you write the letter last night?''

Sarah's stomach clenched at the question. ''Yes. It's in my pocket.''

His wrist came away from his eyes. ''Can I see it?''

''If you like.'' She reached into her pocket and slowly withdrew the note.

Briggs sat up. The seconds it took for him to read it felt more like hours. Finally, he lowered the paper to his lap and let his gaze rise to meet hers. His brow was no longer furrowed. The firm line of his mouth had softened. ''It's a good letter.''

Sarah's shoulders slumped with relief. ''Thank you.''

Everything was quiet for a moment, except for the wind sweeping across the prairie.

''Is it true?'' he asked.

She knew what he was asking her, and the question made her feel suddenly afraid. ''Which part?'' she asked, stalling.

He handed it back to her. ''The last part.''

Sarah gazed down at the words. *I love someone else.* Her heart beat erratically as she considered it, wondering if she even knew what love was. She thought of how Briggs had made her feel over the past few weeks, how he had touched her and how she had shared her body with him and felt closer to him than she'd ever felt to anyone in her life. Was that love? Was it love because she couldn't bear to think of living without him?

When she didn't say anything, Briggs sat up. "You don't have to answer that. I shouldn't have asked."

"No, please, I—"

"I'm sorry I was so hard on you last night, but I was angry."

Surprised, she wet her lips. He was staring apologetically at her, his golden hair whipping in the wind. "It's quite all right. You had a right to be."

"I should have given you a chance to explain." He leaned back on one arm, plucked a blade of grass, and entwined it around his index finger. "Do you think, after we post your letter, we could..." He paused, swallowing. "We could start again? I don't know what Martha told you about Isabelle and me, but it's finished. I've brought the necklace and I'm going to sell it today. Once your letter goes out to Boston, things will be different."

Sarah's heart warmed with hope. "I'd like that."

They sat in silence for a moment, staring at the clouds, and Sarah wondered if this nervous feeling would ever go away. Her husband wanted to start again. Out here on the prairie, so far from Boston, it seemed almost possible.

"Let's unload the wagon," Briggs said, feeling replenished after eating his lunch and watering the horses. He had to admit his wife had been right in forcing him to take a break to eat something. The horses had needed the rest, too.

Sarah helped him unload the cooking utensils, the kettle, the spider skillet and the boxes of butter and eggs she'd brought to trade. Briggs removed his shovel and his rifle. "I'm going to dig us out of this hole, so it isn't so steep. Then you can lead the horses out."

For the next half hour, he forced the shovel into the tough ground, thick with tangled, grassy roots. Growing warm, he removed his coat and shirt, draped them over the side of the wagon bed, and felt some relief from the cool wind on his bare back. The hole was longer now, and he hoped there was enough room to rock the wagon and get it moving. He set the shovel down and turned to face Sarah.

"I'm going to wedge my shovel under the wheel for leverage and try to force it a bit."

Sarah walked to the team and took hold of the harness. "I'm ready whenever you are."

Briggs speared the shovel handle into the dirt to lift the wheel. It came up an inch or two. "Okay, start pulling!" he yelled, throwing his full weight against the iron tire and feeling it cut into his palms. Sluggishly the wagon moved, but stalled when it reached the slope he'd dug. "Harder!"

The horses strained against the impossible weight, stumbling and groaning. The wagon creaked like an old ship, then soon shifted and rolled up the slope. The back wheel plunged down into the hole and the wagon seemed like it was riding the side of a large wave. Only the team's momentum pulled it out again.

All of a sudden, Briggs heard a scream. He scrambled out of the hole but couldn't see Sarah. "Whoa!" he yelled, groping for the reins. Where was she?

The team came to a sudden stop. "Sarah!" he called out, then he saw her trapped under the wagon. He dropped to his knees and crawled under, into the dark shade where she lay on her side, clutching her wrist. "What happened?"

"I fell. The horses couldn't stop. I think my arm is broken."

"Let me see." He tried gently to peel her hand away. A muddy hoofprint dirtied her long sleeve.

Why had he let her do this? Why hadn't he done it himself? "Can you move it?"

"No."

Leaning up on his elbow beside her, watching her face go pale, Briggs carefully rolled up her sleeve. "I need to see it." His hands were shaking as he closed his fingers around the tiny, wounded wrist, feeling for any broken bones. "Am I hurting you?"

Stiffening, she stared straight up at the bottom of the wagon and nodded. "Do you think it's broken?" she asked.

"I can't tell for sure." But he was lying. He could feel a ghastly lump on the thin bone and it made his stomach turn.

Clenching her fist, Sarah awkwardly tried to sit up. "Maybe it's just bruised."

"I don't want to take any chances. We'll go straight to Doc Green's office when we reach town. Can you move?"

"Yes, but I'll need help getting out from under here."

Briggs inched his way out, skimming over the prickly, dry grass. He reached back to guide Sarah out. A few throaty groans escaped her as she clumsily slid along the ground, gritting her teeth together, her face drawn and pallid.

After helping Sarah to her feet, he swept her into his arms like a new bride and set her gently onto the wagon seat. He tried to appear calm, but his heart was battering his rib cage. What if something worse had happened to her? What if the horses had crushed her? She could have died right there in his arms, all because he was too impatient to wait on posting that letter.

Sarah clutched her arm as she settled into her seat. Briggs's body ached at the sight of her, hunched over in pain. The bumpy ride ahead wasn't going to be pleasant.

He glanced at the sun and realized it was late afternoon. It would be dark when they reached town and Doc Green's. He began to reload the wagon, swiftly and haphazardly tossing things over the sides. He could barely think. This was all his fault. Surely, Sarah knew it.

By the time they drove into town, it was dusk, and the pain in Sarah's arm was so excruciating, she could barely tell where it began and where it ended. Her shoulder? Her back? Her hips? Every time they'd hit a bump along the way, fresh spasms had shot through her and she could have leaned over the side of the wagon and retched. Instead, she'd forced herself to withstand it. When she wanted to cry out, she focused on controlling her breathing, keeping it steady and even.

"We're almost there," Briggs said, steering onto Front Street. "You look cold."

"I'm fine." But in fact, her teeth were chattering and she could not stop them, even when she tried to clamp her jaw shut.

Briggs shrugged out of his buckskin coat and draped it over her shoulders. As she wrapped it around herself, fresh pain shot up her side, but the coat was warm...thank heavens it was warm.

They pulled up in front of a building on the main street, but all the windows were dark. "Wouldn't you know it," Briggs whispered. "The doc must have gone out."

They sat in the wagon for a moment while Briggs decided what to do. Sarah pulled the coat tighter around her shoulders.

"I'll tell you what. I'll drive you to George's place and get you settled. Then I'll look for the doc and bring him over." Briggs slapped the reins and drove to his brother's house. Thankfully, a lantern was flickering in the front window. Briggs leaped out of the wagon, ran up the steps, and pounded on the front door.

A few seconds later, it creaked open and George stepped into view. "Briggs! What are you doing here?" He looked past Briggs toward the wagon. "Is Sarah with you?"

"Yes. We came in for supplies and got stuck on the prairie. She's hurt and we need the doctor."

George's eyes widened in shock. "Bring her in!"

Briggs ran back to the wagon to help her. Feeling weak and sick, Sarah leaned on his shoulder to step down. Before she knew what was happening, she was swept into her husband's strong arms. She buried her face into his neck, wanting to disappear into a deep sleep there, but knowing it would be impossible to ignore the pain long enough to slip away. He carried her inside, his strides smooth and fluid.

"Take her upstairs to the spare room," George instructed, following. "I'll light the lamp."

In a matter of minutes, Sarah was being set down

on a soft mattress and her husband was drawing a
quilt up to cover her. He touched her forehead with
the back of his hand. "You'll be all right till I get
back?"

She nodded sleepily.

"George, look after her. I'm going to look for the
doctor."

Sarah listened to the sound of her husband's boots
pounding down the stairs and the squeaking of the
door as it burst open and snapped shut. She lay in the
bed, staring at the white-painted ceiling.

George approached the bed. "How did it happen?"

Sarah hadn't even realized he was in the room.
She'd been concentrating on fighting the pain, and oh,
to talk was such a distraction....

"We got stuck in a hole," she answered. "I was
leading the horses out, but Gem slipped and I fell. I
should have been more careful."

"Nonsense. Accidents happen. Where was Briggs?"

"Behind the back wheel." She paused to breathe.
"Pushing. He was in such a hurry to get into
town...."

George frowned. "Is everything all right between
you two?"

Confused and disoriented, Sarah tried to sit up.

"No, don't...you must lie still." George hurried to
the bedside and pulled the covers up to her chin. "I
know about the situation. You mustn't worry."

She tried again to sit up. "What *situation?* Do you
mean the locusts?"

He backed away, bumping into the rocking chair
and stumbling slightly.

"George, what's going on?"

"Nothing's going on. You need to rest."

Her agitation caused another spasm of pain. She clutched at her arm and dropped back down. "Don't tell me to rest. I'll rest when you tell me what's going on."

George pushed his spectacles up along the bridge of his long narrow nose. "It's nothing to be concerned about."

"Please tell me," she said, her tone softening. She didn't have the energy to persist. "If you don't, I'll lie here imagining all kinds of things, probably worse than whatever it is you're hiding."

After a brief hesitation, George let out a sigh of defeat. "Like I said, it's nothing to worry about. It's just that an old…an old friend of Briggs's is in the middle of a scandal again."

"Scandal?" Sarah's thoughts came back into focus. "An old friend? Are you referring to Isabelle?"

George relaxed a little. "You know about her, then?"

"Yes, of course. What has happened?"

"I'm afraid her husband has left her."

Sarah felt an uneasiness spread through her body. "Where did you hear that? Perhaps it's just gossip."

"It's quite true."

"How can you be sure?"

He stared at her, directly. "Because she came home to her father's house and she called on me the other day to ask about Briggs."

Chapter Twenty-One

Briggs burst through George's front door with Doc Green right behind him. "She's up here."

They quickly climbed the stairs. When they walked into the bedroom, Sarah looked at first as if she'd fallen asleep, but her eyelids fluttered open at their approach. George was sitting in the rocking chair, watching her.

The doctor leaned over and felt her head. "How are you feeling?" he asked, opening his brown leather bag.

"I'm all right, really."

"Let me be the judge of that." He pulled the covers back. "Which arm is it? Ah, this one."

Briggs stepped forward. Sarah's hand had turned blue.

Dr. Green tried to roll up her sleeve but found it too tight. "We're going to have to remove this." He darted a glance at George in the rocker.

"I'll wait downstairs." George rose and took Briggs by the arm. "Why don't you come, too? I have something I need to talk to you about."

Briggs looked down at his brother's firm grip. "I'll be down later."

"I'm going to need his help," the doctor said.

George hesitated a moment, then left the room and closed the door behind him.

The doctor carefully but quickly removed Sarah's bodice, leaving her under the covers in her chemise and corset. "I have to examine you. It might hurt a bit."

Briggs approached the bed and took her other hand.

The doctor touched her wrist. "Does this hurt?"

"Yes."

The doctor's grip inched up a little. "How about this?"

Sarah's whole body wrenched. "Ahhh!" She squeezed Briggs's hand and clenched her teeth.

The doctor felt around a bit, then looked at Briggs. "It's broken, all right. Judging by the look of her hand, I'm going to have to set the bone right now. There's no circulation."

Briggs met Sarah's frightened gaze. "What about something for the pain?" he asked.

"No time to wait for it to take effect. She could lose her hand. Grab her arm right here."

In a panic, Briggs moved around the bed and took hold. Sarah looked up at him, fear evident in her pleading eyes. He wanted to hold her, to protect her, but he knew this had to be done. His stomach churned with dread as he gave her a regretful look.

The doctor closed his hand around her wrist, feeling with his fingers. "This is going to hurt, Mrs. Brigman, but I'll do it as quickly as I can."

Suddenly, he yanked. Sarah screamed. Briggs held on to her arm, biting back the urge to shove the doctor away. He was pushing and pulling and pressing down on the bone with all his might. Screaming in agony, Sarah writhed like a dying creature on the bed. Briggs gasped for air, holding her arm while the doctor yanked some more. He could not do this. He could not stand to see Sarah suffer!

"Please stop!" Sarah cried. "I can't take it!"

The doctor suddenly set down her arm and took a step back, wiping his forehead with his sleeve. Sarah squirmed on the bed, crying.

"Did you do it?" Briggs asked.

The doctor shook his head, his eyebrows drawn together in defeat. "I couldn't get it in place. There's a lot of swelling. I'll give her a break, then I'll have to try again." The doctor went to the door and called down the stairs. "George! Do you have any whiskey?"

Briggs leaned over Sarah and brushed her hair off her forehead. She was lying still now, a thin film of moisture covering her face. "I feel sick," she said.

The doctor grabbed the chamber pot from the dresser and brought it over to the bed. Sarah retched into it, then collapsed, trying to catch her breath. Just then, George hurried into the room with a bottle. "What's going on?"

"I'm setting the bone," the doctor replied, taking the whiskey from George. He tipped it over Sarah's mouth and she gulped down as much as she could.

"I have to try again," he said, giving the bottle back to George.

"No, please, not yet," Sarah pleaded.

"I'm sorry, Mrs. Brigman. But your hand…" He nodded at Briggs to take her arm again and hold it steady. "Courage, now," he said to Sarah.

Briggs held on to her, steeling himself. His heart ached at the sight of her, gritting her teeth and squeezing her eyes shut. Tears spilled onto her cheeks as she prepared herself.

The doctor yanked against Briggs's hold. Sarah cried out and contorted in pain. Horrified at the degree of physical strength he had to use against the doctor's yanking, Briggs prayed for it to be over quickly. He could not bear to see his wife being tortured much longer.

The next minute seemed like an hour. Finally the doctor set the bone in place and Sarah sagged against Briggs in relief.

"George, get me the splints in my bag."

Doc Green wrapped Sarah's arm while she clenched her jaw. Briggs couldn't help but admire her courage. He leaned down and kissed her forehead. "It's over now, love. It's over."

She nodded weakly.

"Can you give her something now, Doc?" Briggs asked.

"Yes. I'll give her some morphine."

A short while later, Sarah closed her eyes and went to sleep. Briggs breathed a heavy sigh of relief. All this, because he'd been in such a hurry to post that letter.

Briggs and Doc Green went downstairs to the kitchen where George was boiling water for tea. "Is she going to be all right?" George asked.

"She'll be sore for a while," Doc answered, "but she'll recover. She'll keep her hand."

"That's a relief. Would you like to stay for tea, Doc?"

"No, thanks. I have to get home and put the little one to bed."

Briggs showed him to the door. "I guess you heard about the locusts," he said quietly. Doc Green nodded, touching his shoulder. "We've got an impressive mound of butter in the wagon, if that'll do till I can pay you what I owe you."

The doctor held up his hand. "I know you're a man of your word, Briggs. Pay me when you can."

Briggs nodded, appreciating the doctor's patience. At least he had the necklace to sell.

After the doctor drove away, Briggs went to the kitchen and sat down, his legs giving out on him suddenly. He'd been strong upstairs for Sarah, but now all he wanted to do was down some of that whiskey himself. He looked up at George. "So, what is it you wanted to talk to me about?"

George poured two cups of tea and carried them to the table. "I think you better listen. I had a visitor the other day—Isabelle."

Briggs raised the cup to his lips, trying not to appear shaken. "What did she want?"

"Are you ready for this?"

Briggs wasn't sure he was, but he nodded anyway.

"Her husband ran off with a barmaid from The Comique Theatre."

Briggs calmly sipped his tea, set the china cup down on the saucer with a *clink*, trying not to spill any, and took a deep breath. "Is this supposed to matter to me?"

George slumped back in his chair. "I don't know. I thought it might, but I'm pleased to hear it doesn't."

"What did you expect me to say?"

"A part of me thought you might dash out the door to let her cry on your shoulder."

Briggs shifted in his chair. "I have a wife upstairs. Do you actually think I'd leave her here alone in her condition? How would that look?" He sipped his tea, staring over the rim of his cup at his brother. "Why are you looking at me like that?"

George rubbed his chin. "I was hoping it was less a point of appearances."

Briggs set down his cup with a clatter and stood. "I don't care about what's happening to Isabelle, George. I'm sorry for her. But that's all."

Briggs entered the quiet, dimly lit bedroom and climbed into bed next to Sarah. She was flat on her back, sleeping soundly. With that dose of morphine, the doctor said she probably wouldn't wake until morning.

Briggs reached out and let his hand rest gently on hers. A swell of deep regret erupted within him. If he could have traded places with her tonight, he would have, without hesitation. He would have done anything to spare her that suffering.

He leaned up on one elbow to look at her lovely face, peaceful at last, then kissed her lightly on the cheek. Strange to think he was married to Sarah because of Isabelle. He had never imagined anything good would come of her breaking their engagement, but looking back on it, it was the very thing that had made him place a passionless advertisement in a newspaper, and that in the end had brought him Sarah.

Isabelle had been here to see George. Why? What had she said to him? Downstairs, the news had startled Briggs. He had worked so hard to appear indifferent, he'd not allowed himself to ask any questions.

He rolled onto his back and tossed his arm under his head. Perhaps Isabelle regretted her decision to break their engagement. Maybe she wanted him back.

He cupped his forehead with his hand and closed his eyes, dreading the possibility of meeting her again. He would be polite, of course, but it would be awkward. On the other hand, if her visit with George was simply a courtesy, there was nothing to worry about.

He stared through the darkness at the ceiling, listening to Sarah's steady breathing beside him. If Isabelle held on to some hope that he would take her back again, she would have to learn he was married to someone else and had no intentions of breaking his vows. She would have to learn that what had once existed between them was over and done with.

Sarah woke the next morning with her arm throbbing painfully. She groaned and remembered the horrors of the night before—the doctor pulling and yanking at her broken arm. It was like something out of a nightmare. She'd never endured anything so physically grueling in all her life. And it seemed the pain intended to stay a while....

She listened to voices downstairs. Briggs and George were talking, but she could not make out what they were saying. Feeling thirsty, she noticed a glass of water on the bedside table, but when she reached for it, she accidentally knocked it over. It fell to the floor and smashed.

"Drat." She tried to rise, but felt sick and flopped

back down on the bed. She was still in so much agony.

A knock sounded at the door. When she didn't answer, it opened and Briggs walked in. "Sarah, are you all right?" He closed the door behind him and crossed the room. "What happened? George and I heard something break."

"I think you better bring me that washbasin. Now!" Her body heaved. She was going to be sick.

Hurriedly, Briggs brought the large china basin and held it for her while she retched. She felt mortified that her husband was seeing her like this. When she finished, she lay back and pulled the covers up to her neck. "I'm so sorry," she managed to say, wiping the tears from her eyes.

"Don't be silly." He set the bowl on the floor and found a handkerchief in the dresser. He sat on the edge of the bed and wiped her face. "The doctor gave you quite a dose of whiskey last night. And morphine."

"I remember, and I feel terrible."

"I can see that." He smiled, trying to make light of the situation. "How's your arm?"

"Sore."

He reached up to move a tendril of hair out of her eyes. Despite her rolling stomach, her body calmed pleasantly at his touch. "We don't have to go anywhere until you're feeling better. George says we can stay as long as we need to."

"What about your plowing?"

"That can wait a few days. The important thing is that you get well."

"I feel like such a nuisance. I've caused you nothing but problems."

Briggs tenderly caressed her face and gave her a reassuring smile. "I won't have you thinking such nonsense. If this is anyone's fault, it's mine. I shouldn't have been in such a hurry to get to town. I shouldn't have asked you to lead the horses when—"

"Briggs, you don't have to stay just because of me. You could go back and finish your work and I'll come home when I'm better. I'll be fine, really." But in all honesty, she didn't want to be away from him, not even for a single day.

"I wouldn't think of it. The doc said you'll be feeling better in a couple of days. You'll just have to take it easy for a while. I'll look after the milking. I'm sure Martha would be more than happy to help out."

Sarah gave him an appreciative smile. "Did you run the errands?"

"No. I'll go after breakfast."

"Please," she said, holding up her good hand. "Don't mention breakfast."

Her feeble attempt at a joke made him smile. "You should get some rest. Do you need anything?"

When she shook her head, he slowly rose and moved to the door, taking the washbasin with him.

"Briggs? You'll need this." She reached into her skirt pocket and dug out the wrinkled letter to Garrison.

Hesitantly, he moved toward her. He reached out to take it but she didn't let go right away.

"I think I'll feel better when I know you've sent it." She finally released it and dropped her weary hand to her side.

With a smile that seemed tainted with regret, Briggs turned and left the room.

* * *

Bells jingled when Briggs opened the door to the postal office, anxious to send the letter to Garrison and to start fresh with Sarah. All that wretched business about her past had caused enough pain and heartache. Sarah had a broken arm because of it.

When he walked into the building, every man, woman and child seemed to stop what they were doing and fix their eyes on him. Whispers and giggles filled the air. He stood in the doorway, trying to control his breathing. He had a funny feeling the whole town knew about Isabelle's latest tragedy.

Ignoring the gossips, he walked to the postal wicket. "Morning, Roger."

Roger Crosby sniffled and blew his nose. He'd lost some hair since the last time Briggs had seen him. "Morning, Briggs. Haven't seen you around in a while."

"I've been busy on the claim. You heard about the locusts, I reckon."

"It's a darn shame. Folks are having a rough time." He turned around and began sorting through a pile of letters. "There's something here for Martha Whitiker. Came in just this morning. You want to take it?"

"Sure." Briggs dug into his pocket for the letter to Garrison and tapped it on the counter.

"Anything else I can do for you today?"

Briggs handed the letter over. "Yes. You can post this to Boston."

Cupping one lens of his spectacles between his thumb and forefinger, Roger studied the address. "Boston, you say."

"Yes."

"Are you certain? Because there's a Garrison McPhee here in town."

Briggs felt the room begin to close in around him. "Maybe it's a different Garrison McPhee."

"Possibly, but this one just arrived from Boston a few days ago. In fact, he came in to hand deliver that letter Martha picked up. Is he a relation?"

"No, he's not." Briggs turned to walk out, his boots pounding across the floorboards.

"You don't want to post that letter?" Roger called after him.

"No," Briggs snapped as he flung the door open. "I'll hold on to it for now."

Chapter Twenty-Two

Walking back to George's house, Briggs worked hard to keep his anger under control. Sarah didn't know about Garrison's presence in town—at least he didn't think so. God only knew what was in that letter she burned.

As he walked, unseeing, he forced the suspicions down. He had to trust her. He *did* trust her. He approached the house, considering what he would say when she asked if he'd posted the letter. He stopped on the covered veranda and stared down at the unpainted wood planks under his boots. What if she wanted to see Garrison again?

Laughter from the kitchen startled him. Sarah was feeling better, it seemed. Briggs snapped the screen door open and walked in to find Sarah sipping on tea with her shawl pulled over her arm in the splint, listening to George tell the story of Briggs bloodying Little Charlie Tomkins's nose twenty years ago.

Briggs moved into the room. The laughter died and he felt uncomfortably like he'd just walked onto center stage.

George slid his chair back and stood. "Briggs. We were just talking about you."

"I gathered that." He looked down at his wife's curious face and shrugged out of his coat. "You were saying?"

"Uh, I was just telling Sarah why no one calls you Arthur."

Briggs glanced from George to Sarah, and back to George again. The two of them looked like children caught spying on their teacher before school. He draped his coat over the back of a chair. "Little Charlie Tomkins was in bad need of a bloody nose. In fact, he told me afterward it cleared up his head cold."

George and Sarah looked at each other, then began to laugh. Briggs backed up against the dry sink, watching them giggle.

Sarah rose and approached him. She seemed weak and slightly hunched over as she reached around him to set her cup on the counter. Briggs let out a deep breath that seemed to come from nowhere.

Rubbing the back of his neck, he eyed his coat pocket across the room and saw the top of the letter. It wouldn't be long before Sarah saw it, too, and asked why he hadn't posted it. His mind filled with dread as he tried to decide what to tell her.

"I guess you noticed I'm feeling better," she said, sitting carefully at the table again. "My arm is still sore, but I think I just needed to eat something. If you want to go home today, I think I could manage it."

Go home. She wouldn't want to leave so soon if she'd come here expecting to see Garrison.

Briggs felt relief pour through him. They could drive straight out of town and be long gone before he even mentioned Garrison to her. He would have to tell her, of course. He only hoped it wouldn't matter. "Sure, we could leave today. Only if you're absolutely certain you feel well enough."

Sarah stood with care. "I think so. Did you run all the errands? You weren't gone very long."

"I still have a few things left to do." He thought mainly about the necklace and maybe having a word or two with a particular worm from Boston if he could find him.

"We could run the errands on the way out of town. If someone would help me get my things?"

Briggs reluctantly agreed, knowing that if Sarah was with him, he couldn't very well track down Garrison. Wondering what to do, he watched her leave the room to go upstairs, then felt George staring at him.

"What's the matter?" Briggs asked.

George cocked his head. "Nothing. You just look bothered."

"Wouldn't you be if a horse broke your wife's arm?"

"I suppose," George replied, as if he wasn't convinced that was the problem.

Sarah let Briggs lift her into the wagon, but with the movement came a sharp stabbing pain in her arm. She suppressed the urge to complain about it, wondering if she'd made a mistake when she suggested they travel home today. She had honestly felt better at the time and she didn't want to be a bother any longer. She just hadn't imagined how difficult it would be to get into the wagon with one arm in a splint.

Briggs climbed up beside her and freed the brake. They waved to George, who was out on the veranda leaning on the railing, then they ambled down the dusty street toward the business district.

A few minutes later, they were rolling down Front Street, passing other wagons, carriages and roaming livestock. The street itself seemed to play music, like a grand orchestra of *clip-clops,* jingling harnesses, cowbells and nickering horses.

"I'll stop in at Wright's to sell the butter and eggs," Briggs said, pulling the wagon to a halt a few doors down. "Why don't you stay here and rest?"

She knew it would be painful to move, but she also knew the trip home would leave her sitting in the wagon for many hours to come. "I'd like to come in."

"You'd be more comfortable here."

Puzzled by his objection, Sarah said, "I'd like very much to go inside."

After a peculiar hesitation, Briggs helped Sarah down, withdrew the large wooden box from the back, then led the way into the store.

The door jingled closed behind Sarah, the clatter of hoofbeats and wagon wheels now muffled behind her. Everything from saddles and rifles to common groceries, barrels of salt and molasses, canned goods, ashes for soap making, and bolts of calico fabric lined the aisles. People roamed around, looking and considering, inspecting items and chattering constantly, and the air was thick with the scents of tobacco, spices and leather.

She and Briggs made their way to the counter where Briggs set down the box. "Morning, Austin."

"Briggs, my boy." He glanced at Sarah, curiously.

"This is my wife, Sarah Brigman. Sarah, this is Austin Moore. He's in charge of the place."

"It's a lovely store you run, Mr. Moore."

"Thank you. I don't recall seeing you in town before. You must be from away."

"Yes, that's right. I'm from—"

"She's from out east."

Bewildered, Sarah glanced up at her husband. He was already changing the subject, and she could only guess that he didn't want anyone to know he'd ordered her like a catalogue item.

"We have some butter and eggs here, Austin," Briggs continued.

While Sarah watched the transaction take place, a cowboy approached and leaned on the counter beside her. He held soiled, brown gloves in his hands, and Sarah wondered uncomfortably how long had it been since the man had bathed. She raised her gloved finger to hold under her nose, then unexpectedly, she gagged.

Briggs stopped talking and turned his attention to her. "Are you all right?"

Eyes watering, she nodded quickly, unable to talk for fear of gagging again.

"Are you feeling ill?" he whispered.

"I'm fine. I just need some air. I'll wait outside." She hurried toward the door.

"What about picking out the blankets?"

Without turning back, she replied, "You pick them."

Outside, she sucked in a lungful of fresh air. Well, as fresh as could be expected with the stockyard less than a mile away. At least the gagging sensation was gone.

Sarah walked along the boardwalk to the wagon, and climbed awkwardly onto the seat while favoring her sore arm. She sat down and spread her shawl over her legs, waiting. Wagons and buggies rattled by, the gentlemen tipping their hats at her, the ladies smiling. On horseback, cowboys trotted down the middle of the wide street.

Just then, a familiar voice spoke from behind her. "Well, well, well. What a coincidence."

Numb with shock and disbelief, Sarah could do nothing but stare straight ahead. She would know that voice anywhere.

Garrison moved into her range of view and tipped his black hat. "That arm of yours must be awfully sore if you're going to let your husband choose your bedding. Aren't you worried he'll choose the wrong color?"

Briggs stared blankly at the pile of blankets for sale. There were gray ones, red ones and blue ones. He wondered what Sarah would prefer—something like the red blanket she had hung in their house, or something different?

Oh, what did it matter? All he needed was something to keep them warm for the winter and he'd kept her waiting long enough.

He chose a red one and a blue one, and went to the counter. He had to wait a moment while the lady ahead of him paid for her groceries. While he stood there, he found himself searching the store with his eyes, wondering ridiculously if he would somehow know Garrison if he encountered him. He sighed, watching the lady ahead of him count out her money.

He stepped up to the counter and set down the blankets. "I'll take these."

"Fine. I gave you a credit for the butter. Tell your wife I already sold half of it."

"She'll be pleased." He thought of how worried she'd been that no one would want the butter. He couldn't wait to tell her. Right after that, he'd drop the news about Garrison and hope to the highest heavens she wouldn't care.

Sarah instinctively tried to slide across the hard seat, away from Garrison, but winced in pain. "What are you doing here?"

She watched helplessly as he leaned against the side of Briggs's wagon and crossed one shiny shoe over the other. He brushed a fleck of dust off his black suit at the arm. Panic—raw, icy panic—froze her to the seat.

He removed his hat. "What do you think I'm doing here? I came to take you home, where you belong."

"How did you find me?"

"It wasn't difficult, my dear. Didn't you get my letter? The train master in Boston was most cooperative and once I got here... Well, this town is quite friendly, I discovered. It seems everyone knows everyone else's business."

"Then you must know I'm married. His name is Briggs and he'll be out of the store any minute."

"Yes, yes. Briggs. The heartbroken farmer. Sad story, that is."

"You have no right to..." She stumbled over whatever she was going to say, then quickly recovered. "That's none of your business. He's married to me now, and we're very happy."

"Married. Yes, I heard. But aren't you forgetting something?"

Sarah stared at him, unable to speak. He leaned toward her, his eyes triumphant. "You must realize it's not legal."

Panic like she'd never known stabbed at her heart. "It *is* legal. It was done at the courthouse."

Garrison shook his head, amused. "You didn't tell him, did you?"

"It's none of your business what my husband and I discuss."

"*Your husband?* You say it with such conviction. It makes me want to laugh, Sarah."

She faced forward, raising her chin. Her arm throbbed suddenly. "Why don't you just leave us alone?"

He strolled to the front of the wagon and stroked Gem's forelock. "How much longer are you going to keep this up? Are you so angry that you want me to suffer indefinitely?" When she said nothing, he walked along the team and rested his hand on the wagon seat. Sarah slid across to the other side, holding her arm.

"Well, perhaps I deserve it," he said. "But I told you I was sorry for not explaining everything sooner. You know I love you more than anyone else. You're far and away the most beautiful woman I've ever known. I want you to come home. Put all this foolishness behind us."

"I'm not going anywhere. I told you, I'm married to Briggs now."

"But surely, you couldn't love a *farmer*." He glanced at the splint on her arm. "It looks like he doesn't treat you well at all."

"He didn't do this! He would never lay a hand on me!"

Garrison shook his head at her. "As you say. But with all that aside, I'm your true husband, Sarah, and I mean to remind you of that."

"You're not! Our marriage was never legal. It was completely meaningless." She leaned forward and realized too late she'd attracted some attention. Quickly, she sat back.

"Come home, Sarah. Stop all this."

"I told you I'm not going. I'm warning you to leave me alone."

"Warning me, are you? I should think you'd know better than to threaten me."

She slid across the hard seat again, and despite the pain it caused, climbed down the other side of the wagon. She had to get away from him.

"Where are you going?" Garrison asked, following her to the boardwalk.

"Away from you." An unexpected raindrop landed on her cheek.

"But we're not finished."

"Yes, we are."

His shoes tapped closely behind her. "If I thought that, would I have come all this way to find you? To make sure you've kept your mouth shut?"

Sarah stopped, recognizing the controlling tone she'd thought she'd escaped. An unpleasant chill shook her as rain suddenly dropped from the sky in a misty curtain, pounding like a drum on the roof above them. She moved into a doorway. "Get out of my sight, Garrison."

"You know I can't do that. I love you. I live for nothing else."

Sarah's chest was heaving. She wanted to hide her panic, but could feel her face turning red, her expression cringing with rage. "I don't love you."

His lips fell open in shock. "You can't mean that."

She knew this was another one of his great performances, yet she still felt the urge to soften the blow. "I do. I'm sorry, Garrison."

He stared at her in disbelief, saying nothing. He seemed hurt. Genuinely hurt, but she would not give in. He was a liar, she reminded herself. And a good one.

He glanced down the boardwalk. "I see that your farmer is coming."

Fear quaked within her as she leaned out of the doorway to look. She withdrew back in. What was she going to do?

Briggs stopped just outside the store, saw the empty wagon, then looked in the other direction up the street.

"Good God, Sarah, look at him," Garrison scoffed. "That hair. You can't possibly prefer that over me."

Her stomach knotting, Sarah watched Briggs pause, waiting for the pedestrians on the boardwalk in front of him to clear. His golden hair blew across his face. The brown fringe on his coat whipped in the rain-filled wind. Indeed, he was different from Garrison. Less civilized, less polished.

But decent, and most certainly more of a man.

"Will you introduce us?" Garrison asked.

Sarah shot him a glare. "He doesn't want to meet you."

"I doubt that. I think he wants very much to meet me."

Just then, Briggs looked in her direction just as she

peeked out of the doorway. He stood motionless, staring at her. Sarah felt as if she was choking.

"He's seen us!" Garrison said, enthusiastically.

Sarah wondered if she could run to Briggs before Garrison had a chance to say anything. She had to try. She could not let him find out this way.

When Briggs started toward her, she made a move. Garrison closed his fist around her sore arm and jerked her back to him. She winced in pain.

"Not so fast, love," he breathed into her ear. "I want to meet your new husband."

Chapter Twenty-Three

Sarah felt as if she were standing on the edge of a cliff, teetering, about to be pushed over the side.

Carrying a wooden box of supplies from the store, Briggs walked calmly toward them, not once releasing her from his intense green gaze. Thunder boomed somewhere in the distance and rain pattered on the slanted roof over their heads.

Time seemed to slow down as Briggs neared. Sarah tried to take a step toward him, but Garrison yanked her back by her injured arm again. He'd always been brazen, but this was beyond belief.

Briggs drew his eyebrows together. "Sarah?"

She shook her head frantically, trying to tell him with her eyes that she hadn't planned this, that Garrison was her enemy, that she had not known he had followed her all the way from Boston. *Help me,* she tried to say.

Briggs shifted a narrowed gaze to Garrison. "What's going on here?"

She felt the grip on her throbbing arm loosen. She immediately moved closer to Briggs.

"I don't believe we've been properly introduced,"

Garrison said, holding out his hand. "You must be Briggs. I'm Garrison McPhee. I've heard a lot about you."

Briggs looked down at Sarah. Her heart tightened with dread.

"It seems we have a great deal in common," Garrison remarked, lowering his hand.

"I doubt that," Briggs said. "What do you want?"

"What do *I* want? I should think that's obvious."

Briggs set his box down on the boardwalk and took a step forward, crowding Garrison against the wall. Sarah had not known her husband to be a violent man, but at this moment, she feared the worst.

She touched his sleeve. "Briggs…"

He didn't seem aware of her. He was glaring down at Garrison, who had by this time backed into the wall. "It's all right, Sarah," Garrison said. "He just wants to intimidate me."

"You're damn right I do." Briggs said nothing more. The seconds ticked by and he simply stood there, towering over Garrison.

"Briggs, let's just go home," Sarah said, touching his arm again.

At first, he didn't respond. Then, thankfully, he took a step back. "Sarah doesn't want to see you anymore," he said. "So why don't you go back where you came from."

"I didn't travel all this way to be bullied by you."

"I don't care what you came for. You're not to lay your hand on my wife again."

"What was that?"

"I reckon you heard me fine."

The challenge between them hung in the air while the rain beat down on the overhang. Sarah's heart thumped wildly in her chest. Her breaths came in short gasps.

"Briggs, let's go," she pleaded one more time.

He started to back away from Garrison, but Sarah couldn't relax just yet. She'd do that when they reached the wagon and could finally discuss this mess calmly.

Briggs stopped again. Sarah's fears bubbled to the surface. What was he going to say next? Why couldn't he just let it be?

He jabbed a finger at Garrison. "Stay away from my wife."

Oh, God.

Sarah shot a look toward Garrison, begging him with her eyes. *Please, don't say anything. Not now. Just let us go....*

A slow, crooked smile played across his face. "*Your* wife? I think you're mistaken."

"Oh, you do?"

"Briggs, let's go," Sarah said. "We need to talk about this—" They moved along the boardwalk, the raindrops bouncing off the street beside them, but Garrison followed.

"It's unfortunate that *I* must be the one to tell you this," he said, "but she's not your wife."

Briggs stiffened noticeably. "That's ridiculous. We were married a month ago."

Garrison shook his head in mock pity. "I'm afraid you weren't. She isn't your wife."

"Why the hell not?"

Garrison's dark eyes flashed triumphantly. Sarah thought she was going to faint.

"Because she's *my* wife."

* * *

Briggs felt like he'd been struck across the chest with a wood plank.

He laughed once, thinking this conversation absurd, but somewhere beneath the denial, he knew something was wrong. He tried to make sense of it, wanting nothing more than to believe his wife over this scoundrel, but all his thoughts were scrambling together. For some reason—and it shamed him to admit it—his instinct moved him to doubt her.

"You don't look as surprised as I'd expected," Garrison said. "No more arguments?"

Briggs felt Sarah's uneasy presence at his side.

"Let me explain," she pleaded.

He couldn't look at her. He knew he should hear her out, but he just couldn't listen right now.

"There's nothing to explain," Garrison said. "It's quite simple. She married me, then perhaps a little hastily she married you."

Briggs wanted to say something. Anything. But the words would not come.

He heard Sarah's voice like an echo. "Briggs, please listen—"

He cut her off by holding out his hand. "This can't be true. I have the marriage certificate."

Garrison dug into his breast pocket. "And so do I." He unfolded a piece of paper and held it up. "See for yourself."

The print blurred before Briggs's eyes. He saw Sarah's signature and he saw Garrison's. A sickening feeling engulfed him.

"You see?"

But Briggs could not see. He could not accept this. Sarah was *his*. They'd spent the last month together on his farm. They'd grown to care for one another. They'd made love. They'd made promises....

"Briggs, there's more you don't know," Sarah said, her voice wavering. "If you'll let me explain..."

Finally, he looked at her. All he saw was the woman who had deceived him on their wedding day. He had asked her if she loved this man, and now, to learn she had *married* him? Sarah touched his shoulder but he shrugged her away.

"Are you all right?" she asked.

Turning, he glared down at her. "No, I'm not all right."

He could not stay here. He had to leave. If he didn't, he might do something he'd regret.

He hopped down into the wet street, splashing and sinking into the mud. He could feel the cold hard rain slamming onto his head, soaking his hair so it clung to his neck and shoulders. If this man was her true husband, then so be it. Truthfully, it wasn't all that surprising. He'd been expecting something like this from the beginning. When had anything he ever loved stayed with him?

Briggs climbed into the wagon and reached for the reins, staring straight ahead. He would not look at her again. He couldn't. He slapped the reins, flicking water into the air as a damp chill invaded his clothing. Raindrops trickled from his eyelashes onto his cheeks.

As he started to pull away, he heard a muffled cry from somewhere beyond his barely functioning consciousness. He tried to block it out, but it cut through his fury like a blade.

Don't look back, he told himself over and over as he turned his wagon toward home. But the scream punctured his resolve again.

He pulled the horses to a slow halt.

He sat there, staring, water streaming down his face. He felt like he was in a thick fog trying to find his way forward. The muffled screams were coming at him from somewhere outside this debilitating stupor. *Sarah*. She was crying for him to come back.

He swung around in the seat. Garrison was dragging her by her broken arm, pulling her along the boardwalk while she struggled and pleaded for help.

Good God—what had he been thinking?

Leaping from the wagon, Briggs sprinted toward them. His boots splashed through the mud. Rain battered his face, but he had to get to her. He could not leave her behind.

He flew up onto the boardwalk before Garrison had a chance to realize it. Sarah was sobbing and crying, her arm outstretched toward him. He grabbed her hand just as Garrison turned around.

Briggs drew back and punched Garrison in the face. He stumbled backward, then fell onto the boardwalk. A deathly silence surrounded Briggs's thoughts as he swept Sarah into his arms and carried her into the street, through the mud, then lifted her into the wagon. In a matter of seconds, the horses were galloping away, mud was splattering everywhere, and Briggs had no idea what to do next.

Sarah tried to control her tears, but couldn't. Cold rain stung her cheeks as they sped into the wind. Sobbing, gasping for breath, she clung to the side of the wagon as they skidded around a corner. She said a silent thank-you that he had come back for her. *He had come back.*

Turning her gaze toward him, she wondered miserably if it mattered. He was staring straight ahead, all emotion absent from his dark expression. Yes, he had rescued her from Garrison, but had he lost all feeling for her in the process?

"Briggs, I'm so sorry," she cried over the noise of the clattering hooves.

"Why didn't you tell me about this?"

"At first, I was afraid you'd send me back. Then, I became afraid of what Garrison would do if you exposed him."

He wouldn't look at her. He focused on the road ahead and slapped the reins. "Yah!"

Sarah, swiveling in the seat to face him, clutched his sleeve in her tight fist. "Can you honestly say you wouldn't have sent me away? You almost left me behind just now, after everything we'd been through these past few weeks. I thought we'd fixed things. I thought there was hope for us, but you almost left me behind!"

"I'm not the one who should be defending myself. You are."

"If you'd given me a chance to speak back there, I would have told you what *really* happened. Now, I'm not sure it even makes any difference."

She saw the muscle in his jaw tighten. After a few seconds, he pulled the reins and slowed the horses to a walk. For the first time since they'd leaped into the wagon, he looked at her. "What do you mean, 'what *really* happened'?"

Sarah let go of his sleeve and wiped the wetness from her eyes. "It's not as simple as Garrison made it out to be. I didn't just marry him and then marry you. I wouldn't do that."

"Are you telling me you're divorced?"

She shook her head, wishing it could be so. "No. But when I married you, I honestly believed I was free to do so."

He pulled the wagon to a stop on the edge of town. "What are you trying to tell me?"

"I'm trying to tell you that my marriage to Garrison was never a true one."

His eyebrows drew together in confusion. "Why not?"

"Because...because he already had a wife."

Briggs sat stone-still, blinking from the rain. "You mean bigamy?"

"Yes. But I didn't know it when I married him. He told me on our wedding night, just after we'd..."

"Why didn't you tell me this before? If you were innocent, you could have turned him in. It could have been straightened out before you ever came here."

"You wouldn't have wanted me if you knew. And besides that, Garrison threatened me. He said if I told anyone, he'd say I knew what I was doing, that I was after his money. Then I saw your ad and I had the chance for a decent life with an honest, hardworking husband like my father. Someone to start a family with. I didn't think I'd ever get the chance to have those things if anyone knew. I thought if I could keep the whole thing a secret—at least until some time had passed—I could straighten things out later. But I made a mistake when I got on the train in Boston. I should have used a different name."

"You make it sound like your only mistake was getting caught."

"I don't expect you to understand. I wish I could go back and undo everything."

They sat in silence a moment, both of them soaking wet. Sarah couldn't stop her teeth from chattering.

"So what does this mean?" Briggs asked, looking down at the leather strap he squeezed in his hands. "Are we married or aren't we?"

She didn't want to answer that question, but she knew if she wasn't honest with him now, all would be lost. The time for secrets had ended. "I'm not sure of anything anymore."

He locked her in his gaze. "Why should I believe you after everything you've kept from me?"

"Because I love you. I wanted to say it yesterday, but I couldn't. I wasn't sure you felt the same way. I didn't think you wanted to love anyone. Or for anyone to love you."

He bowed his head.

"In my *heart,* I'm your wife. Isn't that what's most important?"

"You tell me you love me, but all along you knew you were lying to me. What kind of love can there be without trust?"

"Briggs—"

"No, answer me. How do you expect me to reply to this—" he paused and waved his hands in the air "—this sudden confession that you love me? How can I believe you when you're pretending to be someone you're not? Our whole life together over the past month has been a lie. Would it be real for me to love you, when I don't have the slightest idea who you really are?"

She shuddered at his icy tone. "You say there can't be love without trust. But I trust *you.* With my life."

He tore his gaze away from her. "Maybe that's

because I never lied to you. I never played any of the charades *you're* so good at.''

With growing resentment, Sarah thought about everything they'd been through, how she'd been treated after their wedding night, how he'd been so cold. ''Never lied to me! What about Isabelle? You didn't tell me any of that. I had to find out from Martha!''

''I don't want to talk about that.''

''Why not?''

''Because that was different. I didn't lie about Isabelle. I just never mentioned her. There was no point.''

She felt her blood quicken with anger. ''Yes, there was. She's the reason you sent for me. I was just a way to forget her. You were using me just as much as I was using you.''

Briggs squeezed the reins in his hands.

''I know you've never gotten over her. So if Garrison finds a way to destroy what we have, will you order another wife and forget about me, too? As if the past month never happened?''

''Of course not.'' His voice was low and controlled.

''If you were truly over her, you wouldn't fight so hard against trusting me.''

He dropped the reins and stood up in the wagon, towering over Sarah. ''I am over her. I'm just not over the—'' It was as if he were only now understanding the emotions he'd worked so hard to ignore all this time.

''The what?'' she asked, pressing him. ''You're not over the what?''

Rain rapped against his coat. ''The things I care about always getting taken away.''

He sat down again and his expression shook her with its openness. "I watched my family die. My mother, my father, my baby sisters and little brother. There was nothing I could do to stop it."

Fighting tears, Sarah covered his cold hands with hers. "Oh, Briggs."

"I didn't want to love you, Sarah. I worked hard not to, but then I gave myself permission to hope, and now I find out you were never mine to begin with."

"I *am* yours, Briggs."

"You were Garrison's before you were mine. You took vows, you said you'd love him until death parted you. Did you really believe you would? Did it mean anything to you when you said it?"

Ashamed, she tried to find a way to answer him. But how could she, when she didn't even know the answer herself?

"Did it?" Briggs asked.

Unable to look him in the eye, she nodded. "I wrongly believed in him."

"You promised him a lifetime."

She quickly looked up. "And you promised me one, too, when you didn't know me at all."

He did not respond. He just stared at the gray horizon, blurred with rain and mist.

"Please, believe me. I thought I was free to marry you. I was certain my marriage to Garrison was not valid, and over the past month I've grown closer to you than I ever was to him. To anyone."

"The past month…" He gazed up at her, despondently. "In all that time, I never really knew who you were."

His dark tone sent a chill down her spine. "But you know now. I promise, you know everything."

"Maybe so. I'm just not sure I like what I know."

Panic shot through her as he picked up the wet reins and flicked them against the horses' broad backs, turning them around.

"Where are we going?" she asked.

"Back to see George. I want a lawyer's advice, and I want it now."

Chapter Twenty-Four

Drenched to the core with cold rain, Sarah and Briggs pulled into George's yard. They had not spoken a word since Briggs turned the wagon around. Sarah felt the tension surrounding her shivering body like a cloak of ice.

Without waiting for Briggs to assist her, she climbed down and hurried toward the front door to escape the downpour. Her arm ached with every move she made, but the ache in her heart was more painful by a long shot.

She pulled the front door open, and shivering, entered the warm, dry house. George walked into the foyer. "Sarah, you're soaked. Come in by the fire." He led her into the kitchen. "Where's Briggs?"

The front door squeaked open and she heard her husband's boots tap against the step. George immediately went to meet him. "What's wrong with you?" he demanded. "Sarah could have caught her death out there."

As much as she could tell from the kitchen, Briggs didn't answer. She wondered if he even cared. He walked into the room and didn't waste a single moment on civilities. "George, we have a legal problem and we need your help."

George followed behind Briggs and gave Sarah a questioning glance. "Maybe we should go into the parlor."

Briggs gestured for Sarah to lead the way. She went in and sat on the sofa in front of the window, but the two brothers stood.

"I suppose you should be the one to explain it," Briggs said. "You know what happened better than I do."

She hesitated, wondering how she would ever get through this. Her stomach felt like it was bleeding fire. "It's something very private, I'm afraid."

George removed his spectacles.

"I have a problem—*we* have a problem," she said softly.

"You have my utmost discretion," George assured her.

"Thank you." This was proving more difficult than she had expected. She kept her eyes lowered. "I—I made a mistake before I married Briggs and now I'm afraid it's going to ruin everything."

"What kind of mistake?"

She stood and walked to the fireplace, staring numbly at the empty white china vase on the mantel. How could she say this to George, her brother-in-law, who had always made her feel so welcome? But if she was going to set things right with her husband, she had to find a way.

Closing her eyes, she began. "I was involved with another man before Briggs and I were married, and the involvement progressed to the point of—" Hearing Briggs clear his throat, she stopped, unable to go on.

Sarah tried to find the right words, but gave up, deciding there was no respectable way to put it. "I married him."

She heard George whistle in shock. "You're divorced?"

"No, George. That's the problem. I'm *not* divorced."

She faced the two brothers. George merely stared, his mouth open. Briggs stood in angry silence.

"Sarah, I don't understand," George said.

"I didn't get the divorce because I never believed my first marriage was legal. I still don't, but I'm not certain. If only I'd had the courage to seek legal advice right away, but I was afraid I'd be arrested."

George stopped pacing and shot her a horrified look. "Arrested! Why?"

"Because he—he already had a wife."

George sank into the rocking chair by the fireplace and rested his forehead in his hand. "My God. This is unbelievable. You mean he never divorced his first wife before marrying you?"

"No."

"And he wasn't a widower?"

"No."

"You're telling me you married a bigamist?"

"Yes."

He buried his forehead in his hand again. "Briggs knew nothing of this?"

She gazed apologetically at her husband.

"I knew nothing about it until today," Briggs said, his voice flat.

"At first I didn't tell him because I was ashamed

and afraid he would turn me away. I had no idea what I was getting into when I met Garrison. He was charming in the beginning, then he turned cruel. I had to escape the marriage.'' Sarah was desperate to salvage what was left of George's opinion of her. ''I had no idea he was already married, and now he's followed me to Dodge and wants me back. I'm afraid of what he might do if I don't do what he wants. He told me he'd never let me go, and now he knows I'm married to Briggs. You should have seen the way he looked today when I told him I didn't love him. It was as if I'd plunged a knife into his chest.''

George sat forward. ''He's here? You spoke to him? Did anyone see you?''

Briggs finally spoke up. ''George, you're missing the point. Are any of her marriages legal?''

His detached tone made Sarah shudder inwardly.

George scratched his head. ''I'm not sure.''

''What do you mean, you're not sure?'' Briggs shouted. ''You're a lawyer.''

''I don't know everything! Bigamy law isn't my expertise. I've never dealt with it before. I'll have to look it up.''

''How long will that take?''

''I'm not sure. If I don't have the information in my library, I may have to wire a colleague.''

''Wonderful,'' Briggs whispered, heading for the door.

''Where are you going?'' Sarah asked, feeling the remaining fragments of courage rush out of her.

Without looking back, he replied, ''For a walk.''

''Can I come with you? We could talk about this.''

''I want to be alone.'' He walked out and slammed the door behind him.

* * *

Briggs sloshed through the mud in town, hardly aware of how deeply he was sinking. The rain had stopped, but the dark-gray sky prevailed. He could still smell moisture in the air, feel its coolness on his skin.

Looking up at a passing cowboy atop an impressive black horse, Briggs realized with some despair that he'd walked all the way from George's house, stepped up onto a boardwalk and couldn't remember anything he'd seen along the way. His head was pounding with tension, his muscles stiff. It pained him to remember the nights he'd spent with Sarah when she had been hiding a part of herself and keeping secrets. Why hadn't she trusted him enough to tell him? Had he been that much of an ogre in the beginning?

He supposed with some regret that he had.

Just then, someone called his name. That voice. That singsong voice...

"Briggs? Is that you?"

He stopped dead on the boardwalk. His heart leaped into his throat, and he wanted to thrash it for doing so. Slowly turning, he did his best to appear relaxed. "Hello, Isabelle."

She smiled and moved toward him. Hesitantly, he did the same, staring, trying to think of something other than the fact that they had once been engaged.

"Hello, Briggs. It's wonderful to see you."

"You, too," he replied, working hard to hide the turmoil in his throbbing head.

"I heard you were married last month. I had no idea it would make you even more handsome than you already were."

He looked around, wondering how many gossips were feeding on this. "Her name is Sarah."

"I know. George told me. Congratulations."

"Thank you."

The twinkle in her blue eyes slowly disappeared. "I suppose he told you about my—" she paused, then whispered "—my situation."

Briggs nodded. "Yes. I was sorry to hear it."

"And I was sorry that..." She stopped herself, and his desire to hear her finish was disturbing, to say the least. He swallowed the urge to prompt her on, but she did so anyway. "I was sorry that I left without saying goodbye to you."

Briggs tore his gaze away from her face and stared over her head at nothing in particular. "It's in the past now."

"I hope you don't have any hard feelings toward me, Briggs."

"Of course not. Like I said, it's in the past."

"Yes, you're right. So much has happened since then. I'm glad you were able to get on with your life."

He thought he heard her voice quaver. What would he do if she began to weep here in the street? He stared down at his boots, refusing to acknowledge it if it was happening.

"What's she like? George told me she was the exact opposite of me. Dark hair, dark eyes, rather short."

"She is a tiny little thing, yes," Briggs said, wishing she was here.

"You must be happy, then, Briggs. Is she everything you've always wanted?"

He stood for a moment, pondering that question,

realizing Sarah was not what he'd *always* wanted.
Until recently, Isabelle had held that position. "She's
what I want *now*," he answered truthfully.

Isabelle's smile faded. "I do hope we can be
friends."

"Of course."

Her eyes darted to something in the street. Briggs
turned to see George approaching in his buggy with
Sarah beside him.

"That's your wife, is it?" Isabelle asked.

"Yes, it is."

"Then I must go. I wouldn't want her to catch us
together."

He turned to tell her to stay and be introduced, but
she was already walking away. He stared after her,
watching that familiar gait.

He turned again, back toward George and Sarah.
The buggy pulled up alongside the boardwalk. "What
are you two doing here?"

Neither one answered. George stared at him, his
lips pressed into a tight line. Briggs looked back to
see Isabelle disappear around a corner and realized
uneasily that Sarah was watching her, too.

Chapter Twenty-Five

Briggs stared into his wife's dark, wounded eyes and chastised himself for feeling the urge to explain himself. He'd done nothing wrong.

George jumped down from the buggy. "Sarah needed some fresh air so we thought we'd go for a drive and look for you." He frowned with disapproval, then spoke to Sarah. "I'll head over to the office now. Briggs will drive you home."

Slowly, not knowing what to expect, Briggs walked toward her and climbed into the driver's seat. Without a word, he flicked the reins and turned them around. His palms were clammy and it irritated him that he should feel so guilty about a simple conversation. It wasn't as if his wife hadn't done the same thing less than an hour ago, with far worse implications....

A few minutes later, they pulled up in front of George's house. Briggs set the brake and hopped down. Sarah didn't wait for him to come around and help her. She began to climb out by herself, wincing at the pain in her arm.

"Wait," he said, hurrying around the horse. "Let me help you."

He wrapped his hands around her tiny waist and gently lowered her to the ground. She looked up into his eyes as if asking a question.

"It was a chance meeting," he said, his hands still gripping her waist. "I didn't plan it."

He saw the hurt lingering in her eyes just before she turned and walked toward the house.

"Sarah, wait."

She climbed the steps. "You don't have to explain. I believe you." She let the door snap shut behind her. Briggs whipped it open, following.

"Just listen, please? I bumped into her. It couldn't have been helped."

Sarah went into the kitchen, poured water into the teakettle and set it on the stove.

"I wanted to introduce you, but she walked away before I got the chance."

Saying nothing, Sarah set a china cup on the small pine table, then went looking for the sugar bowl.

Briggs couldn't take it anymore. He reached out, grabbed her around the waist, and whirled her to face him. "Sarah, you have to believe me—I don't want Isabelle. Anything I might have felt for her is long dead."

Eyes wide with shock, she stared up at him and nodded.

He pulled her into him, felt her soft, heaving breasts flatten against his abdomen, and suddenly wondered why *he* was the one trying to explain himself when *she* was the one who had been married to two men in the same month.

But none of this made sense, he realized, feeling his body grow warm with an insurmountable need for her. The only thing that mattered was that she was *his* now. She belonged to him and he to her. He wanted no one else, and if he had anything to say about it, no man would ever touch her again.

He dropped his mouth to hers and felt her lips part with longing. Their fiery heat turned his muscles to liquid.

She would not go back to Garrison. She would not.

Her hands slid inside his coat...he had to get it off....

Tearing it from his body, he dropped it onto the wood floor. He scooped Sarah into his arms and carried her up the stairs, taking two at a time while she clutched at his neck, kissing his cheek and whispering his name. He kicked the bedroom door open with his boot. It slammed and bounced off the inside wall.

He carried her to the bed and gently laid her down. Her bodice—it had to come off. One button, two buttons...his fingers trembled uncontrollably, and he felt an odd mixture of desire and a disturbing, confusing impulse to weep.

Trying to ignore his jumbled emotions and concentrate on what he was doing, he tugged at her corset hooks and slid her chemise off her shoulders until her beautiful breasts were bare and calling to him. She pulled his head down and he took what he could into his hungry mouth, more than willing to give her as much pleasure as he was capable of giving.

At her urging, he ripped his own shirt from his body, kicked off his boots and pulled off his trousers.

As he came down upon her, she whispered, "I need you so much, Briggs...."

With one swift thrust of his hips, he entered her. Heavy rain pelted the roof over their heads, roaring steadily.

They moved together, Sarah digging her nails into his back, while Briggs raised himself up on his arms to look down at her—her face so exquisitely beautiful in the murky light of the afternoon rain. Soon she reached her peak and cried out as lightning flashed in the window. Clenching his jaw, Briggs felt his seed explode into her.

For a moment, he could not breathe. All he wanted was to remain here in this bed forever while time stood still around them.

But time would not stand still, he knew with regret. Life didn't work that way. There was so much left to resolve between them, so many secrets he needed to understand. How long would that take? he wondered, breathing deeply and feeling Sarah also take a deep breath beneath him. His heart tugged painfully and he hugged her in his arms, then wondered when he would ever feel certain of anything again.

With that old familiar urge to protect himself, Briggs rolled off her and sat up. Damp air chilled his skin and he shivered. He could barely speak. What was the right thing to say?

"I have to go," was all he could come up with. It was all he could *ever* come up with.

He dropped his feet to the floor and pulled on his trousers, then his shirt.

Sarah reached for the quilt to cover herself. "Where are you going?"

"Nowhere. Just downstairs. I need to think about things." He touched her on the forehead, gently brushed her hair away from her eyes with his thumb, then walked out of the room to leave his wife to dress alone.

* * *

As the lace curtain billowed inward from the open window, a rain-scented breeze blew inside the bed-chamber where Sarah lay on the bed, clutching the quilt at her neck and knowing in anguish that Briggs had needed to be away from her.

What had just happened? she wondered hope-lessly—and in the middle of the afternoon, no less? But after seeing Briggs with Isabelle, the idea of los-ing him made her need him more than ever. The de-sire to touch him and be touched *by* him had been overpowering. She simply had to have him.

That was her motivation. In a way, she needed to stake her claim. What was his? He'd pulled her against him with all the force of a winter gale, and she'd seen the arousal in his green eyes. He, too, had wanted her in a way that was different from the other times in their sod house. Why? Had he closed his eyes and imagined he was with Isabelle?

That thought sent a hot current of jealousy through her and she had to force herself to banish it from her heart.

Suddenly aware of the excruciating pain in her arm, she rose from the bed and clumsily buttoned her shirt with one hand. She hobbled to the window and pulled it closed, shutting out the noisy rain, then she stood in front of the mirror and straightened her tousled hair and wrinkled bodice.

Sarah jumped at the sound of the front door open-ing. Was Briggs leaving the house? she wondered anxiously. Gathering her skirt in her fist, determined to stop him, she charged out of the room, only to look down from the top stair and see George hanging his overcoat on the hook behind the door.

He looked up and removed his fogged spectacles. "Sarah, are you all right? Your cheeks are flushed."

Embarrassed, she touched each of them with her good hand. "I'm fine. I was just resting." She started down the stairs. "Did you learn anything about the marriage?"

Briggs appeared from the kitchen, holding a cup of water in his hand. Sarah stopped halfway down the stairs, but he did not look up at her. "What did you find out?" he asked.

George folded his spectacles and slid them into his breast pocket. "Why don't we go into the kitchen?"

All three of them went in, and Sarah sat at the table. Pockets of dread burst like spasms under the surface of her skin. All she could do was grit her teeth and prepare herself for the worst. "Please tell us, George. I can't stand this any longer."

He stood just inside the door, looking down at her, his hands cupped in front of him as if he were about to recite the Lord's Prayer. "Well, you're married. There's no question there."

"To whom?" she whispered.

George nodded at his brother. "To Briggs."

Sarah leaned back in the chair. "Oh, thank God."

"But there's more."

"More?"

"Yes. I think Briggs should sit down."

Briggs set his cup on the table and sat down across from her, never once making eye contact.

"The good news is, your marriage is valid," George told them.

Briggs glared up at his brother as if he were about to argue the fact that he'd just delivered *good* news. Something inside Sarah died a little.

"It seems a bigamous marriage is considered void, whether or not either party moves to end it with an annulment or a divorce. So you were right in your assumption that it was void, Sarah, when you agreed to marry Briggs."

Sarah nodded, wondering why she wasn't happier about this news. But with Briggs sitting across from her, hardly seeming to care what George had to say, she found herself fighting tears.

"You said there was more?" she mentioned, working hard to keep her voice from quavering.

"Yes." George reached behind him for a document that he'd laid on the counter. He put on his spectacles, reading some of it over to himself. Those few silent moments seemed like an eternity.

Finally, he set the page down. "In 1862, an Antibigamy Act was set forth. It's a federal statute making bigamy a criminal activity."

"Will Garrison go to jail?"

"Yes, once he's reported to the proper authorities, but so could you, Sarah."

Heart suddenly racing, she felt Briggs look at her. She couldn't bring herself to meet his gaze. "But I didn't know," was all she could say.

"That being the case, you would be innocent, of course, but if Garrison says otherwise... Do you believe he would try to incriminate you?"

"Yes. He told me if I ever revealed any of this, he would say I knew what I was doing because I wanted his money."

"But you left him without taking anything, isn't that right?"

"Of course."

"Then he'd have a difficult time proving you wanted his money."

"So you think I have nothing to worry about?" Sarah asked, afraid to even hope.

"I would certainly do everything to help you."

Through all this, Briggs said not one word. His silence troubled Sarah more than anything.

"But this is good news," Sarah said to George. "Why are you looking so—so worried?"

"Because there is still one other point."

Sarah steadied herself.

"It has to do with your marriage to Briggs."

Briggs leaned back and folded his arms. "I thought you said our marriage was valid."

"I did say that, but there are some complications."

"Because we didn't know each other?" Sarah asked. "People do that all the time."

"Yes, they do, but in this case, it was more than not knowing each other. There's the issue of fraud."

"Fraud," Sarah repeated.

George cleared his throat. "On the day you arrived by train, Briggs let me read your letter. Don't be angry, he was just trying to convince me he was doing the right thing. I distinctly recall that you wrote you had never been married before."

"But I hadn't been married. Not legally."

"I understand that, Sarah, but a court might see it differently if Briggs were to bring it forward."

Sarah shot a glance at Briggs. He was sitting calmly, listening to it all. "What do you mean, bring it forward?"

"I mean Briggs has grounds to seek an annulment."

Sarah's stomach turned. She laid her trembling fingers across her abdomen. "An annulment?"

George nodded. "If he wants to." He looked down at Briggs, questioning him with his eyes. "He may not want to, of course, in which case everything would remain as it is."

Staring across the table at her husband, Sarah swallowed nervously. Perhaps the worst of it was she couldn't begin to guess what he was thinking, despite the fact they'd shared so much over the past few weeks. Would she ever really know him? she wondered. Would she even get the chance to try?

"Why is everyone staring at me?" Briggs asked, flipping his hair back off his shoulder. "I suppose you both want me to say I don't want to end this marriage."

George stepped back and set the paper down on the table by the stove. "I think we'd both like to know what you—"

"I don't know. If you're looking for an answer, I can't give it to you." He grabbed his coat and strode out of the room. Sarah sat frozen in her seat staring helplessly at George.

The front door opened and slammed against the inside wall. George hurried to the foyer. "Where are you going?"

"Somewhere to think."

Heartsick with dread, Sarah listened to her husband's boots pound down the veranda steps. *He will never forgive me,* she thought miserably, then buried her face in her hands and wept.

Chapter Twenty-Six

Rain-drenched and exhausted, Briggs pushed through the swinging doors at the Long Branch Saloon. He stopped just inside, inhaled the thick scent of cigar smoke and removed his waterlogged hat. The place was uncommonly busy for this time of day. Must be the rain, he thought as he strode toward the bar and dug into his pocket for a few coins.

"What can I get you?" the bartender asked, wiping his hands on a damp cloth.

"Whiskey." Briggs didn't take a drink often, but he reckoned if there was ever an appropriate time, this was it.

The bartender poured him a glass, then turned to set the bottle back on the shelf.

"Leave it," Briggs said, knowing he wasn't going to be ready to return home for a while yet. He had a lot of thinking to do and he wasn't about to do it in the same house with Sarah. She'd cloud his judgment with her mere presence and he had an important decision to make. He should have known something like this would happen a month ago when she'd first told him about Garrison and about her parents being dead for four years instead of four months. The lies had started then, but he'd felt obligated to stick to their agreement.

Raising the shot glass to his dry lips, he took the first drink, tasting the bitter liquid for a moment before he swallowed. He carried the bottle to a table and sat down.

After everything that had happened with Isabelle, he should have been more careful. He should never have let himself fall for Sarah so quickly without knowing her better. He should annul the marriage. It was quite simple, really.

He tipped up the glass, downed the rest of the sour-tasting whiskey, then poured another. He watched as the amber liquid gushed into the glass. What the hell was he going to do?

His head was telling him to end it. The law was clear; he was justified.

But the idea of leaving Sarah behind and returning to the farm without her was unthinkable. Just the thought of it made his whole body ache. Never see her again? Never touch her? Smell her? Could he go on knowing he'd never be able to bury himself in her warmth again?

Laughter erupted in the back corner of the saloon. Briggs jumped, then tossed back another mouthful of whiskey, welcoming its numbing effect. He pinched the bridge of his nose and shut his stinging eyes. What were the chances this would all work itself out? What were the chances he'd be able to trust her? Ever?

If he was smart, he'd never trust anyone again.

Briggs heard heavy footsteps approach and felt

someone's unbidden presence behind him. He swiveled in his chair.

"We meet again," Garrison said, bowing slightly.

"Not by choice." Briggs had to force himself to stay seated when all he really wanted to do was toss Garrison out face first into the mud.

After a short pause, Garrison pulled out a chair. "Mind if I sit?"

"Yes."

"Oh, come now. You're being a bit hard on me, don't you think? Sarah's the one you should be angry at."

Something inside Briggs jolted. He downed another mouthful of whiskey.

Garrison sat down across from him, despite Briggs's earlier protest. "Bartender, I'll have what he's having."

The bartender brought a second glass. "You want a bottle, too?"

"No, just a glass. I'm not in need of it like this gentleman is."

The bartender poured, then turned his back on them and returned to work. Briggs felt Garrison's gaze upon him and tried to ignore it. The last thing he needed was to get into a saloon brawl and spend the night in jail.

"Ah. The drowning of the sorrows," Garrison sighed.

"It's none of your business, McPhee."

"I'm only trying to make conversation. We got off on the wrong foot, it seems."

"There is no right foot where you and I are concerned."

"I don't blame you for being angry. I would be,

too. But like I said—it's not *me* you should be angry with. I'm only trying to help.''

"Help? You're helping?"

Taking a slow dignified sip from his glass, Garrison crossed one leg over the other. ''I'm here to talk to you, aren't I? You look like you need some helpful advice.''

"As if I'd take that advice from you. You're my problem, McPhee, not the solution.''

"That's not very neighborly of you.''

"You're not my neighbor. I'm surprised you're even willing to come within ten feet of me.''

Garrison chuckled with too much confidence. ''We're in a public place, Mr. Brigman. If you lay a hand on me, there are plenty of gentlemen here to come to my aid.''

"That's not what I'm talking about.''

Garrison took a drink, staring straight ahead. ''No?''

"No. I could talk to the sheriff. You'd be locked up before you even knew you'd left the room.''

"Locked up? And how may I ask would the charges read?''

"They'd read exactly as they should. Bigamy with a capital *B*.''

Garrison nearly choked on his drink. ''Is that what she told you? I must admit, that's not one she's used before.'' Garrison swallowed another mouthful, then smiled and dropped his hand onto Briggs's shoulder. ''Bigamy. How original. But in this case, I'm not the bigamist, Brigman. She is. I suppose that makes you one, too.''

"I'll have you know my brother is a lawyer. He's

checked into things for me. My marriage to Sarah is valid. Yours isn't.''

"I'm sorry, I'm sorry," Garrison said, chuckling and holding his stomach. "I shouldn't laugh. This is very serious."

"You bet it is. I think it's about time you tell me what's so funny."

Garrison reached for Briggs's bottle of whiskey. "May I? Perhaps you should have another, too." Briggs watched as Garrison filled both their glasses. "This is indeed difficult. It always is."

"What do you mean, *always?*"

"I've had to do this before. It's not the first time Sarah has gone off for a new life and I've had to bring her home, and you're not the first man she's married."

Briggs tried to keep his stomach from rolling.

"I can see you're surprised," Garrison said.

"I'm surprised you're fool enough to make any of this up."

"I'm not making it up. She's my wife and she's got a problem."

Briggs downed the rest of his whiskey and slammed the glass onto the table. He wiped his sleeve across his mouth and stood up to leave. "Why don't you go back to Boston and take your lunatic stories with you?" Briggs walked toward the door. The confident sound of Garrison's voice stopped him.

"I suppose she told you her parents were dead."

Briggs froze. He stared out over the swinging saloon doors at the curtain of rain cascading from the roof. Slowly, he turned around to look at Garrison. The man had risen and moved to stand at the bar.

"Did she say they'd died in a train accident? Or was it the pox?"

Every thought in Briggs's head was humming with disbelief. This couldn't be. Why had he stopped to listen? Why hadn't he just ignored Garrison?

"Well?" Garrison asked. "Which was it?"

Briggs regarded him coldly. "They *are* dead. They were killed in a carriage accident."

Garrison moved toward him. "Ah, yes, the carriage accident. Now, was this when she was a child? Or was it recently?"

Swallowing his unease, Briggs searched his brain for an answer. Before they were married, she'd written him and told him they'd died four months ago. She'd later told him four years. Which was it?

Garrison poured more whiskey into both glasses. "Maybe you should have another drink."

Briggs didn't want another drink. He didn't want to let his guard down. He didn't want to look at Garrison another minute. But something inside him was screaming for answers. Most likely, Garrison was playing him for a fool. At least, that's what he wanted to believe.

Slowly, cautiously, he returned to the bar and wrapped his large hand around the glass. "What else?"

Garrison reached into his breast pocket and withdrew a cigar. "I'm assuming she told you they were dead, then."

"Aren't they?"

He cut off the tip of the cigar and lit it, shaking his head as he puffed a few times in succession. "Alive and living in Chicago."

Briggs felt his chest throb.

"You must have had a feeling something wasn't quite right," Garrison said. "Instinct? She would have come to you with some obvious experience. Didn't that suggest anything to you?"

Unwilling to confide in this man, Briggs stood in silence. His head was pounding with confusion and near dizziness. Yes, his instincts had been to doubt her, but he'd told himself at the time it was his own problem. He'd come to the relationship a skeptic. Even George had tried to convince him of that.

But perhaps it had not been because of his experience with Isabelle. Perhaps his instincts had been right....

He gulped down another mouthful of whiskey and felt it sear its way down to his knotted stomach. He looked at Garrison. "If it's as you say, why do you keep taking her back?"

Garrison puffed on his cigar. "You should know the answer to that. You've been with her a month. Surely you feel for her, just a little."

Briggs stared at his glass and worked hard not to reveal anything.

Garrison continued. "There's something about her, don't you think? Something that makes you want to protect her, even when you know she can take care of herself, better than anyone, in fact. I suppose I'm no different from you. I want her still, after everything she's done. The thought of letting her go, well, I can't easily live with that. Isn't that how you feel, too? Aren't you trying to justify all this, figure out a way to fix it and put it behind you?"

Briggs didn't answer Garrison, but the question flapped wildly in his brain. Sarah had deceived him from the beginning, saying she'd never been married.

Then, to trick him on their wedding night as she had...

Briggs prepared himself for the question he was about to ask. "Do you have children?"

"No. Sarah doesn't want any and she knows how to prevent it."

Briggs's head was spinning...his limbs felt shaky. It wasn't the whiskey.

He tipped back his glass to finish. Laying his money on the bar, he pushed away from the counter.

"Where are you going?" Garrison asked.

"I'm going home."

Garrison's hand snaked out and clasped Briggs's arm. "What are you going to do? I won't stand by and let you beat her to a pulp. Just let her go, that's all you have to do. Bring her back to me and I'll take her home where she'll be safe. You can forget any of this ever happened."

Briggs hesitated, glaring down at this man before him.

"You'll give me your word? You won't mark her?" Garrison implored.

Briggs's gut wrenched with disgust. "That ain't how I handle things."

Walking out of the saloon, disillusioned, Briggs wondered how he *would* handle this, when all he wanted to do at the moment was put Sarah on the first train back east and never lay eyes on her again.

Walking back to George's house, Briggs had to concentrate on staggering around the cow patties and not falling face first into the mud. In fact, in his pathetic, intoxicated condition, he wasn't sure he could distinguish between the two.

He flipped his wet hair out of his eyes so he could see better. The rain had finally stopped but the road remained a sticky pool. With each step, he sank down at least four inches, the dark muck pulling at his boots.

And oh, his head…pounding like a drum. He should have known better than to accept that last drink. He should have known better than to take the first one. He'd never had much of a head for liquor.

By the time he reached George's house, it was sufficiently dark. He stopped on the veranda to scrape the mud off the soles of his boots, and paused there, gazing blurry-eyed at the lighted windows. He didn't want to go inside. He didn't want to do what he had to do, but the time for indecision was over. He just didn't want to get Sarah into trouble with the law….

Nearly losing his balance, he reached out to grasp the door handle, and kicked himself again for drinking that whiskey.

He entered the dimly lit house.

No one came to greet him.

The silence pulsated around his garbled senses.

Standing unsteadily in the foyer, he heard a chair slide out from the kitchen table. George appeared. "You're back," he said softly.

"Yes. Where's Sarah?"

"She's resting. I'll get her." He made a move to go upstairs.

"No. Don't."

George stopped at the bottom step. "I promised her I'd wake her if…*when* you returned."

"I don't want you to."

Suddenly, the room began to spin and Briggs

stepped sideways. George grabbed his arm and drew his eyebrows together. "Are you drunk?"

"No. Well, I had a few drinks, but I'm perfectly fine."

Wearing a disapproving frown, George went into the parlor and lit a second lamp. "It's not like you to take a drink, Briggs."

"I know, and believe me, I regret it."

The room brightened and George sat down on the sofa. "Sarah was upset after you left. She didn't eat any supper. She went straight up to bed."

Briggs leaned against the door frame and folded his arms. "Are you trying to make me feel guilty? I'm not the one who lied."

"I know, I know."

"Whose side are you on, anyway?"

George raked a hand through his hair. "I'm not on anyone's side. I just think Sarah needs—"

"*Sarah* needs. *I'm* your family, George. Me. She lied to me from the beginning and you act like I'm the only one to blame here, like I'm causing all the problems."

"I don't think that."

Briggs moved into the room with deliberate care. "Then what *do* you think?"

"You can't turn your back on her, Briggs. She has no one."

Briggs tried to push away the throbbing sensation in his head. "No one? Did she tell you the story of her poor deceased parents?"

"Yes. Why are you looking at me like that?"

"So you lent her your sympathetic ear, did you?"

"You're not making sense."

Briggs stood and walked to the mantel. He leaned

one elbow upon it, resting his temple on two fingers. "George, you don't understand everything that has happened."

George rose and rested his hand on Briggs's shoulder. "Sarah really does love you, you know."

Wincing inside, Briggs stepped away from his brother. "I don't want to hear that."

"But you care about her, Briggs. I know you. You're just angry."

"Damn right, I'm angry. And you don't know everything, big brother. You think you know her because you've spent a little time with her, but you don't. She's a beautiful woman and she uses that to get what she wants. You're playing right into her game."

George backed away, retreating into the dark kitchen. Briggs followed. "Don't walk away from me."

"You're drunk and you're being foolish."

"Am I?"

George said nothing. He went to the kitchen window and slammed it closed.

"You're always taking her side," Briggs continued, "like I'm the one who did everything wrong. I haven't always been easy to get along with, I admit, but dammit, George, I'm your brother! We really don't know anything about Sarah."

George sank into one of the kitchen chairs. Leaning both elbows on the table, he said, "I'm sorry, Briggs. I just can't accept what you're saying."

"I know. You were taken by her the moment you saw her at the train station. Weren't you?"

George shook his head. "No, Briggs. She's your wife."

"That's not the point." Briggs sat down and stared at his brother for a few minutes. "Funny, you were the one trying to convince me not to marry her in the first place. You wanted me to get to know her first."

George leaned back in his chair. "I remember. I had a bad feeling about everything."

"And you were right. You have no idea what I learned tonight."

"Are you going to tell me?"

"I suppose I'll have to...."

A half hour later, George sat back in his chair and sighed. "You believe him?"

"I don't know what to believe. I just know this marriage is not meant to be. I thought I was avoiding trouble by getting a mail-order bride. I thought it would be simpler."

"What are you going to do?"

Briggs rested his forehead in his hand and squeezed his eyes shut. "I should do what any man in my position would do. But the idea of it..."

George looked up. "The idea of what?"

"The idea of..." He couldn't believe this was happening. "God, George, I really do care for her, but I can't let how I feel about her change what has to be done. I know it'll be hard, but I have to do the right thing. I need your help."

Chapter Twenty-Seven

Sarah lay awake in the darkness staring at the ceiling. Her throbbing arm had awakened her an hour ago, and she'd tiptoed into the hall only to find herself alone in the house.

Her mind had already created an alarming number of unpleasant scenarios. What if Briggs and George had gone out to find Garrison? What if something terrible had happened to them? What if they'd reported everything to the sheriff?

Back in bed now and turning onto her side, she rested her cheek on the back of her hand. If only she could sleep through this uncertainty and awaken when they returned.

About a half hour later, she heard a wagon pull up in front of the house. She leaped out of bed and hurried to the window.

They were back. A sigh of relief escaped her. She stood at the window, one hand resting on the sill. George and Briggs spoke for a moment. Then George hopped down from the wagon and came to the door.

Briggs drove away.

A sick feeling crept into Sarah's stomach. Where was he going?

Sarah wrapped her shawl around her shoulders and hurried downstairs. She met George in the kitchen. "Where were you?" she asked, unable to restrain the desperate tone in her voice.

George laid some papers on the table, refusing to look at her. "I think you better sit down."

Her heart began to thump in her chest. "Why? What's happened? Where did Briggs go?"

"Why don't you sit down?" George suggested again, finally making eye contact. His face was pale, his eyes red with exhaustion behind his spectacles.

Sarah hesitated, then slowly made her way into a chair. She sat there waiting while George flipped through the papers. "Would you like a cup of tea or something?" he asked, distractedly.

"No! I don't want anything—except for you to tell me what's going on!"

He sat in the chair across from her and laid his hand flat on the papers in front of him. "I have bad news."

A jolt of fear left her paralyzed in her seat. She could not speak.

"I'm sorry to be the one to tell you this, but Briggs has decided on an annulment."

Everything seemed to grow dark around her as George's words pounded against her skull. Annulment? Had she heard him correctly?

"Are you all right?" he asked.

"No."

George wouldn't look at her. "I'm sorry, Sarah. He was quite firm. He wants you to go back to Boston."

Tears flooded her eyes. She swallowed, trying desperately not to cry. "Did he say anything more? Did he tell you why, exactly?"

"It's his legal right."

The coolness in her brother-in-law's voice stung. It seemed the whole world had turned against her.

"Does he still love Isabelle?" she asked, her voice cracking.

"It's not my place to discuss these things with you. I'm acting as Briggs's attorney."

Sarah felt like she'd been hurled against a brick wall. She tried, but could not stop her eyes from filling with tears.

George picked up the papers. "Everything's right here. Briggs has already signed it."

Staring in disbelief at what George held in his hand, Sarah wiped her cheek dry. "What does it say?"

George kept a stony expression. "It doesn't implicate you as a bigamist if that's what concerns you. We discussed it at great length to come up with a phrasing that would—"

"I don't care about that," she blurted out. "I just want to know what his reason was."

"It says you misrepresented yourself. Led Briggs to believe things about you that were not true."

She shoved her chair back and stood. "This annulment won't make me go back to Garrison if that's what Briggs thinks. I'll make my own way. I want you to tell Briggs that."

George stared at her, his face pale. "I will."

"And if Briggs can walk out on me knowing that I love him, I'll welcome this annulment. If he's incapable of trusting me—of loving me!—then I'm better off alone.''

Heart racing, she turned and walked out of the kitchen, but stopped at the bottom step. The papers. She hadn't signed the papers....

She squeezed the railing. Should she sign her name? Should she let Briggs go so easily?

Sarah took a deep breath, feeling a cold rage grow inside her. How could he leave her without saying goodbye? He'd sent his brother to do it for him.

As she stood at the base of George's staircase, trying to see her future, she realized with sorrow that this sudden end to her marriage had been inevitable from the beginning. As desperate and frightened as she had been on her wedding day, she was wrong to have deceived Briggs, and this was her much deserved comeuppance.

Fighting unfathomable grief, Sarah spun on her heel, walked into the kitchen, and hastily scrawled her name.

The sun was just rising when Briggs drove into his yard feeling sleepy, sore and very much alone. He'd driven all night in a blank stupor, brooding over Sarah's lies and deceptions. At the same time, he'd fought the urge to turn around and bring her home with him. Though now he had to wonder what there was to come home to. Dry, dead fields? A tiny structure made of sod? A bitter cold winter on the way?

He pulled the wagon to a gentle stop, set the brake and hopped down. The chill of night had not left his bones with the advancing dawn. Autumn would soon be here. With the sky growing lighter, he could see his breath floating from his lips in small, quick puffs.

The barn door suddenly swung open, lantern light spreading like spilled water on the ground. Briggs stared until little Frank Whitiker appeared in the doorway.

"Briggs! You're back!" the boy shouted. "I was looking after Maddie for you. She's milked and the pigs are fed."

Briggs walked toward the boy and messed his hair. "Thank you, Frank. I knew I could count on you."

The boy's face beamed with pride. Briggs smiled, but noticed how much effort it took to do so.

"I should be getting home. I still have my own chores to do before breakfast." He bolted across the yard, but stopped suddenly and turned back. "Wait till I tell Ma and Pa you're back! They'll want to come over again for more dancing."

Briggs frowned. He wasn't looking forward to explaining any of this to Howard and Martha. "Mrs. Brigman isn't with me, Frank. She stayed in town."

Frank scratched his head. "Oh."

"You can tell your folks not to worry, though."

The boy hesitated, then slowly turned and took off across the barren field.

An hour later, Briggs sat at the table staring at the dirt wall, listening to the wind roaring eerily over the ocean of endless prairie. Why didn't he feel relieved? He'd just cut loose a deceptive wife, gotten out of it legally, yet the only thing he could think about was how desperately he missed her.

After accepting George's offer to pay for a train ticket anywhere, Sarah went to the train station and chose her destination. Caldwell. It was as good a place as any. Then, not feeling very well, she went out for a walk, thinking the fresh cool air and sunshine might help. She stepped up onto the Front Street boardwalk, her heels clicking in a steady rhythm as she walked by Mueller's Boot Shop. The smell of fresh bread emerged from the bakery next store and an unexpected wave of nausea moved through her.

Not again, she thought, holding her gloved hand up to her mouth. Her eyes searched frantically for a place to go, but where? She gagged, then turned and ran into the fenced-in alley beside the boot shop. With one hand on the tall fence, she bent forward and retched.

A moment later, she was wiping tears from her eyes and sniffling. What else would she have to endure today? Making her way back onto the boardwalk, she tried to ignore the curious stares. She waited for the sick feeling to go away, but it lingered. When she imagined getting on the train and rocking and swaying for the entire journey, she nearly retched again.

"Are you all right?" an older woman asked her. "You don't look well at all."

"I'm fine."

The woman stared sympathetically. "Why don't you let me take you to the doctor? I couldn't live with myself if I left you here."

Sarah was about to decline the lady's offer, but thought better of it. Perhaps she did need some help. She would put the visit on Briggs's account.

"Thank you," she said, her voice shaky, her body weak as she tried to walk. The kind woman held Sarah's good arm and led her slowly down the street.

* * *

"Pregnant!" Sarah shouted, staring wide-eyed at Doc Green. "Are you certain?"

"Yes, I am."

Sarah collapsed into a velveteen upholstered chair by the door. The doctor knelt in front of her, his brown eyes full of compassion. "Is there a problem?"

A problem? Only if one considered it a problem to be pregnant and not know who the father was.

She stood up and touched her fingers to her lips. Did the baby belong to Briggs? If so, she could not dispute what she felt—a joy so intense, it could not be matched by anything in this world.

Something inside her told her it was his....

She whirled around and yanked the door open, her skirts spiraling outward.

"Mrs. Brigman! Where are you going?"

"I'm going to tell my husband!"

From where he sat in the barn milking Maddie, Briggs was exceedingly aware of the late afternoon silence. The wind had died down; the grass had gone still. If not for the rhythmic streaming of Maddie's milk into the wooden bucket, he would have questioned whether or not his ears still worked.

He hunched forward under the cow and remembered all the days during the past month when he'd looked forward to returning to the warm house after a long day's work. It's true what they say, he thought, squeezing the last drop of milk from Maddie's udder—you don't appreciate what you have until it's gone.

He gripped the bucket's rope handle and rose to his feet, wondering if what he missed was simply the smell of hot corn bread and pork roast. Any woman could prepare a meal and create a cozy feeling in a sod house. All it took was a few flowers, a tablecloth, a curtain hung on the window.

But would another woman make this empty feeling go away?

Suddenly he wanted to hop on one of the horses and ride back to town, get down on his knees and beg Sarah to forgive him for being such an ass, such a coward. When had he ever just let himself love her without fretting about it? When had he ever given her what she'd given him?

He turned to carry the bucket outside, but stopped when he heard something. Hoofbeats?

Anticipation rippled through him. Had Sarah come back to give him another chance?

His heart flooding with hope, he bent forward to set the bucket on the ground. The hoofbeats came to a halt just outside and someone hopped down.

Briggs moved to the door. His mood began to rise. He was beginning to shake with joy, with the urge to laugh! The orange sun came into view as he stepped outside into the light, ready to break into a run.

He stopped dead in his tracks.

Approaching him with her long flowered skirt sweeping to and fro was Isabelle.

Chapter Twenty-Eight

Clutching her purple skirt in a tight fist and holding on to her hat, Sarah burst out of the doctor's office and ran up the street toward the livery. She would hire a buggy and find her way to the farm. She would tell Briggs she was expecting a child. A child!

As she ran, each long stride sent a jolt of pain up her arm, enough to make her feel faint. How would she steer the horse with this miserable splint on her arm? Maybe she could ask George to help her. She just couldn't give up. This news had to change things. She raced into Ham Bell's Livery and skidded to a halt, panting.

"Hey there, what's your hurry?" a man in blue denims asked.

"I need a horse and a buggy."

"Well, okay. We got that. How long do you want it for?"

Sarah struggled to catch her breath. "I need to drive out to the Brigman farm."

He stared at her, his face lighting up like the Fourth of July. "Are you the one that left him for the gentleman from Boston?"

"How in heaven's name did you hear about that?"

"Everybody knows. Aside from that, the reverend's daughter was here this morning, hiring out a horse. Seems like Briggs is finally going to get her back."

Sarah staggered back a step. "Wh-when did she go?"

"This morning. I reckon she's there by now."

Defeat held Sarah immobile. She tried to catch her breath. Had she lost Briggs forever?

"You still want that buggy?" the man asked.

For a long moment she just stood there, the world shrinking before her eyes. Could she dare to hope that Briggs would give her a chance when Isabelle had finally come back to him?

And the baby? Wouldn't he think she was now using her condition to get what she wanted? Hadn't he always been quick to think the worst of her?

Sarah looked up at the wood rafters, searching for answers. A meadowlark flew back and forth, trapped high in the peaked ceiling. When it swooped down and found its way out the wide barn door, Sarah took a deep breath and stared directly into the man's small, round eyes. "I want that buggy. If you please."

A few minutes later, Sarah paced back and forth in front of the livery, waiting for the little man to bring the buggy around. Her courage cracked slightly when she pictured herself pulling into the homestead. What if Isabelle was inside the cozy dugout preparing a meal? What if Briggs was there, too, sliding his hands around her waist and pulling her to him? Burying his lips into her neck?......

If Sarah walked in on that scene, her courage would surely dissolve like embers in the wind.

Biting her thumbnail, she decided to see what was taking the man so long. She walked around the side of the building and collided hard with someone.

Taken aback, she looked up. "No, not now."

Garrison grabbed her broken arm. Sarah shrieked, the pain so intense she sank to her knees. "It has to be now, my love. Otherwise, we're going to miss our train." He dragged her toward the station.

"No! Somebody, help me!"

Garrison whirled around and pulled a pistol from beneath his black coat. He pressed his cold palm over her mouth, cupping the back of her head with the hand that held the gun. "One more peep and I'll shoot you right here. I'd rather you be dead than in the arms of that savage you call a husband."

"Hello, Briggs," Isabelle greeted, her long strides fluid and graceful. Stopping a mere foot away, she smiled warmly. "I heard about everything. I couldn't imagine you out here all alone."

"You heard? What did you hear?"

"George filed annulment papers at the courthouse this morning. I'm afraid Dodge has a distinct talent for spreading news of people's personal affairs. We both can attest to that."

He buried his hands in his coat pockets. "You came all the way out here by yourself? That wasn't a wise thing to do—"

"Oh, hush. It was early in the day and I remembered enough not to lose my way."

He remembered the last time she'd been here, and the way she had left....

"Still, it's not exactly—"

"Not exactly what?" she challenged, in that melodic tone she used whenever she wanted her way. Funny, how he used to crumble into a hundred pieces over that voice.

She raised an eyebrow. "Appropriate? These days, I hardly think my reputation is worth protecting. I've been married and deserted, and now I'm going to be a mother." She lowered her gaze. "A mother without a husband."

"I didn't know."

"No one does. Not even my father." She wandered toward her horse and stroked his muzzle. Briggs felt an odd sense of pity—something he hadn't imagined he'd ever feel for Isabelle. She'd always gotten everything she'd ever wanted. Even at his expense.

"I'm sorry about all that," he said, taking a step forward, then stopping himself.

"I know you are." She turned to face him, masking any emotion with a smile. "But I didn't come all the way out here to talk about me. You're the one who needs a sympathetic shoulder today. I don't suppose you've eaten."

He gestured toward the barn. "No, I was just finishing up some chores—"

"Well, I have just the thing for a hungry man." She reached for her saddlebag. "I brought enough sandwiches for an army, plus a bag of my own home-cooked sweets. I remember how much you loved my molasses cookies."

He stood in the yard, staring. As much as he would like to believe she was just being kind, he knew she wanted something. Something he wasn't, and would never be, prepared to give. He wondered how he was going to handle this. He gestured toward the house, and together they went inside.

Briggs set the bucket down in the dark dugout, accidentally kicking a chair as he moved toward the window to open the curtains. When he turned, Isabelle was still standing on the bottom step, looking around the one-room house.

While he knelt to light a fire in the stove, she moved all the way in and set her saddlebag on the table. "I see a definite improvement over the last time I was here. Sarah certainly branded the place." She walked to the window. "What lovely curtains." She rubbed the fabric together between her thumb and forefinger and noticed the dried flowers in the vase. "I'll have to replace these first thing."

Briggs's stomach lurched.

"Yes, a new bouquet tomorrow," Isabelle chirped.

Tomorrow. He hadn't thought of that. Of course she was going to have to stay somewhere overnight. She couldn't very well ride back to town in the dark. Maybe Howard and Martha would be kind enough to provide a bed for her.

Isabelle clasped her hands behind her back and wandered around the room, looking at everything. "Shall we dig into those sandwiches?" he asked, rising to his feet and wanting to put an end to the awkward evaluation.

"Oh, of course! Pardon me for snooping around. You must be famished."

She laid the sandwiches in a decorative circle on a tin plate, and set it down on the table. Briggs sat down and began to eat immediately, thankful for a reason not to talk.

Afterward, Isabelle cleared away the empty plate and wiped the crumbs off the table, then began to make coffee. Within moments, its rich aroma filled the house, and Isabelle poured them both a cup. "So, I heard Sarah's old beau came to take her back."

Old beau. Obviously, the more degenerate parts of the story had somehow been concealed. "That's right. The man came all the way from Boston."

"They must have loved each other very much. I'm sorry, Briggs. You must know I can't bear to think of the way *we* parted. Yet here we are, sitting together as friends. You're not angry at me?"

Why, he wondered, did the conversation always come back to her? "Of course not." Yet the truth of it was, he hadn't given it much thought. It wasn't so much a forgiveness. It was a gradual fading of anger, or more accurately, a growing indifference.

Isabelle sipped the last of her coffee. "You know, Briggs, it doesn't have to be so painful for you. I could come back. We could finally have what we both wanted before things got so messed up. Since we've been apart—" she wiped a single tear from the corner of her eye "—I've missed you." Her voice cracked on the last word.

Briggs dutifully reached across the table and patted her hand.

"You're so kind, Briggs. So caring. I was a fool to leave you. Zack was so unpredictable and so vulgar sometimes. He always wanted to be the center of everyone's attention. But you were always calm and settled. I realize now that to be settled is exactly what I want." She raised her lids to reveal blue eyes now drowning in tears. *"You're what I want."*

Briggs sat staring at her, his pulse pounding inside his head. Here she was. Isabelle. Returned to him. Every night for two full months after she'd left him, he'd lain awake wondering where she was, how she was, and hoping beyond hope that she was missing him, just a little.

He leaned back, watching her slowly rise from her chair. Reaching into her bag, she withdrew a hand-kerchief and dabbed her eyes, then walked to the window. Briggs pinched the bridge of his nose and closed his eyes. Even in the heat of this situation, as he faced the fulfillment of an old fantasy, he was thinking of Sarah.

"Everything's going to be all right," he told her, approaching. "You're strong, Isabelle. You'll manage."

"But must I manage it alone?" Her hand glided along his jaw and slid under his hair to cup his neck.

Then she rose up on her toes to kiss him.

Chapter Twenty-Nine

Briggs looked down at Isabelle, her eyes closed, her lips parting in their approach. Her mouth touched his, and what should have been heaven, felt like hell.

Hands on her shoulders, he gently pushed her back down and shook his head. "I'm sorry, Isabelle."

Her arched eyebrows came together in confusion. "What do you mean?"

"I can't be with you."

"Why not? I'd stay this time. Zack can jump off a cliff for all I care—"

"It's not about Zack."

She stepped away.

"I did want you, Isabelle. Once. But I married someone else."

"You may have gotten married, but everyone knew you'd placed an ad. You just married her to get over me." The sparkle in her eyes died, as if she suddenly realized she'd said the wrong thing.

Briggs hated this. "Maybe at the time I did it to get over you, but I care for Sarah now."

"But you annulled the marriage. Why did you do

that if you loved her? I thought you did it because I was free again."

He backed away from her. "I made a mistake. I never should have signed those papers."

All at once, Briggs knew what he wanted, and this time, he would get it.

Isabelle began to gather her things. "Zack will come back for me, you know."

"I know. I'll drive you back to town."

"I should hope so."

Briggs dropped Isabelle off at her father's house later that night. It had been a long drive through the darkness. They had both felt the chill of autumn on their cheeks and hands, and Isabelle seemed more than thankful to be returned to civilization.

Briggs returned her horse to the livery, all the while feeling rushed, as if he were running from a fire someone had lit behind him. He had to find Sarah and apologize. A silent prayer rose up inside him—a prayer that she would forgive him, that she might give him another chance.

He pulled up in front of George's house, set the brake on the wagon, and glanced up at the bedroom window. A fluttering of butterflies erupted in his stomach. He couldn't wait to see Sarah, to hear her voice, to smell the rosewater he'd come to associate with only her.

Dear Lord, let her be here, and let her hear me out.

He hopped down and raced up the porch steps. Without hesitation, he reached for the copper door handle, but the door opened wide before he could touch it. He looked up. George was standing there, his face flushed with anger.

"What's wrong with you?" Briggs asked.

George didn't answer. Instead, he took a step forward, hauled back his fist, and punched Briggs in the nose.

Pain spread through his cheeks like wildfire. "What the hell did you do that for?"

George turned away and strode back into the kitchen. Briggs followed, realizing with shock that his brother had never hit him in all their lives. He'd never had reason to, Briggs supposed.

He walked into the kitchen. "You gonna tell me what the problem is?"

George sat down, his face suddenly pale.

"Don't worry," Briggs said. "I'm not going to return the sentiment. I grew out of fistfights a while back. I'd rather you tell me what this is about."

George flung a piece of paper toward him. "It's about this."

With one hand cupped over his nose, Briggs used the other to pick up the paper.

"It's a telegram from a colleague in Massachusetts," George said. "I wanted to be certain that I'd done the best thing for you with that annulment. So this morning, I wired him and asked him to look into your little legal problem."

Briggs read the telegram. "When did you get this?"

"About an hour ago. It seems Sarah was telling the truth all along."

"I already know that, George."

"Well you don't know this—Garrison is wanted in three different states. Not just for bigamy. For polygamy, under a number of different names. Sarah was wife number four, poor thing, and she had no idea.''

Briggs sank into a chair.

"Sarah tried to do the right thing," George said. "She tried to work things out with you, but you just assumed she was lying from the beginning, and I let you talk me into it.''

Feeling sick, Briggs dropped the paper onto the table. "You don't have to tell me I was wrong. I know that. Where is she? Can I talk to her?''

George stood, giving Briggs a glare that could stop a stampede in midtrample. "I'm afraid you're a little late.''

"I know you already filed the annulment papers," Briggs said impatiently. "That doesn't matter. I just want to see her. Talk to her. We'll straighten the other stuff out later.''

George leaned back against the dry sink and crossed one ankle over the other. "If I wasn't such a rational person, I'd think you wanted me to punch you again.''

"Why?" Briggs was speechless. George had never acted like this before.

"How the hell did you know I filed the papers? Did a little bird tell you?''

Briggs stood, letting his hand come away from his throbbing nose. "I can explain that—''

"I'm sure you can. Everyone in town knew Isabelle was riding out to see you. She told the widow Harper that you two were finally going to be together, and no one tells the widow anything they don't want spread all over town by noon.''

"What are you saying?''

"I tried to find Sarah after I got the telegram. I was

going to bring her out to you. But I found out she'd ordered a buggy to go see you herself, then changed her mind when she heard about Isabelle. She just disappeared. The train master told me she got on the train to Caldwell. I'm sorry, Briggs. I did everything I could, but she left town tonight.''

Briggs couldn't accept that. He just couldn't. ''Was Garrison with her?''

''I don't know. The train master said a lot of men got on.''

''I'm going after that train, George. Right after I report Garrison to the city marshal.''

Briggs and George hurried to the wagon. There wasn't much time. Once they turned Garrison in, they would ride to Caldwell, but there was no guarantee they would get there before the train did.

They pulled up in front of the city clerk's office and Briggs hopped down. ''You wait here, George.''

''Are you joking? I wouldn't miss this for the world.''

They knocked once on the door before entering. Marshal Peavy sat behind his desk, his long legs stretched out on the top. ''Evening, George. Briggs. What can I do for you?''

''You know that fella who came up from Boston?'' Briggs said. ''You might want to arrest him.''

The marshal lowered his legs to the floor and leaned forward. ''You mean the fellow who came to fetch your wife? I heard all about it, Briggs. You have my sympathies. She was a beautiful woman. You don't have much luck in love, do you, son?''

''No, sir, but forget about that,'' Briggs said irritably. ''George has a telegram from a colleague in Massachusetts, and he says Garrison McPhee is wanted for polygamy in three states.''

"Polygamy, eh? Federal offense, if I'm not mistaken.''

George moved forward. "That's right, Marshal, and Briggs's wife, Sarah, reported it to me.''

The marshal eyed Briggs carefully. "Didn't I hear from old widow Harper that you got an annulment today?''

"Yes, sir, and you may have heard something along the lines of me taking Isabelle back, but that's just as tall a tale as you're likely to hear around these parts.''

Briggs and George looked at each other. George nodded in encouragement.

"My wife was one of Garrison's wives, sir," Briggs said. "But she didn't know he'd been married before. She was completely taken in.''

George added, "All the women were, as I understand it.''

Marshal Peavy shook his head. "Terrible thing. Your wife must be beside herself.'' He rose and fastened his gun belt around his hips.

"Do you think you'll need that?'' Briggs asked.

The marshal donned his black Stetson. "You can never be too sure of anything around here. Do you know where this man is?''

"He's been staying at the Great Western Hotel,'' Briggs answered.

The marshal checked his gun for bullets and clicked it shut. "Let's go give these ladies some justice.''

Briggs and George accompanied the marshal into the dark street and they walked side by side to the hotel. Garrison was finally going to get what he deserved—and Sarah, too. This would clear her of any wrongdoing, and she would be free—free to marry again if Briggs got what he wanted.

They approached the front desk clerk. "Evening, Marshal," the man greeted, closing his register book.

"Evening. I hear you have a guest here by the name of Garrison McPhee."

"Garrison McPhee..." He opened the book, running a long, crooked finger down the last few pages. "I'm sorry. He checked out this afternoon."

"What!" Briggs exclaimed.

"He checked out," the clerk repeated, uneasily. "He was planning to catch the evening train."

George laid his hand on Briggs's shoulder. "You mean the one to Caldwell?"

"I believe. Said he was going to be with his wife."

"Hell," Briggs uttered. He whirled around to face George.

"She didn't say she was going back to him, Briggs. By what she said last night, she despised him more than ever."

The marshal removed his hat. "What are you two going on about?"

George turned his gaze to the marshal. "I believe Sarah got on the same train as McPhee this evening."

Marshal Peavy scratched under his beard. "Maybe she changed her mind about him."

A tremor of rage shook Briggs. "You're wrong, Marshal. If she's with him, it's not willingly."

"You talking about kidnapping?"

"Yes, sir." Briggs turned on his heel to leave. *Sarah would never go back to Garrison,* he told himself. No matter how devastated she was. This time,

Briggs had to trust her. He only hoped she wasn't in danger.

He slammed the door of the hotel and raced down the steps, two at a time, crossed the road and climbed into the wagon.

"Briggs, wait!" George called, running after him.

"I don't have time to wait. I have to get to Caldwell before that train does."

The marshal approached. "You ain't gonna make it in that old box."

Briggs swallowed, refusing to give up. "It's all I've got."

"Why don't you borrow my deputy's horse? I'll take mine. I'll ride with you to Caldwell and take McPhee into custody."

"You can't leave me behind," George said. "I'll get my horse from home."

"Hurry up, then. We're wasting time."

Chapter Thirty

It seemed she had come full circle. One month ago Sarah had sat expectantly in her seat watching the Kansas countryside pass by outside the train window, wondering what her new life would be like. Now she was doing the same, only this time—this time, her worst fear had become a reality.

Drained of tears and fighting the harsh pain in her arm, she turned to look at Garrison beside her. She must pull herself together and be brave. She had to find a way out of this mess and return to Dodge to tell Briggs about the baby. She couldn't lose hope. Even if he was with Isabelle.

Garrison stared at the seat in front of them, the tip of his pistol nudging her in her side. "My God, this part of the country is monotonous," he sighed, shifting to make himself more comfortable. "Nothing but grass. Miles and miles of it."

"It's magnificent," she said, refusing to look at him.

"Magnificent? Trust me, you'll be glad to see civilization once we get there. Though for now, I should think we'll end up somewhere in Texas. If nothing else, I admire the spirit of gambling out here.''

''I thought you wanted to go back to Boston.''

''Too many bad memories there. We need a fresh start.''

Sarah closed her eyes, feeling utterly miserable. ''You can't make the memories go away. A different city won't erase what's happened.''

His expression softened with his perfected mask of affection. ''I know what happened between us was unpleasant, but—''

''I'm not talking about us. I'm talking about what happened to *me*. I love another man, and nothing you do or say will change that.''

She winced as the barrel of his gun jabbed her in a rib.

''I told you, I don't want to hear another word about that.''

She glared at him, her chin rising defiantly. ''Just because you don't want to *hear* about my feelings doesn't mean they don't exist.''

''Oh, hush. You don't know what you feel.''

Sarah ground her teeth together. She tried to feel pity for this man who knew nothing of real love, but it was hopeless. Garrison would never receive her pity. Not after what he'd done to her life.

Oh, how would she ever get out of this?

She sat in silence after that, jostling back and forth with the train's easy rhythm, thinking of her unborn child and trying not to lose hope.

Briggs, George and Marshal Peavy galloped into Caldwell the next morning, just behind the arriving train and the black cloud of coal dust that sputtered out the front chimney. The horses were winded and so was Briggs after riding all night with little time to rest. It was the price he would pay for a second chance—a second chance he hoped he would receive.

The train, chugging ominously into the station, hissed and blew white steam onto the platform. The three men trotted alongside, Briggs standing up in the stirrups to peer in the windows at the passengers milling about in the aisles, picking up their bags. His head ached with the possibility that Sarah was not even on board. How would he ever find her again?

The locomotive's wheels scraped noisily along the rails as it ground to a halt. Steam shot out again and the brass bell rang as Briggs and the marshal dismounted from their horses. After handing the geldings over to George, they ran to the back of the train, feet crunching over gravel, and climbed aboard.

Briggs led the way up the aisle, pushing his way through the passengers already standing. He and the marshal walked through two cars and found nothing, but when they reached the third, Briggs froze, his heart galloping at a frenzied pace. There it was. That purple feathered hat.

A noise escaped from deep inside his chest. She was here. He'd not lost her. Taking an anxious step forward, he suddenly remembered Garrison was supposed to be here, too. He looked at the man beside Sarah, and though he could only see the backs of their heads, he recognized the black top hat.

A new realm of horrible possibilities yawned in Briggs's face. What if she wanted to be with Garrison after everything Briggs had put her through? He'd annulled their marriage. He could only imagine what tales Garrison had told her.

He felt the marshal's hand touch his shoulder. "Do you see him?"

Heart racing, Briggs pointed. "That's him. Beside Sarah, the lady in the purple hat."

Marshal Peavy moved past Briggs. "That's some hat."

He walked up the aisle which had by now cleared of passengers, and reached their seat near the front. "Are you Garrison McPhee?"

Briggs watched from the back, needing to see how Sarah would react. She turned her head to look up at the marshal, her sweet profile revealing full lips parting in surprise.

Garrison paused, eyeing the marshal's silver badge. "Yes. Is there a problem?"

Marshal Peavy reached down and grabbed his arm. "You're under arrest. Come with me."

Sarah stood, panicking, "No!"

A spark of grief ignited inside Briggs. She was trying to protect Garrison....

In the next instant, he saw clearly what she was yelling about. Garrison pulled his other hand up to reveal a large caliber pistol. He pointed it at the marshal and fired.

Briggs didn't think. There was no time. As the recoil thundered in his ears, he lunged forward.

Garrison saw him out of the corner of his eye. The marshal fell back into the seats across the aisle. Garrison turned, cocking and pointing the gun at Briggs who heard Sarah's cry, muffled as if from a great distance. "Garrison, no!"

Briggs reached Garrison and tackled him. They both fell into the aisle; Briggs landed on top and his chin impacted with Garrison's forehead. Twisting and writhing, Briggs tried to grab for the gun. Passengers screamed and yelled. Noise and confusion rebounded off the walls. The barrel of the gun was jabbing into his gut.

Terror coursed through Briggs. His life was hanging on a jagged edge of time. He grunted as he jerked his hand to turn the barrel away.

Something clicked. The sound echoed inside his head.

Then the gun went off.

Garrison and Briggs stared at each other. Bewilderment filled Garrison's eyes. In a breathless moment, his head tipped back and rested on the aisle floor. Then his eyes slowly closed.

All the chaos and screaming of seconds ago retreated. Silence wrapped around Briggs's head; his body and mind felt drained. A hand touched his shoulder. He knew that touch. With a start, he scrambled to his feet, realizing he'd been lying on a dead man. Sarah took him by the arm and pulled him around to face her.

"Are you all right?" Her face was pale and tight with worry.

"I'm fine." But his hands were trembling.

A groan sounded from the seat behind them. The marshal...

They turned, just as George came running up the aisle. "What happened?"

Briggs leaned over Marshal Peavy. Blood had stained his shirt at the shoulder. "You're going to be okay."

The marshal's cheek twitched. "I think I'll need a doctor."

"George, fetch help," Briggs said.

White-faced with shock, George turned and ran out. Sarah moved in close and took the marshal's hand. "Can I do anything for you?"

He blinked a few times, worked hard to suck in a breath, then said, "You might want to reconsider that hat."

After telling their stories to the local marshal, Sarah and Briggs watched with relief as the doctor took Marshal Peavy away on a stretcher. Sarah carried her hat in her hand and stepped off the train into the clear light of a sunny day. She could smell the scent of coal smoke in the air and the familiar animal smells that told her this, like Dodge, was a cow town.

Other passengers milled about on the depot platform and there was a low hum of curious conversation, undoubtedly about the recent disturbance. She felt Briggs step down behind her, and her heart tightened with longing. She could not turn around. She could not look at him. She was too afraid to hope…

George hopped off the last step and stood on the platform. "That was close. You both could have been killed."

Sarah finally turned around. Briggs stood tall and strong, his hair resting lightly on his broad shoulders, his expression unreadable. Oh, how she wanted to feel his arms around her….

Sarah lowered her head, wanting to tell Briggs about the baby, but not in front of George. What if Briggs had already planned to marry Isabelle? What would happen then?

The three stood in awkward silence for a moment or two, staring at the wood planks beneath their feet.

George scratched his head. "Maybe I'll go check on the horses."

Briggs called after him. "Check the train schedule, too, George."

"Will do."

Sarah felt her hopes die a little. Perhaps he meant to see her off.

All of a sudden, Briggs wrapped his hand around her good elbow and led her around the side of the building. "Where are we going?"

Stopping by the depot wall, he faced her, taking both her shoulders in his firm grip. "When you told the marshal you'd never intended to leave Dodge with Garrison, that you wanted him out of your life for good—was that true?"

She gazed up at him, seeing the concern in his eyes, the tension in his forehead. Fighting the urge to reach up and smooth away those deep lines, she answered, "Of course it's true. I told you before. I don't love him."

"I was afraid you'd left town together."

She shook her head.

Briggs closed his eyes. "When I think what could have happened if we hadn't caught up with the train when we did."

"But you did catch it, and everything is fine now."

Slowly, he opened his eyes. Her gaze met with his, steady and unyielding. What was he feeling? she wondered, her stomach rolling with doubts and nervous knots. She had to know. She had to know before she told him.

She parted her lips to ask, but her words were cut short. His mouth came down upon hers, hard and wet with desire. Her head began to whirl. He swept her off the ground and into his arms, into the place that had become a fantasy these last agonizing hours. Feeling his warm tongue touch hers, she moaned with pleasure.

He broke away and gazed into her eyes. "I'm so sorry, Sarah."

All the possible meanings contained in that single statement swam in her head. "Sorry for what?"

He shook his head, lowering it, as if in shame. Was he saying he was sorry to hurt her, sorry for going back to Isabelle? Or was it something else?

"I'm sorry for not believing you about Garrison. I should have been able to trust you."

Still uncertain, she tried to find the right thing to say. "It's not your fault. I should have trusted you, too. If I'd told you everything from the beginning, things might have turned out differently."

"No, you had every reason to keep things secret. I was impossible. I shut you out when you needed me."

Tears formed cool webs through her lashes when she blinked, glistening, blurring her view of the man before her. She wiped her eyes, trying to focus on him.

"I want you to know I never meant to hurt you," he said. "But I think we were right to annul the marriage. When we spoke our wedding vows, they meant nothing."

Sarah's heart shattered. Grasping desperately for strength, she slowly filled her lungs with air and held on. Was he going to tell her he still loved Isabelle?

"All aboard!" the conductor called.

Harnessing all the courage she could find, Sarah

posed the question directly. "Are you going to marry Isabelle?"

"Isabelle!" he blurted out. "I don't want Isabelle."

"But she came to visit you."

Panic whisked across his face. "I drove her right back to town."

Sarah stared at him, afraid to believe it.

"She wanted to work things out, but I told her…"

Sarah touched his face with her hand, forcing him to look at her, forcing herself to look into his eyes. "You told her what?"

"I told her I love *you*. That I always would."

"All aboard!" the conductor called again.

"But the annulment… You said we did the right thing."

He cupped her face in his large, warm hands. "Yes, I'm glad we annulled it, because the second time around, our vows will mean something."

"What did you say?"

He dropped to one knee, holding her hand, kissing it again and again. He wrapped his arms around her hips, pulling her against him, burying his face in her skirts. "I love you, Sarah. Please, marry me. Truly, this time."

Joy and rapture flooded through her. She, too, dropped to her knees, drove her fingers through his thick hair and pulled him toward her for a deep, soul-reaching kiss.

A minute later, the train whistle blew. As it chugged noisily out of the station, hissing and blowing huge clouds of black soot that quickly disappeared in the wind, Briggs and Sarah stared at one another. Sarah felt the sun on her nose. There was one last thing to confess....

"I have something to tell you. I'm not sure how you're going to feel about it."

"No matter what you tell me, I could feel nothing but happiness at this moment."

She appreciated his reassurance, but couldn't help feeling shaky. "I found out yesterday that I'm— I'm—"

How could she say it? What if Briggs couldn't accept that the child might be Garrison's?

"I'm in the family way," she said, without further hesitation.

Briggs stared blankly for a moment, and Sarah's heart stood still.

"Is it...is it mine?" he asked.

Something crumpled inside of Sarah. She had hoped, fancifully perhaps, that it would not matter.

The answer she had to give ripped her heart in two. "I'm not sure." Ashamed and filled with remorse, she squinted through tears. Six months ago, who would have thought she would ever find herself in this predicament?

Head lowered and weeping in silence, she was startled by Briggs's warm finger under her chin. Gently, he raised her face, urging her to look at him. His eyes were filled with tears.

"Sarah, I will love this child more than any father ever could. No matter what."

Her body shuddered with a sob. "Briggs, I'm so sorry!"

"Sorry!" he bellowed, laughing. "You have nothing to be sorry for. You've just made me the happiest man in the world!"

Sarah drew back in dismay. After everything she'd done, after all the lies, how could she be so blessed? "I love you," she cried.

He gazed intently at her, his green eyes sparkling. "And I love you, too. It's time to go home."

Epilogue

Feet crunching over a thin coating of morning snow, Briggs paced by an upturned barrel outside the little sod dugout. He rubbed his cold hands together and blew into them. He could see his breath.

The labor had come early. What was taking so long?

A painful scream cut through the early morning air. He stopped, chest heaving. *Good God, let her be all right. I can't lose her, not now.*

Another cry stabbed at him. He approached the door. He had to go inside. He couldn't wait like this. He couldn't stand to hear Sarah in such pain.

Just then, a different cry sounded. He sucked in a quick breath. A baby. It was a baby's cry!

Waiting there, listening, he heard Martha's gentle laughter. Hope and wonder moved through his swirling insides. The seconds ticked by like hours while he stood there, frozen with excitement, waiting for Martha to come out. Was everything all right? Was Sarah okay? He couldn't bear to think what he'd do if she wasn't.

He took an anxious step forward when the door

swung open. "Congratulations," Martha said, wiping her hands on a bloodstained cloth. "You have a son."

His shoulders relaxed as a paternal glow warmed him. A son. He had a son. "Is Sarah all right?"

Martha smiled and nodded. "She was very brave. She wants to see you."

A lump filled his throat. He rushed by Martha, touching her on the arm in thanks. Taking two steps at a time, he reached the dimly lit interior of their warm little house. Sarah lay on the bed with the babe in her arm, smiling. Her long black hair was damp around her face, her cheeks flushed. She'd never looked more beautiful.

"Hello," she said, softly.

Briggs stood at the foot of the bed, staring at his wife and child. "Hello."

"Someone wants to meet you."

He walked around the bed, never taking his eyes off the two of them.

The child, red-faced and gently wiggling, was wrapped in a small white quilt Martha had brought with her as a gift, and tucked close to Sarah. Briggs knelt down to get a closer look.

"Do you want to hold him?"

Unable to speak, Briggs took the infant into his arms. The boy held up his wee tiny hand and grasped Briggs's large thumb. *What joy could be greater than this?* Briggs wondered, staring blissfully down into the sweet face, noticing the full head of black hair. "He has your fine looks."

"Not entirely."

Briggs raised his questioning gaze to see his wife smiling at him.

Carefully sitting up, she folded the quilt back from the child's tiny head. "It seems he has your ears."

Briggs shouted out in laughter. "I hadn't thought you'd noticed my ears!"

"Your hair is beautiful, my dear husband, but it doesn't hide everything."

Sinking back into the pillow, Sarah giggled for a moment, then gestured for him to sit beside her. Briggs held the child in his arms and felt his eyes fill with tears. There would never be any doubt about it.

The boy was a Brigman.

* * * * *

Harlequin Historical

is delighted to introduce author

Julianne MacLean

and her terrific new book

PRAIRIE BRIDE

Harlequin Historical #526—August 2000

DON'T MISS THESE OTHER
TITLES AVAILABLE NOW:

#523 THE SEA WITCH
Ruth Langan

#524 THE PAPER MARRIAGE
Bronwyn Williams

#525 PRINCE OF HEARTS
Katy Cooper

HARLEQUIN®
Makes any time special ™

HEAR YE! HEAR YE!
Harlequin Historicals does hereby invite
one and all to partake in five adventurous
stories of Merrie Olde Englande!

In September 2000 look for

HALLOWEEN KNIGHT
by **Tori Phillips**
(England, 1542)

THE DUKE'S DESIRE
by **Margaret Moore**
(England, 1800s)

DRYDEN'S BRIDE
by **Margo Maguire**
(England, 1423)

In October 2000 look for

A SCANDALOUS PROPOSAL
by **Julia Justiss**
(England, 1812)

MY LORD DE BURGH
by **Deborah Simmons**
(England, 1280)

**Harlequin Historicals
The way the past *should* have been!**

HARLEQUIN®
*M*akes any time special ™

Visit us at www.eHarlequin.com
HHMED14

**Don't miss
an exciting opportunity
to save on the purchase of
Harlequin and Silhouette books!**

Buy any two Harlequin or
Silhouette books and save
$10.00 off future Harlequin
and Silhouette purchases

OR

buy any three
Harlequin or Silhouette books
and save **$20.00 off** future
Harlequin and Silhouette purchases.

**Watch for details
coming in October 2000!**

PHQ400

HARLEQUIN®
Makes any time special ™

Silhouette®
Where love comes alive ™

HARLEQUIN

Duets™

JULIANNE MacLEAN

is thrilled to be joining the ensemble of Harlequin Historicals authors with her debut novel, *Prairie Bride*.

Before embarking on the wonderful challenge of writing romance, she earned two degrees—one in English literature and the other in business administration. She then became a financial statement auditor for the Canadian federal government. Julianne now stays at home to write and keep the books for her husband's medical practice, but most importantly to be a devoted wife and mother. She and her husband love to travel, and lived in New Zealand before settling in Canada with their three-year-old daughter.

HH526IBC